TO SANTERIA AND BACK

Mike Beetlestone

Order this book online at www.trafford.com/08-1350
or email orders@trafford.com

Most Trafford titles are also available at major online book retailers.

Note for Librarians: A cataloguing record for this book is available from Library
and Archives Canada at www.collectionscanada.ca/amicus/index-e.html

Printed in Victoria, BC, Canada.

ISBN: 978-1-4251-8859-7

*We at Trafford believe that it is the responsibility of us all, as both individuals
and corporations, to make choices that are environmentally and socially sound.
You, in turn, are supporting this responsible conduct each time you purchase a
Trafford book, or make use of our publishing services. To find out how you are
helping, please visit www.trafford.com/responsiblepublishing.html*

*Our mission is to efficiently provide the world's finest, most comprehensive
book publishing service, enabling every author to experience success.
To find out how to publish your book, your way, and have it available
worldwide, visit us online at www.trafford.com/10510*

Trafford rev. 5/14/2009

www.trafford.com

North America & international
toll-free: 1 888 232 4444 (USA & Canada)
phone: 250 383 6864 ♦ fax: 250 383 6804
email: info@trafford.com

The United Kingdom & Europe
phone: +44 (0)1865 487 395 ♦ local rate: 0845 230 9601
facsimile: +44 (0)1865 481 507 ♦ email: info.uk@trafford.com

AUTHOR'S NOTE

All the characters and the scenarios enacted throughout this book are entirely fictitious and are not based on any known character living or dead.

The exception to that is the description of Che Guevara's capture which is to the best of my knowledge accurate and that Felix Ramos was a CIA agent. He is still alive at the time of writing and is living in Florida. Any actions or statements attributed to him during the course of this book are totally the work of my imagination and no way reflects any of his own opinions or beliefs.

MIKE BEETLESTONE

Santeria

Like the countries on their neighbouring islands in the Caribbean, Haiti and the Dominican Republic, Cuba has a deep rooted religion based on the belief that things in nature, such as trees, mountains, the sky and the elements have a soul and a consciousness. These beliefs were brought in by the slaves from Nigeria and the Congo during the period of Spanish colonialism. In Cuba, the slaves suffered a savage and systematic destruction of their cultural identity. They were forbidden from speaking in their native tongue and from practising their customs and beliefs. Fellow countrymen, ethnic groups and families were systematically dispersed to prevent them from congregating and worshiping in large groups. The Yorubas, the ethnic group from the Niger delta, who were the largest group of slaves in Cuba overcame this persecution and re-established their religion by mirroring their Gods to Catholic Saints. When forced to worship in the churches of their masters, they were in fact praying to their own Gods. Through the generations Santeria has grown in acceptance throughout the population, if not in significance.

Now accepted both by the Catholic Church and the Communist State, largely as a sop to rebellion without in reality posing a threat to either, Santeria plays a huge cultural role in Cuban society, possessing around forty gods, Orishas, which are devotedly worshipped by nearly half the population.

Like the Voodoo of Haiti, Santeria worship involves rituals with statues and dolls along with sacrificial elements. However most ceremonies are spiritual, colourful and emotional, involving music, chanting and dancing with accompanying incense burning and alcohol consumption. There is not the revenge aspect that the media has attributed to voodoo. The ceremonies are public and everyone is welcome to join in whether or not they are worshippers themselves. The services are friendly, encourage audience participation and are generally enjoyed by all who attend, however they frequently last for several hours. During such occasions the Orishas will be called upon to answer the prayers of the congregation, in a similar fashion to Western religions, however in return the congregation will offer a sacrifice. This will generally be food, drink, shells, even money but occasionally an animal will be slaughtered.

PART ONE

Dundrum Central Mental Hospital

Chapter 1

'Do you know why you are here?'

If I had been paying for this counselling I think I would have walked out at this moment. It wasn't that I didn't know the answer; I'd rather regarded that as irrelevant. It was just my unwillingness to talk about the events that had cascaded around me over the past few months, I felt that invasive. Maybe I would have considered facing up to everything in my own mind, but I didn't want judgement from anyone. Least of all this imbecile in front of me.

But of course it wasn't my choice. I was incarcerated in the Dundrum Central Mental Hospital for the criminally insane facing Dr Sissons, a gentle man with a sympathetic ear, whom I was beginning to loathe. I knew co-operation was the sensible option but why would I change the habits of a lifetime? I allowed myself a barely concealed smirk.

'Yes' I responded definitively.

'I was rather hoping for a little more detail from you, perhaps you could try to start at the beginning. There's absolutely no need to rush, Ben. I've all the time in the world. You know the sooner you acknowledge what you have done and why you did it, the sooner we can get you out of here.' Dr Sissons crossed his legs in a rather pronounced movement and opened his hands using his body language to create a relaxed and honest ambiance. It didn't work, I felt I was facing Kenny Everett in a Cupid Stunt sketch.

Even without that thought I wasn't ready for this. I had never been a subscriber to 'It's good to talk' and hated being pigeon holed. I looked at the doctor and read a quizzical look on his face. I was enjoying the fact that he really couldn't label me and I was determined to make things as difficult as I could for him. But then I felt a cold chill of realisation seep over me. I needed this guy. He was my only chance to get out of here, but then what did I care. I was in Dundrum because I had lost just about everything I had ever cared about and nothing was going to bring them back.

Most of all Jenny.

Nothing was going to bring Jenny back.

'Ben, I know this is painful but I promise you it will become easier once you start. Now lets see what I know, you were in Cuba to visit some old friends....'

Shut the fuck up. Nothing is going to bring Jenny back.

'…..and you felt you saw someone you knew, someone you were investigating from Dublin....'

Nothing is going to bring Jenny back.

'……... when you decided to attack him. I think that was totally out of character, Ben. From the little time I've known you, I've seen a sensitive man with a total respect for others. Even caring. Something must have happened to you to decide to........'

Me, caring? I felt another mood change taking over and suddenly viewed Sissons with an urgent venomous distain. Whatever he tried to do for me was only what was required of him as the resident psychologist. I started to suggest that the time was not right for this discussion when I realised it would never be right.

'Why don't we... no... why don't YOU... just' I felt my neck muscles tightening '... get the fuck out of my life.' Dr Sissons reached over with a comforting hand and I pull away sharply. 'Get out, GET OUT...'

'Ben please I can help you' he stood up and looked as though he was going to hug me. I recoiled in absolute and transparent horror.

'Get the fuck away from me you shrink. Leave me alone,' looking him straight in the eye I said as cruelly as possible 'I don't want to see you again.' I think I saw compassion but I really didn't care. He realised I was beyond calming and decided to end the session immediately. Turning he said 'I'll call in tomorrow' and knocked on the door anxiously waiting for a nurse to come and release the lock.

'Yeah OK' I said softly as though nothing had happened. I didn't feel any animosity towards the Doctor any more. I suppose his leaving had removed the threat that I might have had to face up to my problems. I mean how could he know what was going on, I didn't have an iota of an idea of what had happened to bring me here. And how could he understand the intricacies of my mind when I never held the same mood for more than a few seconds.

When the doctor left I reflected rather pessimistically that I probably had not acted in my best interest, my rational alter ego suggesting that loser was a more than generous description of my present status. I had to take stock, I did want to get out of the hospital and he did provide one very viable option I had to achieve that. I called the nurse and told him to get Dr Sissons back; that I wanted to talk. The nurse was in his mid twenties, could have been a gym instructor with a fine build but had little patience for the criminally insane who changed their mind faster than a three year old turning a light switch on and off. He looked at me in total control without any fear of possible reprisals from either me or his superiors 'Go fuck yourself' and walked out of my room.

I considered the impossibility and sat down and wept.

Dr Sissons called to me as promised the next day and suggested that perhaps we should adopt a different approach. He tried to reason with me that I was in Dundrum as a condition of repatriation to Ireland from Cuba after an alleged assault but that there was no court order holding me in custody. I was free to go as soon as I could demonstrate that I was not a danger to myself or the public. He had no doubt that I could do that if I could face up to the consequences of my actions, but he could not do it on his own. I had to help him.

We engaged in a superficial discussion for a few minutes during which he stated that I should reflect what my options were and how I could best move forward. His forward movement was to leave, turning with a final word.

'Ben, contact me whenever you are ready. I can arrange that you visit me in my private rooms away from this environment which can be debilitating and oppressive. You have had a lot of turmoil in your life and you have to let it go. Promise me you'll think about it.'

He paused briefly, waiting for a response that never came and then left me to my own thoughts before I had a chance to abuse him again. I felt numb, partly because I was aware of my childish behaviour earlier and partly because I didn't have any positive thoughts to raise my spirits. I wanted to get out of here but I didn't want to agree to actually doing anything. Why couldn't they just let me go. The nurse who abused me yesterday entered my room and could not have been nicer, making no reference to the incident. Well, maybe I imagined it. I wasn't able to put any relevance on any relationship. He started to talk to me about a young lady who telephoned enquiring about visiting times with genuine concern. I put an end to that conversation by trying to ridicule him 'How could you know she was young. I don't need your patronising interest. Leave me alone,' which rather unsurprisingly, he did.

With instant remorse, I started to wonder who might have wanted to see me who did not know the arrangements already. In fact why did anyone want to see me? I knew I have had my troubles but I was overdosing on self pity and told myself that as soon as Joe, the nurse, came back I would show more interest in my potential visitor.

I started to reminisce about Jenny and lost myself in a delusional day dream of what might have been. I had met her in Madrid just a few months ago in a bar surrounded by friends. Although several years younger, maybe even a generation, we seemed to spark immediately. I was taken first by her demeanour, she was a free spirit but a contradiction. She was caring but carefree, conscientious but fun loving, pretty but unassuming, intelligent but frivolous. I think I fell head over heels in love with her from the instant I met her. Not that I'm the type, throughout the undulating pattern of my life, both in career and family, I have managed to maintain a cynicism common amongst my fellow journalists. This was new to me and despite myself, I liked what I was feeling.

I had gone to Madrid to make my way to Havana and met up with a friend I had known some years ago in Dublin. He introduced me to a few of his drinking companions including Susanna, her new beau Anton, a footballer from South America and to my eternal gratitude, Jenny. After a succession of musical chairs to accommodate toilet runs and taking our turn on collecting the ever quickening rounds, Jenny and I found ourselves tucked away in a corner on either side of a small wooden table. Our arms resting on the table which frequently resulted in our hands brushing against each other. Never intentional nor quickly withdrawn, the merest touch sent an apprehensive shudder through me as we discussed matters more personal. How she had left England after the break up with her boy friend two years previously to learn Spanish but really to get away. She had met Susanna who was deeply involved in politics, but was very infectious and she enrolled her in various rallies and fund raisers. Jenny had known no one like Susanna, warm and genuine. She knew she had found a true friend forever and she was so happy that Susanna had met Anton, whom she thought seemed a really nice guy. She was the one real person Jenny would literally trust with her life. Not really doubting either of them I decided to tease out this devotion a little to draw Jenny out.

'How do you know she would never let you down. Suppose Anton gets drunk and makes a pass at you. Susanna sees it and thinks you are leading him on. That's all it takes, a simple misunderstanding and you never talk again.'

Jenny lifted my hand from the table and looked at me affectionately before dumping me figuratively in a bucket of ice cold water.

'Love is the purest way two people relate to each other. It is independent of any other emotion and of any other person. Just because I love Susanna it doesn't mean I cannot love another. Love is not all consuming but it surpasses all other feelings. I don't know what Susanna would do in any situation, but I do know I would agree with her. She would be the same with me. That is not to say we are predictable nor always right, just that we are together. There would never be a misunderstanding.' She smiled as she continued to pour scorn on my simple scenario. 'I bet you think love and passion are always connected, don't you? They are as independent as a butterfly and a rose. They can flourish together but they can each grow and blossom separately into something beautiful or shrivel and die if not nurtured.'

I felt duly admonished and was lost for a response but she changed the mood instantly by reversing the challenge. She asked me with a huge grin, 'But if Anton did make a pass at me, would you be jealous? Would you hit on Susanna in revenge or would you try to kill him?'

I didn't know what to say, I know she would have had a smart response to anything I may think up, but if I don't say something clever she would think I wasn't interested. Yet I had only just met her and didn't want to sound pushy or silly. Just when I thought I could say something complimentary but non committal I heard Susanna over my shoulder.

'Come on Ben, why wouldn't you want to kiss me?'

Now I knew everyone in the bar was listening. It had to be good. My mind went blank and then inspiration hit me, and I smiled at Susanna, 'And the sunset clasps the Earth, And the mountains kiss the sea, What are all these kissings worth, If thou kiss not me.' I considered giving Shelley full credit but I then felt my delivery and timing were worthy of all the accolades.

Jenny leant over and kissed me full on the lips, softly with a sweetness I'd never felt before and I knew things would never be the same again.

My eyes were still closed and my thoughts still in Madrid when there was a knock on the door and Joe walked in with Trish. I hadn't seen her since my last day in the office before I headed to Madrid. She looked absolutely wonderful, but instantly made me self conscious by reacting ever so slightly at seeing me for the first time in twelve months. I knew I looked a mess.

'Hi Ben, I think you have a story to tell me.' Trish smiled and sat down in front of me without any invitation.

Chapter 2

I looked at Trish, thinking I couldn't imagine anyone better I wanted to talk to. And yes, I did have some story to tell, at least what I could remember of it.

It all began when our boss, Paul rang me on a Saturday evening last November twelve months saying that he had some really important news. He wanted me to come into the office in the morning. I didn't have a problem, he rarely asked favours of me and I didn't want to appear unwilling to be supportive. On the dot of nine I entered Paul's office. He looked elated and I certainly wasn't in the mood to change his demeanour. Not having produced anything of any consequence in the previous three weeks, my mind preoccupied by family distractions, a synonym for over indulgence in drink, I was prepared to go with the flow.

I had been investigating an Irish TD who had been the subject of an inquiry into political corruption. Dennis O'Hara had got away with murder, well possibly not literally but who knows, for years with backhanders and favours. Sometimes from grateful constituents, giving him the solid base for re-election but more often from builders for dubious planning consents and rezoning, favours for wealthy friends easing any speeding or drink driving offences through the system and out the other side. Not to mention the reams of consultancy work to any business man who needed some judicial reform to transform his business into a money making machine by benevolent legislation.

I had spent the best part of a year in and out of the tribunals uncovering a series of exclusives as bit by bit we managed to piece together a few skeletons that were skulking in his wardrobe. Whilst we always knew there was something else we could never pin anything on him that might send him to prison. Just tit bits that kept whittling away at his professional reputation, but I always suspected that I was also adding to his credibility as a politician who got things done, which horrified me. I needed more and I was close. There was a rumour about some property assigned to him on one of his client's death bed which resulted from some gentle persuasion, but we couldn't find out what the persuasion was. There was another case of a banker friend of his being caught with his fingers in the till but no case brought when the Book of Evidence disappeared in the bowels of the Fraud Squad offices. Never proved but everyone seemed to know that O'Hara had arranged something. I had begun to take my inability to hurt him personally and knew this was a bad development. But I couldn't let him get away with holding the Irish public, and more to the point, me, in contempt. I was desperate for help and Paul was appearing on a white charger.

'We have got a real lead on O'Hara. One of the guys from the Florida press following up a story of Cuban illegals came across this Irish guy, Rory Meagan, who has settled in Cuba, married to a Cuban girl. He is only too willing to spill the beans on any capitalist corruption and has discovered that O'Hara has a twenty five percent stake in one of the mega hotels in Valadero. Now how the fuck does an Irish politician buy property in socialist Cuba. He doesn't, he is given it. And why does the Cuban Government OK the free transfer of some of its crown jewels in the scheme of things to bring in bucket loads of US dollars. Because they are eternally grateful that's why.'

My mind was blasted by this sudden onslaught of information. No 'How was your weekend' or run through the results from the Premiership which normally preceded our morning meetings. Those admittedly have always occurred on Mondays up to now, and I should have expected something was special about this engagement. But I was still taken aback by the speed and volume of Paul's briefing. There was no pressure, we have a week before the next edition, I tried to justify my inability to switch on. I had to adjust myself to click my brain into work mode. It was not easy before the morning's first coffee after the obligatory Saturday night's skin full, even if the subject was music to my ears.

'Grateful for what'

'Exactly, grateful for what.' Paul bellowed. I didn't quite understand how he could be complimenting my astute summery of the conversation so far. But he was in full sail and barely paused for breath, 'Our Irish Cuban thinks that O'Hara arranged Shannon to facilitate Aeroflot as a refuelling base when the Americans were putting pressure on the Irish Government to say no, as they didn't want the Russians flying into the States but couldn't say so directly when the cold war was beginning to chill out.'

He must have been rehearsing this speech. 'The cold war beginning to chill out, I hope you haven't been thinking about that for too long,' I prided myself in being able to mount some counter response, no matter how vacuous.

Paul brushed this aside with a derisory 'Fuck Off' as his eyes rolled upwards in total distain and shook his head from side to side. 'Our friend reckons O'Hara smoothed the way for their constructing a fuel base with the help of a slush fund that the Russians were only to happy to provide.' I thought this was relentless. I needed time to assimilate all this information. Not pausing in the barrage he continued, 'To cover his tracks O'Hara didn't want to have any money traceable to him, so the Russians arranged this nice little nest egg in Valadero.'

Panic sets in, I hadn't taken in any of the detail and he thought I was on top of the briefing. Unlike most of the staff I liked to feel I could fool Paul most of the time, but I knew if I didn't somehow encourage him to give me a synopsis, which didn't seem too likely, I would lose browny points.

'Are you saying we have a lead on pinning something concrete...' the thought occurred to me as I was saying it, of the stupidity of the phrase '...on our esteemed member of the Dail. Tell me more.' I knew that was poor and I cringed as I awaited his response.

Not too long 'Are you fucking listening?' he thundered. My concentration lapsed again as I mused that there was something quite enchanting about a rhetorical question, which by definition doesn't need answering, but gets the assumed answer totally wrong. I was still considering over what I should say, I thought flippancy would have been a mistake, when Paul lowered his voice and spoke to me as a delinquent eight year old. 'You have been for the last six months reporting the events of the tribunal into corrupt political donations and you have managed to do little so far other than annoy Mr O'Hara and exercise his solicitor in sending us several writs. What I have just outlined is the basis of an international conspiracy which could blow him out of the water, and you can't be bothered to listen to a word I'm saying. You fucking ask me to elaborate... you're the investigative journalist you arsehole, you elaborate.'

No confusion over the browny points there, I needed to do some serious grovelling. That realisation along with the implications that this story really was mind blowing, I had to try to regain ground by adopting a serious demeanour.

'No, no I'm with you all the way, Paul, what does our Cuban friend definitively have on O'Hara?'

He cooled down a little, sighed, I even detected the faintest of upward movement of his lips as he decided that maybe I was worth the effort. 'Yeah, Meagan, our Cuban source, has proof that O'Hara was in Havana last month to supervise the transfer of funds to an account in the Cayman Islands. He has the transfer documents to an account in the name of Oconco which managed to fall in his lap with the benefit of a few dollars and he thinks he can prove O'Hara is the beneficial owner. What he doesn't have is absolute irrefutable evidence that the money came from a dividend in the hotel, but he does know for certain that it does.'

'This is sensational,' my enthusiasm for what I was hearing suddenly revealed itself if a little belatedly. This could have been the final straw to break O'Hara's back and as my mind slowly begins to shunt into first gear I realise the obvious, 'but there must be more, what about the others he would have had to pay off in Ireland to smooth this over. There has to be a few who knew what was going on.'

Paul finally returned to his normal speaking tone, knowing I'm hooked 'Yeah, I know, I've got Trish working on the sale of brown paper envelopes in 1980 in the hopes we can churn up some more of our brethren we call our Civil Service, Self Service more like. Starting with everyone who was in the Department of Transport then, and the board of Aer Rianta. We probably have to go through the minutes of Council meetings in Clare as well to see who was and more crucially who wasn't objecting to these monstrosities landing usually at night. I reckon we should try and break with this story in three weeks time which should give you enough time to get in and out of Cuba with all the information you can turn up. In the meantime we have to keep it completely under wraps, we don't want anyone else stealing our thunder.'

With lightening quick reflexes I saw the implications building up. This was going to be a lot of research, and I was glad Paul was not looking my way for the spade-work, which has never really been my thing. Trish was in her first year in the job after graduating in journalism in Rathmines College. She objected to being lumbered with the donkey work, but was a willing and effective researcher. She wasn't afraid to ask the awkward questions, I usually had difficulty thinking of them.

Finally it all hit me, Paul was sending me to Cuba for three weeks investigation, this was brilliant. I had never been, was always fascinated and my home life was in such turmoil that three weeks to take stock could be just what the doctor ordered. I just had to act cool. I didn't want Paul to tighten up on the expenses.

'Yeah, OK I can go, when do you want me to leave.' *So much for cool.*

'Time is pretty important because we have to make the most of our head start, don't let anyone – I mean anyone – know where you're going. Tell Katie your going to Madrid, which you will be for a couple of days to get some background detail on the soccer feature you were on last week and that you may have to go on from there as matters develop. You'll ring her every couple of days with your itinerary.'

'She won't be in the least bit bothered,' I sadly commented.

'Good, can you phone the travel agent now and book a flight to Madrid as soon as you can get yourself organised. You can make all the necessary onward flights in Madrid but don't fly for a couple of days I don't want your steps to be traced.' A little melodramatic I thought, but the time was not right for any more smart arsed remarks.

'Can we trust the hack in Florida and this Meagan guy not to look for more shekels from another rag'

'I hope your not suggesting we are a rag' Not pausing for an answer, Paul continued 'No we have a reciprocal arrangement with US Today giving them any scoops that might have more impact in the States for a clear run on this. Obviously we will give them access to everything we find out the day we publish. And Meagan has been given a retainer and a copper fastened agreement on exclusivity. He's more interested on exposing O'Hara than making money, I'm sure he'll probably give it all over to some left wing cause when the time comes to settle up. He comes across as a fairly honourable guy.'

'OK talk to you later,' as I sailed out of the door a pretty excited scribe. Paul had been forgiving but even his patience could not go on for ever. I thought that I had been given enough time to bring home the bacon, but I knew there was not too much room for error. Anyway I owed him a good story. I knew the lads in the news room would have given their eye teeth for an opportunity like this. But what did I care, I had earned this for a lifetime of dedication even if I probably didn't deserve it right at that moment.

I ran down the corridor to the office Trish and I shared, not far from leaping in the air and clicking my heels. When I reached our little, bright but totally dishevelled office I tried not to show too much over enthusiasm but it was difficult. Rather surprisingly, as it was Sunday, I saw Trish. She was sitting with her phone in hand as usual and a bright red tee shirt with a Metallica logo emblazoned on it suggesting rather uninvitingly to 'Eat Shit.' With tight blue jeans, torn around the knees, she took on the look of the student she recently was rather than the hard nose journalist she had become. But I loved her spirit and she made me feel that she thought she could learn from me. I rather thought it was the other way around, but it was good for my self esteem.

'What are you doing here?'

'Same as you by the looks of it. I got the call too. I hear you're going to track down one of O'Hara's backhanders in Cuba while I do all the dirty work in Limerick, God I hope you get pensioned off soon.'

'You wouldn't like it, all that sun, sea and scuba diving. It's not what you need to be doing in November, when there's Council minutes to read.'

'Listen when I get to your age in forty years time I hope I will remember that sarcasm is the lowest form of wit.'

'Forty years – you little tart. And you are very mistaken, sarcasm is beautiful. It is the last refuge of the modest when their soul is coarsely invaded.'

'Very funny, I would never have thought you would describe yourself as modest. Or even admit to having a soul. How did you think that up?'

'Actually I didn't, Dostoyevsky did.'

'Very clever, one up to you, fancy a coffee?'

I did actually but realised that I had better make some forward movement on my arrangements before Paul had second thoughts.

'No I have to go home, see you later'

****

And that was it, now a year later I wanted to tell her my side of the story of what happened to me after I left the office that day. I sat down and reflected how I would start and realised there weren't any details to sort out. I couldn't think of anything to say.

Chapter 3

'So what happened?' Trish looked at me eagerly hoping she was touching base, but as much as I wanted to respond to her I felt a mental darkness. Like a shroud keeping all my thoughts together and secret. I didn't even know if I wanted to delve into the inner recesses. I suspected there was a lot of pain in there just itching to spread its influence. And even if I could, was Trish the right person to share my thoughts? There again there weren't too many options.

I did want to relate to her at some level, I was delighted to see her and wanted her continue to visit. She was my only friendly link with my past. 'Trish it's so good to see you. You know why I'm here don't you? I got into a little trouble in Havana I'm afraid.'

'Yes, I heard, but no one knows your side of the story, what made you attack that guy and how on Earth does any of this relate to O'Hara?'

Never one for gentle protocol, she hits the one button that kicks my mind into a fervour. Whilst I remember O'Hara and knew that I had assaulted a stranger because

I thought he was assaulting a young girl on the back streets of Havana I had not made the connection before. An incandescent white lights somersaults through my mind – I thought he was O'Hara. Almost joyously I repeat it to Trish almost like a mantra. 'I thought he was O'Hara.' I leap to my feet overwhelming any response she may have had. 'I hit the bastard because he was molesting a young girl and I thought he was O'Hara.'

Trish looked at me almost as excited as I was 'Come on, don't stop now.' Pausing for a minute to see if the consequence of this one piece of self discovery was sufficient to unlock all my mysteries, I stalled for time.

'You have to bear with me Trish. I need time to sort my thoughts out, see if I can make any sense of anything. I have a reason for the unprovoked attack I am being accused of but there has to be a reason for the reason, if you know what I mean. I know that I was investigating O'Hara and I discovered something about him I wasn't expecting.' I stalled for a while looking at Trish and another thought darted into my head like a star falling from the sky straight into my mind. I couldn't help myself but laughed at the discovery which was as far from being funny as I could imagine. 'Trish, O'Hara was in Cuba to feed his paedophile habit. The bastard procured young girls for his own gratification.' My euphoria over this breakthrough quickly died when I realised there was nothing else coming.

'Help me Trish, you know why I went to Cuba and why I came back after Jenny died…'

'Hang on, Ben. Who's Jenny?'

'That's what I mean, I don't really know. Just that she was special but I know she's gone and…' the blanket throws itself over my mind again and I feel frustrated, annoyed and helpless. I start to weep pitifully and Trish comes over to comfort me. I knew I definitely did not want that.

'It's OK Ben, hang on in there. We will find the answers.'

I start to mumble 'I'm sorry Trish. I think Dr Sissons wants to try counselling and group therapy and maybe hypnosis as a treatment to see what is troubling me so much, but I don't think I want to know. Whatever is locked up inside me is better left undisturbed.'

'Ben, this is not the way it has to be. I'll talk to Sissons. I don't have a clue about the long term benefits or risks of hypnosis but I promise you I'll find out. Let's face it if it helps you face reality and gets you out of here it has to be worth a try. Look where you are now, you really have nothing to lose.'

She leans over and kisses me on the cheek and I inhale her perfume in an act of self perceived incest and I'm disgusted with myself. I feel the pendulum swinging away from me and before I can check myself I launch into an attack on Trish which is coming from no where I recognise.

'Go away now and don't come back. Don't go anywhere near Sissons, he's my doctor—not yours. Take your pity somewhere else.' I can hear myself saying everything but have no way of stopping it. She turned to leave but inexplicably smiled and winked 'See you soon, Ben.'

After Trish left I tried to re evaluate my position again. I have no control over my feelings. I will have no friends very soon unless something happens and I need help. I know I'm in here because I assaulted a man in Havana, who looked like an Irish TD I was investigating. In between there were twelve months of a blank with the exception of Jenny. She rose from my mind in every exquisite detail, but she was no longer part of my life and I really wanted to know why. I was suffering from ferocious mood swings which meant I cared little most of the time about whether I would ever see the outside of the Hospital. But it was a Catch 22 situation, either I don't care and I happily spend the rest of my life here, or I do care and become so depressed with my psychotic situation that I can not see how I could ever get out. I had to break this cycle.

Dr Sissons, despite my initial misgivings of him, was my only key to rehabilitation. I had to talk to him and remain positive throughout our discussions. My alter ego suggests that I hadn't a hope of achieving that, but fortunately like the rest of me that wasn't working too well either. I knew I had to build some bridges and nothing was going to happen overnight.

During the next three weeks of medication, basically a cocktail of clozapin, zeldox, prozac and anoryn (not all at once I hasten to add, but I did feel the doctors were just giving me tablets because they had them), my mood oscillated between contentment with my progress, to total anger at my incarceration. During my deepest melancholy I felt I had been subjected to a gross miscarriage of justice as the whole legal system seemed to have been bypassed to facilitate good relations with who exactly, the Cuban authorities, the man I assaulted, James Mulroy – surely not, or maybe, the thought occurred to me more and more, Dennis O'Hara.

Dr Sissons took his responsibilities as my consultant psychiatrist as earnestly as I could have wished after our rather indelicate start and during a fairly intimate relationship I began to trust him. He explained that I am suffering from Clinical Depression and that he feared I may have had a slight breakdown, but from various tests he felt I should make a complete recovery as long as I tried to help myself.

'What do you exactly mean Doctor' I asked with a genuine fear that certain things may be beyond my control, 'How can I help myself?'

'It is never easy to suggest a way of life. If it were that easy there would be no mental illness in the world. What I say to you now may seem very reasonable and within your capabilities. But who is to know how your inner self will react when other perspectives are put on your outlook. We would like you to look to the future, build a new life for yourself with the support of your friends and family. You have been through a tremendous turmoil in your life in the last twelve months and you are coping well considering you have little recollection. The prescription is gradually weaning you off the anti depressants which I'm sure you will be free off soon. Then I should imagine you will be released to the care of someone we can maintain contact with. A family member or friend, perhaps, who would be willing to undertake such a role. But it is up to you to define the speed at which this happens. You are going to have to want to get better. That's half the battle, but it's not the only one. We have to be sure that the upheaval in your mind has been pacified. I can raise your expectations of a full recovery but I cannot control it. That is your job. In the course of time your memory will return. But not instantly, you will slowly remember the sections of your life that had most meaning. They may not return in any chronological order and you may have difficulty piecing things together for a while. Be patient, don't be too hard on yourself and trust me.'

He explained how the hospital would help, 'We are going to put you on a fairly rigid programme of counselling and recreational therapy that will occupy your day more or less fully. Each morning after breakfast we will have a group session where you will be able to share your experiences with others who have similar experiences to yourself'

Who has any experiences that remotely resemble mine; I wondered but decide to keep the thought to myself. Self pity should never be shared.

He droned on as I began to get bored, 'You will experience elation and depression at many times through out these sessions which you will counter with anger and laughter. It is your ability to cope with these emotions which will determine your progress. We don't want you to suppress or control your feelings. We want you to feel comfortable with them. Our sessions in the afternoon are designed to place some mental discipline on yourself by committing to a manual task that hopefully you will find enjoyable. We print a newspaper, prepare evening meals, tend to the gardens, engage in art and music classes, learn new languages. We do not measure success in any of these fields in any other way but your commitment to complete them. Again your ability to do this will illustrate your progress in learning to live with yourself. All sessions are voluntary, but we strongly recommend that once you start our programme that you attend every day.'

I couldn't actually make up my mind whether he was saying anything of substance or not, but I was happy for the time being that at least he was being upbeat and vowed as much as possible to match that mood whenever he visited me, and I will give his programme the benefit of some consideration.

Trish came back to visit me every few days and I fear to tell her how much her visits meant to me. She told me of her research into Sissons career and was full of praise from his references. 'You are a lucky man, Ben, to have such a dedicated man on your side.' Then gave me a squeeze to let me know she knows that my own description of my situation would not include the word 'lucky.'

Katie didn't visit me at all and I even wondered if she knew I was here. I knew her well enough to know that our crumbling marriage would not stop her concern. I don't want to see her until I discovered what secrets I had, and how they affected her. Obviously any relationship I had with Jenny had to be ordered in my mind in terms of priorities before I re-established any feelings I had for Katie.

After a couple of weeks of mixed attendance at the Sisson's Sessions, I began to enjoy the routine and start to look forward to telling my story every morning, particularly that most of my fellow patients were rather in awe of me and treated me as some kind of celebrity. Leading a life that they would only see in the movies I raised my spirits as I related more and more detail with more imagination each day. Delusion is only a psychotic problem when your target audience is yourself. It is a positive path to recovery when it is inflicted on others – or so I deluded myself into thinking. Of course I could only go so far with my story, but did feel that every day I managed to go a little further. And I knew my willing audience were eager to join in my political assassination of O'Hara, from which I got a real sense of achievement.

Just as I was feeling at home in my surroundings after ten weeks in Dundrum, I got a surprise call.

One of the nurses came into me and asked if I would like to see Mr O'Hara who had come specially to visit. At first I felt infuriated that he was invading my territory. I was in Dundrum because of him, and I could do nothing about it but then my bravado took over. Why not, I wanted to see what the bastard had to say, there was nothing he could do to me in hospital and maybe I could still shake him up. 'Show him in,' I said with the anticipation of a prize fighter facing up to fun fair wannabes.

The elegantly dressed O'Hara swaggered in looking totally confident, hand extended he welcomed me 'How are you Ben, good to see your making progress. I just called to see if there was anything I could do for you to make your life a little more comfortable.'

Why did I agree to endure this, why didn't I just say no?

'What do you want O'Hara, my being here is just perfect for you. You only demean yourself further, if that was possible by coming here to gloat, just fuck off out of my sight.'

'Ben, I don't want you to feel like that' he was on auto pilot. 'You're one of my constituents and if there's anything I can do for you, it would be my honour. Strangely I feel somewhat responsible for your losing the plot, if you will excuse the vernacular.'

'You're hardly chasing my vote, are you?'

'Please Ben, don't be so cynical. My visit is purely to see if I can help. I really do like you despite everything. I think it's the mutual respect gladiators have for each other,' he tried a compassionate smile which matched his character like a bull taking pottery lessons.

'I find you repulsive to look at, your touch is as slimy as the rattlesnake you have obviously been reincarnated from, your voice drones like a pregnant cow on a mid summers day and the smell that precedes you makes me retch. How's that for mutual respect? Now if you really like to help me you can close the door behind you.' I took a little pride that I could summon up such vitriol at such short notice, but he deserved it. Secretly I was hoping he would stay so I could give him another selection of sweet nuthin's I was sure I could muster, but he took the hint.

'You stupid tosspot, I could have made your life comfortable here but you can't see it, can you? You'll never be released. And you know why? Because I say so. You're in the home of the criminally insane because you're mad. You have to have two doctors to sign you out and do you know when that will happen. Never. Now let me tell you why that won't happen. Because you came so close to actually getting to me I can never afford to let you have any freedom. The longer you stay in here the longer your story will be dismissed as fanciful conjecture. Little did you know when you came to my office with your story that any other newspaper but the Chronicle would have been delighted to publish your investigations on my activities with those Cuban girls. Now the story is dead and buried. If you had only been reasonable and friendly I would have agreed to recommending your release whenever the doctors decided it was OK for you to be back in society. Now you can just fester in this hell hole.' I could see spittle forming at each side of his mouth and was thrilled I'd provoked such a rant.

'Actually anywhere away from you could not be described as a hell hole, now if you would just rewind this conversation about ten minutes I think you will recall that I told you to fuck off, would you be so good as to do just that.' I was delighted I'd annoyed him so much that he made his confession and finally took some pleasure in knowing that I had won this little skirmish. Suddenly a large section of my life fell off the ceiling a struck me hard. I had tackled O'Hara in his office a few months ago and I had got to him. Now he was scared shitless. He thought I had a story on him with under aged girls and it must have caused him a lot of grief. I was absolutely thrilled that the whole story was coming back and he still thought I was a danger. Fantastic. I only wished I knew what he was talking about.

The irony that any success in bringing the story back might directly lead to my institutionalism being possibly lifelong had not dawned on me but even when it did I won't care. I felt as though he thought I had him by the balls and it was worth it. I began to feel elated again and called Dr Sissons immediately to arrange personal one to one counselling. I felt the shroud was beginning to fall away.

Chapter 4

Dr Sissons took my call immediately and was delighted with my up beat response but cautioned against too much optimism. However he did suggest that we could meet in his rooms away from the hospital but he would have to go through all the formalities to be able to arrange this. Four days later I sat opposite Dr Sissons in an extremely comfortable armchair feeling better than I had for months. The four days had passed without any relapse into depression and I felt rested, almost at ease. My euphoria of O'Hara's semi confession to something dark and sinister in his background had evolved into a state of well being. I knew this was going to be the beginning of the end.

'I haven't seen you looking so well and relaxed, Ben and I think now is an excellent time to try to delve a little into your past. Don't be afraid to fail. This is not a competition nor are we trying to break any records. Memory loss can be caused by many things. A drug over dose, a physical blow to the head, an electric shock, a neurological disorder such as Alzheimer's or Post Traumatic Stress Disorder which I feel is what you are now suffering from. My previous diagnosis of Clinical Depression may still be true, but if we can discover that you did suffer a trauma, and I don't think there can be any doubt of that, we can treat it appropriately.

'The brain performs many chemical and electrical functions every moment of the day. But if it is faced with a situation totally out of the ordinary, such as a life threatening situation, a bereavement of a loved one, marital or financial difficulties, trouble in work, witnessing extreme cruelty it reacts. This is normal, a stress breakdown. It is not a mental illness it is a psychiatric illness.

'From what I have gathered from your situation you have suffered all the events that anyone of which could have caused Post Traumatic Stress. Your mind has decided to suppress the horrific memories, it is my job to try to persuade it that it is better to face up to them. Your dissociative amnesia can be treated in a number of ways, I feel we can disregard group therapy as we have seen little improvement over the last few weeks. I know you enjoy the story telling, but I think you are more interested in impressing your audience than to unlock painful memories.' I nodded in agreement while he went on. 'We will now continue with this direct psychotherapy and remove you from all anti depressants. Possibly in time we can introduce pentothal, a mediation to help the brain, but first we have to get all the other drugs out of your system. After I can go as far as I can go I think we should try hypnosis. I have one of the country's leading hypnotherapists, Dr Latimer to call on to treat you, but you have to be comfortable with it.'

Trish and I had discussed this a few times when she visited me and felt that it was ideal to find out what had

TO SANTERIA AND BACK

happened. We had discussed many other things including my capture in Cuba which had made me a minor celebratory for a few weeks, but the detail was flimsy and had caused virtually no new revelations in my own mind. I was ready to go with whatever Dr Sissons suggested.

'Yes, I have to get to the bottom of what I know about Dennis O'Hara and what happened to Jenny. I miss her so much, but I don't know why. Can you imagine how that tears me apart.'

His expression of understanding feed my new found confidence and we went on to say, 'Lets start at the beginning, what do you remember?'

I explained how I had been pursuing O'Hara and that Paul had sent me to Cuba to investigate another scandal of his. On route I had met Jenny, Susanna and Anton in Madrid and we developed a great bond, which took us through a week of partying. 'Can you tell exactly what happened, Ben?'

I was bursting to start.

'I don't know when we first met, but the first time I remember seeing Jenny was at five 'o'clock in the morning in the Central Bar sharing a late night drink with all the usual suspects. I was returning with Dave, a friend from Dublin, and a couple of his Bohemian friends after a night of animated discussions. It turned out that one of them, Geronimo, was a member of the Tropicana dance troupe from Cuba who was on a European tour and he took great delight in enlightening me on the process of enjoying life in Havana. I hadn't suggested that I was heading there, but he just couldn't be turned off once he got started on the injustices that he had to endure.

But he was full of the quality of carnal life he enjoyed in his homeland. He was tall, extremely good looking and quite charming and I found his company totally engaging.' I looked across at Dr Sissons who looked enthralled, which I found uplifting and furthered my confidence.

'I had known Dave when we frequented the same drinking establishments in Lucan and had developed a long friendship based on our joint interest in soccer, golf, palm greasing politics, lust and drink which had survived fifteen years. A couple of years earlier the security firm he worked for bought a Spanish operation which required on the spot supervision for which Dave had volunteered and had enjoyed every minute since. When I rang him to say I had been sent to Madrid to investigate a lead we had learnt of in our quest to expose corruption in the Soccer world, he was quick to invite me for a session.

'Jenny was one of about eight revellers sitting at a long table, to which Dave pulled up a chair and I joined him. Everyone one in fine form despite the lateness of the hour and none were on the point of retiring, the reverse in fact had drinks not arrived I think a contingent were heading downtown. I was grateful that Jenny was not going anywhere and proceeded to try to engage her in fascinating conversation, as fascinating as the level of alcohol in my system would allow.

'She was wearing an ankle length sleeveless red dress and looked sensational. We obviously had talked before in the bar on an earlier visit in the day because I sat next to her and started talking immediately – not something I would usually do with the best looking girl in the room even with a few drinks if I didn't know her. I've been thinking about this since and she was the only person I remember what she was wearing, either the dress was a knockout or she was. Probably both.

'Anyway I managed to isolate her in a corner until Susanna overheard us talking and lay down a challenge which ended up in my kissing Jenny. It really was a lovely moment.' Dr Sissons showed no signs of boredom and I was enjoying piecing things together in a way I hadn't attempted before. I was getting into my stride.

'Geronimo joined us with a certain devilment in his eyes having, during the course of the evening earlier described his favourite pastime, fucking European women, with a certain fanaticism. The delicacy of his pursuits were not something I had wanted to bring into the conversation but it was fairly obvious that he was in no mood for quitting with Susanna being singled out as the evening's target. Susanna and Anton were sitting beside each other and were obviously a couple. Anton was at first quite receptive to Geronimo's interest in Susanna, feeling total confidence in their relationship, but as the evening wore on he began to tire of his intrusion and less than subtle innuendo. I feared that I would have to step in and pull them apart. But then mature reflection negated that thought. If they were going to challenge each other – I would be better to let them at it.

'However Geronimo's hobby does belie an ironic moral authority that he possessed, he was quite charming, sincere and knowledgeable and regarded his habits in a different light to most of us. Well at least in my generation. I think he would view any success he had in the same way a fisherman would look at his catch, quality is great but performance would be judged on the overall numbers and success or failure at any particular juncture would be inconsequential. Not perhaps a unique outlook to the sex game but the difference being their attitude that it was a sport. Geronimo would feel he was involved in hunting. From what I was gathering from his colourful accounts, his Cuban female counterparts largely shared his cavalier attitude. Anyway he was getting nowhere that night which only seemed to encourage his outgoing persona and his sense of battle.'

I looked across at Dr Sissons but he waved 'Go on Ben, as much detail as you can remember, this is excellent.'

Encouraged I continued 'Jenny was oblivious to this or at least I thought so but details of our conversation are completely hazy except that I knew we did banter at length before we all gave up on the evening. I felt we shared a common bond and that I was deeply impressed by her gentleness and somewhat conflicting devilment. What she understood I was contributing was more difficult to fathom.

'One of the other Cubans, like Geronimo, a dancer, annoyed everyone by holding a collection for himself to get a taxi home. Geronimo explained that he felt this was fine, he was asking for a favour from people who could well afford it without any hostility if his request fell on deaf ears. It's what they had to do to survive in his world, where nearly all forms of minor luxury were priced at tourist values way above the reach of his compatriots. Geronimo's insistence that he would not resort to this type of self ingratiation did not stop him from sharing the taxi when the dancer eventually embarrassed enough people to get the fare.

'We all said our goodbyes and I had the opportunity to go over to Jenny and say goodnight directly, but I chickened out. My eternal fear of rejection brought a depression which seams so trivial now. But just as I headed back to my hotel she slid up beside me, sending an electric shock through my arm as she touched. 'Trying to disappear without saying goodnight?' she smiled, kissed me on the cheek and said 'See you tomorrow, Ben.' I was ecstatic.

'I meet Jenny next when she was shopping around midday in the fruit market for provisions for the bar she ran. She suggested a walk along the town after she had completed her errands and I was thrilled to agree to and went off taking photographs, full of the joys of Spring in mid November.

'She arrived about forty five minutes later dressed in a pink polo shirt, open to show a gentle cleavage, comfortable denims and her hair tied back. She had minimal make up and looked totally natural. She was beautiful. Her plan was to take advantage of the Tapas Bars generosity. After several experiments of social intercourse with strangers of a similar disposition, Jenny took my camera and control. She took photographs of any situation that caught her imagination and encouraged me to join our fellow revellers at every opportunity. Some of the photographs of complete strangers hand feeding me with bites of pizza, morsels of chicken, tomato garlic breads, along with others of my embracing the colourfully uniformed road sweepers and even trying to raise a smile from one of the armed policeman left me with wonderful memories of an exuberant afternoon, if I could only find them. All encouraged by glass after glass of draught Cruzcampo, served up in canas, thin tall glasses with a head varying from a quarter of a glass to half, which meant I had no idea how much I was drinking. I did everything Jenny asked and thoroughly enjoyed not only the craic but also her looking out for me. We separated into different groups which just seemed to confirm the free spirit image I had formed of her which made her even more attractive. She never passed an old man or woman or a young child without asking if they were OK and if they wanted anything. Whilst I would have thought such enquiries somewhat patronising in some cases, she never got a hostile response. The opposite in fact, always a smile and either a handshake or hug. I marvelled at her compassion and how absolutely genuine it was. I suppose it even raised another inadequate aspect to my character which even my cynicism recognised.

'I don't quite know why I search for my failings in such depth but I realise that my ranking in the 'Caring Human League' fell way below Jenny's – so much so that I felt embarrassed. I searched my soul for some appropriate sarcasm to shake off this bout of conscience but fail to find any. Jenny sensed my mood change and she teased me with a tirade of swearing, as though she is trying to prove she was not perfect. She failed and not for the first time since we met, I considered just what a wonderful companion she was.

'We completed our foray through the town with a final visit to another tapas bar around five. I start to study her every movement, the rough way she rubbed her mouth after eating, a small mannerism, hardly erotic but it left a lasting impression. The way she adjusted her bra strap under her shirt which not only revealed her shoulder but also a burning desire in me. I was consumed and gratified when she continued to return my interest.

'I was slowly beginning to realise what I really thought about her, she was young, vivacious, wonderfully kind hearted and gorgeous and apparently enjoyed my company. And I loved hers, but she was probably not much more than half my age.

'Anton was just as smitten with Susanna. He met her a couple of days earlier in Joy Madrid, a downtown night club, which had been his haunt for several weeks since his cruciate knee ligament injury had put pay to his football for the following three months. Since his high profile transfer from La Paz two years earlier to Real Madrid he had not established himself as a first team player but had made several appearances from the bench. With time on his hands, he was seriously contemplating his future. He was no longer young and his exposure to the Bolivian International selectors had reduced to zero after a couple of years of peripheral involvement. Other European clubs might be unwilling to take a chance on an injury prone player, so maybe it was the time to go home. At a fraction of his wages of course but at least still a national hero and presumably plenty of opportunity to take advantage of his high profile before his star waned too much.

'Susanna had come into his life when he needed solace, a shoulder to lean on who, he would quickly learn, would offer an unbiased opinion on the traumas that were going through his life. She was passionate and saw Anton like every other female in Madrid as an extremely attractive man with charming manners and lifestyle to die for. Their meeting had somehow seamed preordained, following the accidental bumping into each other on the dance floor of Joy. Since then they had hardly spent a waking moment apart.

'Following my afternoon soiree with Jenny, another long session in the Central preceded a late night in El Sol a central night club that only seems to come to life after three and the live band had finished their gig. Jenny suggested that as she had a few days off and if I was interested we could take a couple of days taking in Toledo which she heard was beautiful and had to see.

'I suppose it doesn't stretch your imagination to much to say I jumped at the opportunity.' Dr Sissons smiled and I was pleased he was so attentive. 'In fact everyone thought it was a good idea and we decided to go first thing the next morning. I gave my journalistic duties a cursory consideration, but another day with Jenny was too good to miss and Paul did tell me not to move too quickly. My mind was definitely in turmoil. I wanted nothing more than this, but I was unsure of what her interest in me was. My alter ego, rarely of assistance to me, was urging me to go with the flow.

'We had a pretty rough bus ride up to Toledo after nearly two days of virtually no sleep and we were all pretty shattered. We arrived at the luxury Parador hotel which apparently is owned by the Government, along with many others around the country. It exuded character and had everything you would expect in decadent surroundings yet is surprisingly moderately priced. After recuperating in our rooms for much of the afternoon, we arranged to go for drinks and the evening took on a life of its own. We ended up in a back street night club where the rhythms were hypnotic. Jenny showed her natural instincts to dance and encouraged me to join in. My best efforts failed to impress but I had fun trying and felt, uniquely in my experience of dancing, total disappointment when it was over. The night came to an end fairly abruptly with the security guards systematically forcing our removal at a quarter to three and we all clambered back to the hotel.

'Throughout the rest of the night the five of us simply told stories and relaxed as the star filled sky offered us tranquillity and a sort of sensual overcoat in the chilly autumn night. Though I suspected the brandy may have helped in that regard. Anton regaled us with stories of his footballing career, the glamour of Real Madrid and the less than perfect conditions in La Paz. I was also interested to learn of stories of the social character of Bolivia as my father had spent some time there in his early days as a doctor and I was wondering if I could retrace his footsteps sometime. He warmly suggested that he would be delighted to take me round and visit his home to which I would be afforded a royal welcome, at any time. He was in full flow at this stage and enraptured about his home land. The view of the foothills of the Andes from La Paz, the grey and yellow sunsets crowning the snow covered mountains. The Sajana National Park, which was taken straight out of the Alamo with the perfect lake, La Cordillera – so beautiful and so peaceful. And then there was Lake Titikaka! Whilst a good traveller I wasn't really interested in what he was saying – just on how I could use his enthusiasm to extend Jenny's company.

'He was winning everyone over before he started to describe the city, which he said took in the best of everything, old and new. The hustle and bustle of modern transport side by side with llama drawn carts. Designer business suits walking with men and women dressed in layers of clothes of every type and colour under the sun. People wearing multiple hats, barefoot kids running everywhere, friendly and full of life. The roads merging from modern highways to narrow cobblestone alley ways before you have chance to blink. There were hundreds of signs, every size, neon, some flashing others plastic, metal, or wooden, handwritten or hand cut, old or new. Then there were the smells, fresh llamas, old exhausts, fresh spices, old perfumes. The constant hum of traffic, the rhythmic beat of street entertainers, the noise of life. It was an explosion for all the senses.

'I thought he had quite successfully sold it to all of us and my mind started working overtime. Maybe this could cover my tracks and also be a lot of fun, a couple of days in Bolivia with Anton and back to Havana. Susanna reflected on this invitation with playful suspicion, 'You invite your new friend to your home but not your girlfriend.

'Anton retraced his steps 'Listen you are all welcome especially the beautiful Susanna' and the idea began to lodge in Jenny's mind that this could be an adventure too good to miss out on. My mind began to race ahead, not only was I going on a trip of a lifetime but also the girl who I was beginning to idolise wanted to tag along. But I still don't know how she felt about me and I didn't know if I wanted to find out. Dave regretted that duty called and that he had to get back to work, but he wished us well on our escapade.

'We adjourned to bed respectfully keeping the same pre ordained sleeping arrangements, though I suspected Anton's single room may well have been visited by Susanna leaving Jenny alone. Whilst the thought of that haunted me, I consoled myself with the fact that I didn't know where this relationship was going but we were going to be together for the next few days so long as I didn't do anything stupid.

'Next day after a very late breakfast we travelled back to Madrid and I made some enquiries about travel to Bolivia. Obviously I should have gone to Cuba first but none of the rest would fancy that so if we travelled to La Paz via Buenos Aires we could spend a couple of days with Anton's family and then head back through Havana, presumably leaving Anton behind. I was sure Susanna would love a trip to Cuba and hopefully would encourage Jenny too. Those travel arrangements would also tie in with my soccer scandal cover if anyone was watching. I was apparently travelling to Argentina to follow up some dodgy transfer agents. Not that I cared at that stage what anyone thought.

'There was a flight to Buenos Aires at ten o clock the next morning and reported all this to our little gang who all say it was a great idea. Anton and Susanna have no difficulty committing themselves, Jenny had to make a few phone calls to extradite herself for a few more days leave. We were on our way and discretion being the better part of valour we all agreed that an early night was called for as we had to be at the airport at eight and crossing the Madrid traffic at rush hour would need plenty of leeway.

'I contemplated what was to have been an exciting working trip playing detective in some Cuban dives had become a wonderful adventure with the work being an annoying distraction. So much had happened and I pondered on the events of the few days and what was I going to do next? I wanted to tell Jenny so much that she was special but I didn't have any ulterior motive because our age gap was too much and she was just too gorgeous for me to consider any deeper liaison. Would she have believed me? I didn't even believe myself – not for a second.

'Then I thought that maybe I should have adopted a different tactic. Try to be Rupert Everett to Julia Roberts in

My Best Friends Wedding, but he was gay, extremely good looking and about the same age as she was. Did I want to be a confidante, a mate, around to pick up the pieces in a crisis, someone to share a joke knowing that's all it will ever be? Or was I prepared to fight for a life changing relationship? I think I settled for a few days in the sun. I knew I was taking this too far, you just don't become life time buddies in three days. I think of what I could say, and then dismissed it as rubbish. But why was I thinking of engineering situations to be alone with her. Why was I being so devious? Why was I thinking of nothing else. Because that's what men do, I heard an inner calling.'

Dr Sissons feigned exhaustion and raised his hands 'Ben, I think you are tired, we've done a lot today and I want you to remain upbeat. We will continue this tomorrow. I can't emphasise enough that this is real progress, but let's not push too hard too quickly. I'm sure you want to go over in your mind what you've said and try and put some order on what happened to you after this. But you should rest. I know that you may feel good now, but we want to be fresh for the next stage.' He was right I did feel good and confident that I was getting closer to Jenny and what happened to her.

Chapter 5

Dr Sissons arranged that we met again the following day and reported his delight at my ability to recall the events in such detail. I was pretty excited about the way things had gone, but I was aware that my mind was in confusion and that my best remedy was to leave as many of my efforts to recall further events to my time with him. I eagerly awaited the next session and sank into his armchair again with an animated anxiety. I picked up from the previous meeting and our arrival in Buenos Aires.

'After our long flight there was only a three hour time zone difference, consequently we had little jet lag to worry about. We discovered there was a connecting flight to Bolivia within the next four hours.

'Initially that seemed to be great news but four hours in the Airport after our long flight passed the same way time passes with toothache in a dentists waiting room, it took an eternity. But the craic was good even if somewhat dulled by constant travelling and partying over the last few days. Eventually we touched down in the early hours of Friday morning, after having another night of little sleep, although Susanna seemed to have taken full advantage of the journey and managed to sleep through all the meals and movies. After all the necessary delays for baggage and Anton signing virtually everyone's shirt in the entire airport, we eventually arrived in La Paz around eight thirty.

'To be honest I remembered that I felt difficult talking to Jenny. Neither of us showed any encouragement to converse and whilst I was disappointed I knew I was tired and not too sharp. Maybe we both needed the rest, at least that was the way I convinced myself of the unfolding events.

'La Paz was different, first there was the killer blow that the altitude gives you, not feeling sick but just not right and a bit shaky on the legs, though the lack of sleep would contribute to that a little I suppose. Then there was a real culture shock. Everything Anton had promised us seemed to just spill out in front of our eyes. Hundreds of Government officials, in uniform of all different colours, the rather severe looking police in grey with knee high jack boots, soldiers in khaki, what seem like military police with sub machine guns, helmets and flap jackets and best of all the scores of ceremonial guards in red tunics, white over vests, grey trousers and red peaked high hats looking as though they've been imported directly from the British army of the eighteenth century. They were all friendly, somewhat belying their appearance, joining surreally with street beggars in waving and crowds formed to welcome us at every turn. I tried to persuade myself that it was our aura that was causing this hysteria but of course it was the presence of Anton that was the centre of the mayhem.

'I could not believe the respect he was accorded, the man was a God. As we travelled through La Paz in a taxi, for which the driver refused to take any money, people waved and ran over to the car whenever we stopped at traffic lights to press their faces into the window and smile madly. Driving down Avenue Busatamante with sky scrappers on either side, horns were screaming all the time, but not just for us. It was a noisy, mad and if my immediate assessment of the driving was only partly accurate, extremely dangerous city. Nevertheless it was easy to imagine we were the centre of the universe right then.

'Our destination was reached in thirty minutes, after driving through street upon street of shanty houses, directly behind the apparent riches of the city centre. There were stalls at every corner selling everything, from a vast range of clothes, including every material, every colour and every shape; hundreds of hats, top hats and bowlers particularly favoured by women and most bizarrely, llama foetuses to ward off evil spirits. We arrived at a huge house in its own grounds with remote controlled gates opening magically as we approached. The extensive gardens had several gardeners tending to their work, waving as we passed and as we approached the house around eight small kids ran over to the car and jumped on Anton as he emerged from the car. He just loved it, who wouldn't I suppose. Then two elderly women appeared from the house and go to embrace him.

'Their Spanish was frenzied and high pitched, presumably something to the effect of 'Welcome home son, why didn't you write to tell us you were coming.' It seemed to last about twenty minutes without their drawing breath. Susanna, Jenny and I just looked at each other with bemused smiles.'

I glanced over to Dr Sissons again and asked if I was turning the sitting into an advert for the Bolivian Tourist Board but he encouraged my detail 'Feel confident in telling me everything you remember Ben, it sounds like a pretty good trip.'

'It was up to a point and I am enjoying reliving it.' He smiled and I carried on. 'Anton told us later when the bedlam settled down that he owned the house, one of the main benefits of earning more in Madrid in a week than the annual GDP of Bolivia, and all his extended family were engaged in the upkeep one way or another. Probably thirty people lived in the house, which was the state residence for a Spanish diplomat in the days of their colonialism, and there was still enough room for a private wing for Anton's use which was not used in his absence. The four bedrooms were more than enough for us, and again the thoughts of which way this was going to develop flooded through my brain. For the time being however we were allocated one each and I took the opportunity to shower and lie down for a couple of hours to try to recharge the batteries for what I knew was going to be a pretty hectic few days, hopefully weeks if I could stick the pace.

'I phoned home and Paul, feeling afterwards that I shouldn't have bothered in either case, Katie was seemingly totally indifferent to any activity I was involved in and my spending a few days with a Real Madrid player in his home in Bolivia held about as much fascination to her as learning one of the Teletubbies was dyslexic. Paul was a little more animated asking what the fuck I was doing in Bolivia, and move my fucking arse into Cuba in the morning or I'd blow the whole story. Or words to that effect. Trish apparently was making massive progress in Limerick. She had discovered that the

Irish Government had actually built the fuel tankers for Aeroflot with a capacity for four million gallons, even though Aeroflot did not pay a penny in landing fees. The benefit for Ireland was that they could buy some of Aeroflot's spare oil and nearly a thousand flights a year would be channel through Shannon. But there was huge scope for corruption. Which country in the world would build facilities and not charge for services to another countries state run airline whose ideologies could not have been more diametrically opposed? I think you could say that he wasn't too keen on Trish working her arse off whilst I was partying.

'I thought he'd overreacted a bit, I was only a day over schedule and I had covered my tracks perfectly. Alright I was having a good time, but he didn't know that. I didn't mention Jenny to either of them of course but neither did I feel guilty about that. I reckoned it was none of their business, though I wasn't quite sure if a divorce lawyer would quite see it that way. As a concession to Paul I did promise myself that I would get back on track as soon as possible. I could see Trish creating havoc in our office, if she only knew what I was up to, though I knew she would have done exactly the same as I did in my position.

I felt again I was digressing too much and suggested that I should cut out my philosophising. 'No Ben, let your mind go. Once you start leaving things out your subconscious might censor other material on your behalf. It's important that I hear everything that's going through your head.'

He made me feel very secure, very confident and for the first time for a long time, good about myself. I don't know why but I suddenly asked 'Do you mind if I call you Aidan?'

He smiled and replied 'Of course Ben – but my name is George.'

'Oh, sorry, I don't know why I thought...'

'No, no only joking Ben,' and we both laughed as though it was the funniest thing we had ever heard.

'Carry on Ben, this is not only good therapy, it is riveting.' I raise my eyebrows. 'Honestly tell me more.'

'Thanks Aidan,' we smiled again as I prepared to continue.

'After making my calls and getting back to full strength, Anton called over to my room and suggested that we should take a run around the city and see what La Paz had to offer. This seemed like a pretty good idea but we had difficulty finding Jenny who was eventually located in one of the outhouses playing with some young children who were absolutely enthralled by her ability to communicate in sign language.

'After extraditing her, not an easy task, the four of us sauntered in the evening sun shine down side streets, main roads, cafes and bars. Everywhere the reaction was the same. People rushing over to buy us drinks, shake our hands and wish us good luck. I've never been anywhere where I felt so much good will and good humour. We were laughing all the time and of course enjoying the hospitality Anton's fame gave us.

'Sitting at a bar one of Anton's friends from his early career pulled a chair over and sat with us for a while. This scenario had been happening all evening and we welcomed him into our company like all the rest before him. Ramon introduced himself and Anton explained that this man was the most popular politician in Bolivia and had almost single handed built a free health care system for school going children but still had managed to look after himself in the process. Ramon wasn't quite sure whether it was a compliment or not but he took it with a bashful raising of the hands and a rueful smile that exposed the most magnificent teeth I had ever seen. Ramon and Anton then proceeded into a double act that had us engrossed in the quickness of their wit and the sharpness of their observations. Ramon took a particular interest in my career and asked many questions as to how the free press of Ireland worked. Being cynical enough I felt his interest was purely professional and confirms my long held theory that a man only asks you what you do for a living because he wants to tell you what he does. Which he did, but in fairness, with a certain finesse. He struck me as being genuine if a little pragmatic, a quality I have found virtually a pre requisite amongst politicians.

'None of us saw the night fall nor felt the venues change from one end of town to another, from bars to dance floors. The five of us were in a whirlwind of socialising. Despite forgetting any mischievous thoughts that were entering my head towards Jenny, I still couldn't help being impressed with the number of seriously beautiful girls who wanted to join our little set. I saw for a while how superstars lived in a bubble. Not required to make any opening gambit and consequently not having to experience the debilitating self doubts that us mere mortals have to suffer. They can be rude imperiously, not that Anton was. They do not have to spend one penny of the vast fortunes they have collected, as somehow we are all only too delighted to shower them with gifts we can ill afford. There could be a downside of course, as they can be victims of the occasional opportunist who try to engineer difficult situations, but not here. Anton received all the benefits with no fear of being set up.

'The atmosphere was superb, we were all laughing, salsa dancing in groups, talking to strangers, drinking anything that's offered, moving from place to place, eating at different times, getting lost and then hearing the group is in another bar down the street. I saw Jenny surrounded by admirers and consider making my presence felt. Before I could think of anything smart enough to say she was by my side, kissed me on the cheek and whispered in my ear 'Let's show these guys how to rock and roll.' The thought petrified me, but I was delighted that we were together and not only that she had her arms around me. In no time at all dawn started to break and Anton suggested that we should head back to his mothers breakfast which would be like nothing we had ever tasted before. He extended the invitation to anyone who could hear and a group of us head back in huge spirits, Jenny and I locked together in mutual support.

'I declined breakfast much to Anton's mother disgust. I had hoped I wouldn't be faced with her hospitality at seven in the morning, but I make my excuses to get some more sleep. I suggested to everyone that I really had to get moving to answer the call of my bosses and that I should try and get a flight to Havana sometime the next day. Anton said he would look after everything and I had no doubt that he would. I looked around to see if Jenny was making similar excuses but she made no movement. I realised that I had to make the first move and this wasn't the right time. I could hardly stand. In my absence my travel companions had a meeting to discuss all that had gone on in the past few days and decided that it would be such a shame to break up the party.

'Jenny knocked on my room at midday with her hair wet from a morning swim and broke the news to me. I was booked on a flight at four and they were all going with me. She looked drained and laid down beside me, but even before I have time to think what I should do, or what I could do, she fell into a deep sleep. The altitude and last four days had finally caught up with her. I was reluctant to wake her as I watch her peacefully recuperate possibly voyeuristically as her breasts rose and fell gently under her polo shirt. I argued with myself that my motives were purely aesthetic, she was beautiful. I woke her an hour and a half before the flight and her reaction wasn't too friendly but quickly regained her composure. She kissed me full on the lips and we held each other without a word spoken for a few moments. Then she jumped off the bed as though she had an electric shock, smiled at me warmly and ran down to her room, waking the others on the way. I was very, very happy.

'Anton called a car and the five of us, Ramon included as he wanted to join us if we didn't mind- hardly-, crushed in. We arrived at the airport feeling at different levels of recovery, as I got the most rest I was designated to take on the responsibility for check in, getting the hand luggage organised and making sure we all arrived at the right gate with twenty minutes to spare. All went without too much difficulty though we almost had to carry Susanna as she failed to reach consciousness with any great belief.

'I contemplated that five days after I had left Dublin, with almost a lifetime spent in microcosm, I was finally on my way to Cuba to start work on digging O'Hara's political grave, certainly a different man to the one who set out. Now with a much larger agenda and a greater fervour than ever before.

Aidan decides that we have done enough for the time being. 'Let's continue this on Monday, Ben. But don't let go of this momentum. You are doing fine.'

Chapter 6

On Saturday Trish visited me again and I tell her about O'Hara's call and how he had referred to my visiting him in his office claiming I had a story on him using child prostitutes in Cuba. I ask her to investigate anything in my files in the office which might have any relevance to his confession.

'I think all your files had been cleared out after you left.'

'Sorry Trish, what do you mean, after I left? Don't I work there anymore?'

'Jesus, Ben. I didn't realise you really have got this so bad. You resigned after you came back from Cuba with your story about the kidnap and the Friends of Che. You went freelance and we lost touch after you hit Paul. Listen I'll bring in the story you wrote in the News of the World and that should help putting a few more pieces together. I could have done this earlier, I just presumed you would remember all that.'

'It's funny Trish, I feel everything coming back but only when I'm with Aidan Sissons. I'm still blank about everything after our last session. I can't wait to see him again, but I would love to see that article. What was that about my hitting Paul?'

'Um, he wasn't too pleased' she smiled her approval. After promising to visit again soon she left me with another series of unanswered questions swirling around my brain.

I tell Aidan about my discovery of my article but he suggests that we should continue where I had left off. Maybe the story would come back to me in order, and that I would possibly remember more personal details than were in the News of the World. If we do come against a stumbling block we could use the article to unlock what happened after the kidnap.

'Yeah, the kidnap.' I thought to myself aloud 'It is coming back. I remember it happened a few days after we had a dinner party in Cuba.'

'Steady on, Ben start with the five of you arriving in Havana, don't jump the gun.'

'Yeah, Ok you're right. We flew in to Havana and spent an age in the Airport between getting through immigration. Passport control was unbelievably slow, each photograph scrutinised for minutes before they are ungraciously returned with a casual air as though it didn't matter – well why the fuck did they just spent five minutes looking at it, you feel like screaming but you knew that would be unwise. Particularly, when we saw a Chinese man being unceremoniously marched away, amid wails of despair, for some clerical oversight. At least that was what he was claiming, I'd love to know what happened to him. Then through baggage claim, which was probably the most appropriately named room in the world, as numerous disputes over who owned what reign over the proceedings. After dropping dollar notes to virtually every Cuban in the building, I was pre warned to bring of small change, we took the half hour taxi drive into the centre of the city before checking into the Habana Libre Hotel. I was pleasantly surprised, it was a large opulent hotel which apparently was the HQ of Castro during the revolution and had every modern convenience including a swimming pool on the roof. After dinner and a couple of very relaxed mojitos we all retired and let the last few days catch up on us. I can say quite honestly that I went to my room thinking of absolutely nothing else but collapsing.

'After a late breakfast with no sight of the others, I began to think maybe they continued partying after I retired. I made all the necessary arrangements to meet Rory Meagan to get down to my work, definitely a couple of days later than Paul had planned. I knew I should have rang him and let him know what was happening, but I deluded myself into thinking that I should only ring him when I had something positive. After all the shit he had given me on my last call, I decided to let him sweat it out for a while.

'Rory was affable and witty. He had come to Cuba several years ago to live his dream of a pure socialist regime and hadn't regretted a minute of it. He managed to eek a living out of his contacts throughout Ireland and the UK facilitating the import of Irish Whisky and the export of cigars mainly, an under the counter operation due to trade embargoes. He ran the risk of being caught, but it was only the Americans who were bothered by the illegal trade and they weren't in a position to stop a small time operator. To stay in Cuba he had to marry a Cuban girl, a task he had easily accomplished and found very rewarding. His young wife, Leonie, I later discovered, being both beautiful and charming. The price he paid for such home comforts was being 'Persona Non Gratia' in the States for life. There are really bigger sacrifices to make.' Aidan smiled his approval.

'Rory gave me a run down on all the information he had on O'Hara. He had documents proving the transfer of various moneys to his Oconco account which coincided with exact dates and amounts taken out of a Brisas hotel account in Valadero, as far as the accounts show, for consultancy fees. This had been going on for over twenty years and the payments made had been rising annually to reach a figure now of $200,000 per annum. Rory felt he must almost have had Castro by the balls to pay that sort of money. He had come across these payments by one of Leonie's brothers who was an accountant for the hotel group's head quarters in Trinidad on the south coast. He had alerted Rory because he learnt of the ownership of Oconco by O'Hara and thought he would be interested because of his Irish roots. And he was right.

'I suggested Rory join us for dinner that evening to introduced him to everyone, which he thought was a brilliant idea. However I hadn't quite anticipated that he was going to lead us through another wild procession.

'The plan was to travel to Trinidad and have a chat with Leonie's brother. Rory said he would be happy to bring me down and when I mentioned to the others what my plans were they were very anxious to accompany us. I can't say I was in the least bit disappointed. It meant an early start but that would not deter my colleagues who were still very much up for another night on the town.

After all this was Havana the home of decadence and self indulgence. Even if it were all a generation before. They still know how to party and I was in the company of graduates from the school of Rolling Good Times.

'My first impressions of Havana were those of contrast, beautiful colonial buildings with wonderful arches, pillars and balconies bedecked with jeans and under-wear hanging from clothes lines. Well preserved na-tional monuments and stately homes under the Unesco Preservation Scheme surrounded by urban decay not ex-perienced anywhere to my knowledge in the West.

'Away from the preserved areas, the city was literally falling down, even main thoroughfares were pitied with potholes, buildings were held up with wooden beams that extended over the paths on to the road surface. Some streets had no lighting, others had lights every ten yards. On the narrow roads the lighting canopies were attached to the buildings arching over the traffic with the electricity cables criss crossing the street like a wire tunnel. The paintwork on all the metal lamp posts was peeling to the extent that they had become an art form in themselves and I didn't see one man hole that wasn't damaged in one way or another. I suppose the truth is that you only notice the broken ones, but the perception remained. And of course the cars, whilst quite superb, wonderful colours and styles of five decades ago but I estimated the ratio of isopan to original bodywork was about fifty fifty.

'On every corner children, teenagers, young men or women, elderly people and most surprisingly the mid-dle aged congregated in groups which were potentially hostile but in reality were totally the opposite. I remem-ber being greeted by a group of men in their forties, huge waistlines supported by decades of drinking. Their dirty colourful vests exposing their muscular arms as they shouted to us, raising their plastic beakers full of luke warm beer and toasting our wellbeing. One of the men came over clasping what appeared to be a handful of change. He told me that they were authentic treasure trove. Gold coins taken from sunken Spanish galleons and I could have one for $10. No thanks very much. Not to be put off he suggested, as he only has a few left and had to go home, he could let me have two for $10. No, not really my cup of rum. He slouched off with a shrug of the shoulders.

'The younger people were more anxious to see if they could squeeze a few dollars from us, but whilst they would be persistent and inventive in their suggestions (my sister's in hospital, needs drugs, has a baby, studying dance in college, needs a man etc) they were never unfriendly, nor overbearing and could be easily persuaded to go away if given a good humoured put down. Round another corner my first assailant struck again offering the coins for $3 each. Beginning to get tiresome I just turned away. Two for $5 he called down the street. I think they were as authentic as chocolate money!

'And of course the girls were beautiful, friendly and self assured without any arrogance. Despite my profession I am singularly unfamiliar with the trappings of theirs – my knowledge limited to Hollywood and bar room vanity, but they didn't appear to be in the same league as their European counterparts. They looked real and as though they were having fun, but some of them were just too young and depression set in as I thought of the sleaze balls they had to deal with.

'After dinner we went down to a music bar called 'Red' and suffered the indignity of being ripped of by one of the waiters who claimed I hadn't paid him for a round of drinks. There was a Mexican standoff as the six of us faced the bouncers and bar staff. Rory was laughing, 'Let it go, it's only $50, you will never win, just be more careful next time.' I wasn't aware that I was careless and didn't see why I should let the $50 go, but the lesson was learnt, you had to be alert all the time. We tried another bar which was swamped with girls and beat a hasty exit with Anton feeling he was missing something and Susanna determined that he should. In his defence he must rarely go into any bar where he wasn't recognised by all the punters so I understood his reluctance to leave.

'Moving from the bars of La Mina to the racy nite club in Monserrate, the music was hypnotic. I noticed women dancing around their seated partners as what looked like serious deals being undertaken. However mistaken the illusion might have been, I did feel I was witnessing the Cuban underworld, as smoke shrouded the tables, bottles of Havana Club scattered around and women of all ages trying to please their men, who remain totally disinterested.

'During the course of the evening we were split up and I found myself alone surrounded by Cubans delighted to practise their English. I found more about them as they discussed their politics, to my surprise quite freely, without any fear of what they were saying. All that concerned was day to day living. They had their basics from meagre pay but any extras had to come from the dollars extorted from the tourists. But no one was homeless, none were envious, all were happy and bloody good company. However as the time passed I still couldn't bring myself to trust anyone and decided I should find my own way back to the hotel, not being able to locate my fellow revellers. Making my excuses I extradited myself with some difficulty from the company of my new found Havana friends and wandered into the street to realise I was totally lost.

'An elderly woman came up to me, grabbed my hand and started reading it in Spanish. Maybe that's why I've never had it done before, it needs to be translated!'

'Oh, dear God!' Aidan feigns horror with his first words in nearly half an hour. I think his style is absolutely superb, I know this just wouldn't happen with anyone else. The story was revealing itself to me as I spoke and I don't know where each sentence is leading. I feel as though I am on a voyage of discovery. Aidan notices my hesitation.

'Ben, don't try to hide anything. Every detail you remember will trigger your next memory. Keep going.'

Encouraged, I was actually enjoying myself, and could not wait to continue.

'I looked benignly on the woman and after she finished she gestured for payment. I try to pull a couple of dollars from my pocket but two fifties came. She grabbed them and immediately another two girls arrived, both pretty but rough looking. All three were screaming at me, I was conscious of my other money in my pocket, but didn't want them to get away with my hundred dollars. So I held onto the woman's hand gesturing for her to open her clenched fist with my notes inside. Eventually she did and she apparently started ripping up the money. The other two pulled out crucifixes and started a high pitch decade of the rosary. I was being mugged by prayer. The hag, my tolerance level had sunk a little, threw the torn paper in the air and the three disappeared into the crowd that has formed before I had a chance to realise what had happened. I looked at the torn newspaper on the ground and marvelled at the precision of the act, palming my notes and tearing the concealed newspaper. After my anger had subsided, I reasoned that I'd been had, but I'd spent a hundred euro on theatre tickets in Dublin and hadn't seen as good a performance. I checked my back pocket and everything was in place. I had just received my welcome to Havana, but it was late, I was on my own and lost in a strange town. I had to start looking out for myself.

'At my most suspicious I felt a hand in my pocket. It was just a kid, about twelve, but he started screaming at me, as though I'm robbing him, in perfect English. This was another set up and I didn't need it, I could see someone threatening to get the police and offering an amicable solution by my paying a few dollars to help the poor lad get over the trauma. Acting instinctively I pushed the young lad to the ground and brushed pass his accomplices with a feeling of supreme satisfaction. No major achievement but I felt as though I was fighting back. Still two one down in confrontations with the seamier side of Havana life but I felt I should look for an equaliser.

'But it was still only early in Cuban terms but ever mindful of another long journey ahead the next day I decided it was safe and sensible to take the offer of a taxi that was proffered by a rather athletic looking hustler. I welcomed the thought of escaping the tensions of the street and felt the taxi was a safe bet with my new confidence. Not so, I couldn't believe my own stupidity as I followed him around a block to a rather beaten up Lada which had a broken windscreen, no bumpers nor wing mirrors and a driver who was distinctly disinterested. Apprehension took over, this was dodgy but I couldn't get out of this situation without appearing rude. Who gives a fuck about being rude; I argued with myself without any success and clambered into the back of the covered skip with wheels. As my procurer jumps into the passenger side I get decidedly anxious, what was going on? I decided to check my escape routes and discovered that the door handle was governed by a child lock, or just didn't work, and then the window handle fell off in my hand. There's nothing I could do but hope that everything was above board, which had hardly been the case up to then. Trying hard to see any familiar landmarks to get my bearings, I was despairing that all that is pretty useless as I was only in the city a few hours, I hadn't a clue where I was being taken. The one sided idle conversation from the passenger seat as he leant over to ask, ...where was I from?...how long was I staying?...Did I want to meet his sister....Was I enjoying myself?...seemed so insincere and I wanted to ask where the fuck were we going as the journey appeared endless. Surely the hotel wasn't this far, we only were walking a few hundred yards. After I considered virtually every possible outcome the hotel came into sight. Never in doubt. I told my inner doubting instincts, but they were not always wrong.

'I let my mind wander back to Jenny and to wonder what had become of the group when I heard a voice shouting 'Ben, we thought you'd gone to bed, come and join us for a nightcap.' Rory happily pointed to a bar across the road from the hotel absolutely packed to the brim with party people. I was delighted to find everyone there and in good form and relayed my experiences of the last couple of hours. They gave their movements which were closely aligned to mine, without the confrontations and congeniality reigned supreme. Eventually common sense prevailed for around four minutes as we get up to leave, but then quickly disappeared as we decided we needed a good night pizza. Back up the street for another couple of beers and an hours conversation with just about everyone who came into the take away café before reason at last knocked in. We were going to Trinidad in four hours time, lets get some sleep. Conversations with Jenny were limited to general points but I was slowly realising the depth of my feelings as she occupied most of my thinking. From time to time this caught me out as my mind wandered only to be brought back to earth with a bump by a question from someone which I hadn't heard. I blustered my way through looking forward to our trip to Trinidad. I had heard of it's colonial splendour set in a town with virtually no motorised traffic, no signs nor street furniture. A true step back in time, I couldn't wait and my conscience was clear as progress was being made on my journalism even if it had been a little side tracked.

'As we wandered back to the hotel in a group Jenny slipped her hand in mine and smiled saying nothing. I knew I was in love with her and that she was happy with me but my eternal self doubt prevented my making the one step further that I was aching to make. We kissed good night gently with my alter ego giving me a really hard time.

'The next day we started another long journey. It took us eight hours in Rory's rather attractive, but short on modern comforts, 57 Cadillac. The one exception being the exquisite leather bench seats which allowed three to sit both front and back in reasonable comfort. Any pleasure that the seats extended us was more than compensated by the non existent suspension which combined with the less than perfect roads to make a lasting impression on various parts of our anatomies.

'However the previous evening's extravagant behaviour did make sense as each one of us slept at least part of the journey, Anton managing to be comatosed throughout. How Rory kept going I do not know but perhaps it was as well we all did sleep and didn't witness the near death experiences we doubtless had. Eventually we registered in the rather luxurious Brisas Trinidad del Mar Hotel, and after welcoming drinks, a short rest and shower we prepared for dinner with a couple of drinks. After our meal all six of us decided, though I'm not quite sure what my contribution was to that decision, to go into town and head to the first night club we found. Successfully achieving that, the girls were immediately devoured by the local Casanovas trying to impress and I did feel some envy as they were beautiful movers. We guys, in our sense of good humoured tolerance (totally superficial in my case) enjoyed the craic and were occasionally called into action to rescue the situation when the locals tried fairly obviously to lure Susanna and Jenny away. I was beginning to appreciate Cuban life more and more, you were never apparently in physical danger but my God you had to keep your wits about you. It was stimulating.

'After salsa dancing the night away, with some pretty nifty steps of my own (self delusion was a great thing), the evening ended by our getting a taxi together. It appeared to drive for miles through the back streets before finding the road to the hotel. Everywhere was in pitch darkness and in literally the middle of nowhere we got a puncture. Our taxi driver was upset because he was inconveniencing us, and was reluctant to accept my help (he was well prepared for such eventualities having two spare tyres). However the others took advantage of the break by lying full out on their backs in the middle of the road looking up at the stars. It probably went without saying the road wasn't too busy, but it was an indication of the real bonding that was taking place between us, we were beginning to think alike, even if it was in a relatively unconventional if not to say non sensical manner.

'Eventually we got started, returned to the hotel and headed straight for the bar – we were so predictable. The barman prepared pizzas for us all (the beauties of an all in package at four thirty in the morning) and eventually Susanna, Anton, Ramon and Rory give into the call of the bed leaving Jenny and myself alone. We strolled down to the swimming pool and sat at the waters edge with our feet dangling in the water. We seemed to cover every topic under the sun, or more accurately the moon before the conversations get more personal. I wasn't quite sure if she was flirting but with the benefit of hindsight I now know that of course she was, but she started asking what I saw in her that I liked. I stumbled; it was a long time since I had to think like this. I ventured her sense of humour, her compassion, her openness, her vitality, her good looks; I began to feel as though I was going over the top and started to hesitate. Jenny was enjoying my discomfort and wasn't taking notice of any of the compliments I was trying to bestow on her. She took my hand and said 'The reason you like me is because you are at ease with me and you know you don't have to impress. And you like me because you can make me laugh.' She turns and smiled and I'm temporarily fulfilled but brought back down to earth by the thought that I didn't have the courage to ask her why she liked me. Maybe she didn't! I responded with my best smile, longing to kiss her but just chickened out.

'I cannot understand how women always seem to have the psychological advantage but they do. Anyone who suggests that it is just my lack of self assurance is deluding themselves.'

Aidan nods his agreement but suggests I try to keep to the story, my observations were not too relevant no matter how profound.

'When day light broke we eventually sauntered home, with nothing even approaching a resolution regarding the status of our relationship in my mind, I walked her to her door. Another mental conflict but I knew I had missed the moment. We were both exhausted and I didn't want to give her the opportunity to decline any advances because she was literally too tired. I might never recover from the rejection even if it wasn't one.

'Breakfast next day was spent on my own with work upper most on my mind but Jenny was bubbling away just below the surface. I was aware that she was around but I didn't want to chase her too much, the thought that she might think I was stalking her was just terrifying me. I had business to do and had to meet Leonie's brother who was waiting for me at reception. We walked outside to discuss his employer's records that he had uncovered. He was full of information; definite proof of payments made to Oconco amounting to almost two million dollars over twenty years, but was unwilling to release the actual documents for publication, feeling even if it were published five thousand miles away he would be implicated and would lose his job at the very least. Without it there was not enough for the Irish courts, but maybe enough for the Chronicle if I could get something tangible even if it wasn't backed up with documentation.

'Coming back to the hotel, I spent a couple of hours phoning the results of my delvings so far to Paul who didn't seem to be displeased but was hardly over excited. He rather obviously explained that we need more black and white detail pinning O'Hara to the payments. I would get something I reassure him, but I wasn't too sure I convinced him. I was not too sure either if I cared. Out of a sense of duty I rang home, relieved to find the answer machine on. I left a message explaining I was still in South America and that phoning was difficult. The thought depressed me that my lying was almost a prerequisite to all conversations home.

'After lunch we all met up and someone suggested that we take a minibus back into town to look around which I thought a great idea. My inner self was screaming for a break and I really needed to start putting pen to paper, but I knew my stamina was good and I didn't want to waste a moment with Jenny.

'Trinidad was everything I had heard about it. It was stunningly beautiful, full of history and a walk back in time. We arrived at a mini market selling pottery, lace etc which wasn't of the least bit of interest to me and returned to the bus to see Jenny talking to an elderly lady, giving her a lip balm and a few other things she had in her bag in exchange for profuse thanks and an invitation into her house, which she graciously accepted. Afterwards she emerged from the house we rambled into town and go our separate ways. She headed into an art exhibition whilst I went further up the town to taste the atmosphere of the street sellers. I was happy to be on my own taking photos but got caught with the rest of our group bartering at the stalls and I went along with the flow for about half an hour. Then a strange thing happened, as though there was some divine intervention, I lost everyone unintentionally. I was surprised to be on by own, but on reflection, delighted, I consider that I have subconsciously engineered this and if I was watching anyone else I would have had my doubts. I wandered back to the art museum Jenny had entered, not particularly looking for her (my self delusion was still holding up) but just wondering what she had seen. To my surprise she was still there comprising the entire audience listening to a salsa group, who presumably were playing for their own enjoyment.

'She welcomed me, offering the only chair whilst she sat on the floor and asked if I was looking for her. I thought I honestly replied that I wasn't, considering the stalking scenario again, but then went onto say untruthfully that I was looking for any of the group. Having said that I wasn't looking for her I was absolutely delighted to find her and thrilled to get a really friendly reception.

'We were both thirsty and decided after nearly an hour listening to the band to go and look for a bar. They were not too common, or maybe obvious would be more accurate, but eventually we found a café with another salsa band (they were all technically superb and the rhythms were so infectious).

'My memory of this café, which I think was an small square room with around a dozen tables all with red gingham check plastic table clothes, was rather squalid. Across the room the loos were manned by a woman sitting at a card table with an empty saucer and what seemed to be a thirty foot length of scarf she was knitting. We took turns to sample the facilities and on returning

Jenny commented that they were spotlessly clean, due presumably to the knitter. My trip took a little longer which required the explanation that the cistern failed to flush and I had ladle over cups of water from the sink to force a manual flush. While I was telling this story I felt as I do now that I was giving too much detail.

I looked across at Aidan expecting a reaction, but he just gave me a half smile which instilled me with confidence. I realised just what a good counsellor he is – not only does he listen attentively but also he restricts his contributions to encouragement

'Outside we resumed our tour of the town, randomly cruising around the town taking an abundance of photographs. This was heaven to me, every corner was so photogenic. A woman sweeping the dust track outside her home, a man getting his haircut on the street, another in the window of the hairdressers (a very loose description), men playing dominoes on the street, women talking in huddles, cars being repaired, flies chewing the meat on sale, children running amok, teenagers in immaculate school uniforms, families watching TV together in front of an open window, the bicycles, the goat and trap, all the classic cars, modern buildings painted in pastel colours we wouldn't normally consider and historic buildings of splendour. And the babies, Jenny could not resist talking to any that passed by and took the opportunity to give one that was particularly cute a cuddle. She befriended everyone and they all took to her openness. I felt totally accepted because she was with me, and marvelled at how much goodness shone out of her.

'We met one of the guys from the disco the previous night who gave us a 'High five, my man', welcome and

I honestly felt it was genuine. Back up to the open air disco of last night which doubled as a café in the afternoon, we passed countless people in doorways all free with a smile, no matter what age or sex. Darkness was beginning to set in but for some reason Jenny decided to do a bit of sunbathing on the stone terracing in the setting sun. I managed to capture this rather surreal scene on camera as she lay in total discomfort, virtually upside down, across the steps looking paradoxically ridiculous and erotic.

'Leaving the café we decided to look round the church and the priest entered at the same time to say the evening mass to a congregation of around thirty. We, or rather Jenny, decided to stay and we listened to the priest welcome us all and sing most of the scriptures which was really quite moving as he had a wonderful voice enhanced by the uplifting acoustics. During the 'Peace be with you' he made the point to come down to us to shake hands and we were encouraged to greet everyone on our side of the church, all of whom had a smile for us. A tourist took a flash photograph from the back of the church and the priest illustrated the other side of his character with a withering look at the offender, who quickly retreated. The half hour quickly passed, pretty rare in my mass attendance experience and we drifted outside to discover the night had fallen and it was pitch black.

'It was around seven and we were both exhausted (we've been travelling, walking, dancing and drinking for the past five days with only a few hours sleep). After the smallest of discussion, when we discovered we had no money, we opted for the taxi home. It was not difficult to find a suitable Chevy and I was certain I would be able to find one of our colleagues quickly enough to pay the fare when we got back to the hotel. Although that proved to be true I forgot that the taxi driver had to drop us three hundred yards from the door, part of the self imposed apartheid the Cubans have inflicted on themselves whereby they are not allowed in tourist hotels. Not only disturbing it was bloody inconvenient and our driver had to wait fifteen minutes for his fare.

'After an hours rest, a shower and quick dinner I went down to the bar and joined everyone except Jenny and enthused over our day. I loved my photography and the town offered so much in the way of unspoilt beauty particularly, I think, of the human spirit. Difficult to explain but I knew I was getting through to a few that we were in a special place. I wonder how many of them realised that my vision, if not entirely awoken by Jenny, was certainly inspired by her. I had a great day and it showed. I wondered virtually all the time if she experienced any of these warm feelings as she recovered. Of course I would never dare to ask her.

'She joined us a little later and we decided that in spite of the allure of another night out in Trinidad, we should take it easy and head over to the bar for a quiet drink. Back into the bar, second wind (or is it the twenty second?) gave enough energy for more conversations. After so much partying there was little reason to anything we were saying but covered virtually every topic with a deep understanding and concluded with an ephemeral observation. Eventually tiredness and boredom took their toll on one by one until there were only the two of us left around two o clock.

'Jenny leaned over, kissed me and ran down to the beach. Without a word she peeled off her clothes and I followed her lead and jumped and I was immediately comforted by several thoughts. Everything was so peaceful; the sky was a dark navy blue, clear with a magnificent moon and a full display of stars. The water was warm, calm and heavy. It was so easy to float without waves splashing in your face. There was a sweet smell of fauna and no noise not even the lapping of waves on the shore. It was really perfect and then there was Jenny just looking beautiful. I knew she was naked but couldn't really see her except for the sweet, smiling, honest, fresh face that filled me with desire.

'The two of us messed around, looking away from the stars it was totally dark and she had moved away and couldn't be seen in the pitch black and nothing, really nothing could be heard. The quiet was interrupted by Jenny's inevitable but ridiculous Jaws impression, and then we tried some aquatic gymnastics which she performed with reasonable aplomb, but her attempt to spin me through a backward summersault was less than graceful, though it ended with our collapsing in each others arms. Smiling she kissed me and without warning she locked her legs around my waist in a moment I will never forget. We made love at the water's edge without thought of anything or anyone. If I had a description of paradise this was it. As we lay together on the warm sand she whispered 'I love you' and I think I cried for the first time in my adult life. I felt stupid, I've got used to it recently, but I was ecstatically happy but realised my life was a mess. She knew I had problems and said 'Come on lets get a shower' and we went back to her room where we slept in each others arms for eight whole hours.'

'How do you feel now, Ben? I think you've come across a point of discovery. A memory that we treasure, the first time you make love to a woman you are passionate about. A moment you never forget, but you did. At this point of recall are you elated or further confused as to what happened next?'

For the first time Aidan has asked a question that requires some soul searching and I wasn't quite sure if I was ready for it. 'I don't know, it doesn't seem new to me. It's not like watching a film for the first time, just a rerun of an old movie I was in years ago. Does that make sense?'

'Ben, you are making complete sense and I don't want to interrupt your thoughts, but I do feel this is a critical point in your relationship.'

'That's it, I don't think it was. It just happened but nothing really changed. I was still totally unsure of where I was with her. She was aware of my home life and what happened that night just happened. I still didn't have the confidence to take it further. I didn't have anything to offer but the present and that could end at any time.'

'Ok, that's fine, carry on if you feel Ok.'

'Erm... I do. The next day suitably revived by our good night's sleep, it was almost midday when we surfaced; we planned our journey back towards Havana. The target was Valadero on the Northern coast to follow up the leads I had on O'Hara. Leonie's brother came with us to facilitate my investigation but his presence did leave the back seat very crowded. He enthralled us all on the journey up on Cuban life, so different from the West, the good humour, the contentment, the good will and the lack of greed, but also a lack of ambition. Money has a lot to answer for.

'A new hotel and a new resort, still four days left and yet so much has happened. I decamped in my room and ponder on the events of the last few days and what was I going to do next? I was thinking about Jenny constantly, about what I should do next and I really had no idea. That evening and most of the next day whilst trying to concentrate on tracing O'Hara's footsteps, was spent thinking what to say to Jenny, how to say it and how could I manoeuvre a suitable time and place to do it.

'The confusion, which was rapidly enveloping my life, could have been sorted by the obvious solution. This was ridiculous, just get back to work and forget her or face her with a direct question. But I could not think straight. On one hand she was fun to be with and I was experiencing thoughts I haven't had for a long time. On the other I was much older, had enough baggage to fill a plane and I really didn't know how she felt about me.

'After a shower and a beer I headed down to the beach where every one else was and decided to take a long walk to try to capture the impending sunset from a unique vantage point. This took over an hour and by the time I got back to our end of the beach it was completely deserted, except for Jenny reading on a sun bed in the twilight of dusk.

'Every thought rushed through my mind. I hadn't engineered this but it was happening. We were alone. Was it fate? Or maybe she was waiting for me – to say what, possibly that I was giving her the creeps, oh God I hoped not.

'Somehow I just thought she was going to say that she wanted to cool the situation that she had to get back to Madrid fairly soon and that we shouldn't see each other again when she got home, Realising that circumstances were really out of my control I got up to go, devastated by the possible outcome. We ended up talking on our evening plans without once mentioning where we were going beyond the next twelve hours. My indecisiveness only added to my despair. I agreed to all her suggestions and headed back to my room for more analysis of all that was churning up my mind.

'I realised I had to contact Paul again. To say progress was slow was rather the understatement of the year. But that didn't really concern me. I got through without any difficulty on the outrageously expensive phone line and waited for Paul to tear strips of me. But his mood was conciliatory and insisted that getting the facts right was the major concern. Time was not the essence, no one else had the story and when it does come out, it will blast O'Hara out of the water. He went onto say Trish had done great work digging up the dirt in Limerick. She had discovered that Aeroflot did not pay for any in plane services they took from Shannon and a multitude of Irish suppliers. All that was provided by the Government in return for a couple of million gallons of fuel Aeroflot had lying around in the huge facilities the Irish had built for them. No wonder the Russians were so grateful for the arrangements made for them by … guess who? She had gone through Dail records and minutes of County Council meetings to discover who said what and had realms of supporting evidence that O'Hara did all he could, along with a Fergus Browne from Clare County Council and a Sheila O'Callaghan in the Department of Transport. And surprise, surprise they all attended Trinity at the same time. Paul then asked me what sort of guy Rory was and if he was trustworthy. Sound, I say, which was a fairly accurate assessment of how I felt about him. For the first time in a while I got off the phone feeling better than when I started the call. I didn't risk the mood by phoning home.

Aidan nods his understanding but I can see he is tiring. I don't know why the patient should be concerned for the doctor's well being, but I did feel I should try and finish. But I was feeling good, it was like seeing the rushes of a film you've starred in for the first time. I couldn't wait for the next bit even though I had already lived through it. I told myself not to stop now.

'To my relief the next night we settled for a quiet dinner together on the self service buffet which appeared delicious but somehow always disappointed. I wasn't in the mood for any meal or conversation for that matter after I thought Jenny had killed off our romance just after we had got past the first hurdle. But I realised I was the focus of the group and I couldn't just disappear to go and sulk on my own. It wasn't just me, the whole mood was sombre, somehow we all need a battery recharge. However that did not stop our full compliment heading down afterwards to the swimming pool bar where there appeared to be a bit of tension between the Canadian and German tourists. Both groups comprised of men and women built like small marquees, and possessing no sense of humour, no style and no class. There wasn't one solitary reason for getting involved with them but Rory couldn't help baiting the Canadians who thought everything should be judged by its physical attributes.

'The Germans felt that Rory's sharp intellect was siding with their arguments for order and control, discipline and patience in all things, but Rory turned his attention to them, ridiculing their lack of flexibility, dourness and more damning their lack of integrity and character. I had this feeling that like Basil Fawlty he was going to mention the war either on purpose just to really stir things up or accidentally which actually might be worse. For the sake of World Peace Rory avoided falling into the trap, but with the benefit of a few drinks I could see the merits of an ethnic row in the middle of paradise, maybe a few scores might have been settled. Even without that happening, the situation was actually getting quite tense, with both the Germans and Canadians both turning on Rory whilst the rest of us were beginning to find the conversation tedious.

'After a series of derisive remarks one elderly Canadian lady felt she could take no more saying she had been a visitor to the hotel for thirty years and had never been so insulted. She insisted she would make it her business to have us evicted. 'Go and fuck yourself', was Rory's less than sparkling repartee, though in his defence his slow delivery did put a certain emphasis on his full understanding of what he was saying. It all proved too much for the recipient and she stood up, breathing fire and said she was going to get the manager, no one ever spoke to her in that language.

'Jodete y aprieta el culo' was Rory's more incisive response but it went over her head.

'As she left a dark, tall man probably in his sixties but very sprightly with leathery skin spotted by black liver marks from too much sun stood up and applauded Rory. He went over to him saying she got just what she deserved but his companion, a very attractive women with raven black short straight hair, of Latin extraction with unblemished olive skin and impeccably dressed in a pale blue silk shirt draped outside Gucci faded jeans, grabbed him from behind and pulled him back into his seat saying 'Felix, behave yourself.'

'Rory acknowledged the humour of the situation took Felix' hand and introduced himself. Felix responded by introducing Maria Rodriquez, his travelling companion. Rory took Maria's hand and introduced Jenny, Susanna, Anton, Ramon and myself. Unbelievably we spent the next couple of hours chatting as all our fellow residents who were enjoying the banter as much as ourselves, fell off one by one unable to stick the pace but very appreciative as to the way the arrogant Germans and loud Canadians had been dispatched. On our own again with the exception of our new friends, Maria and Felix, we eventually adjourned to take a midnight Jacuzzi bringing our drinks with us. So much for the good intentions of an early night and my depression over Jenny had seemed to have lifted.

'One of the hotel managers came down to us and suggested that we could tone down our criticisms of our fellow guests, pointing out that we were all on holiday trying to enjoy ourselves. Rory was on the point of rebuttal but thought the better of it, realising the difficult job of appeasement the staff have. I think Chamberlain gave it a bad name. It's an art form.

'He encouraged us to stay in the Jacuzzi and sent down a bottle of champagne to show no ill will. It transpired that Maria was heading back to Mexico in a couple of days and the next day would be her last full day. Susanna suggested that we should throw a decent dinner party in her honour in a restaurant a little better than the buffet meals we have been subjected to over the past few days. We all agreed that it was a brilliant idea and commissioned her to set up the details. The night ended at the almost respectable hour of four o clock with the cumulative effects of the past week slowly catching up on all of us. Circumstances prevent me from advancing my cause to Jenny, and she did not appear too concerned that I had not been able to talk to her on her own. I would have loved to know if she was hurting as I was but I had never been too perceptive in these matters.

'I woke up late the next day realising that I had to make some progress on O'Hara and decided to visit the hotel he was reputed to have a share in. Taking photographs, asking staff if they had ever seen him but without any luck. However the background was useful information and I visited the offices with Leonie's brother. He was unwilling to show his hand too much in front of his colleagues but did manage to photocopy bank statements showing cheque payments cashed and also some rather dubious invoices from a management consultancy company which cross referred to times payments were made to Oconco. Nothing too specific but if I could tie down this consultancy firm with O'Hara as being the beneficial owner then I would be making progress. It would all help to satisfy Paul on my next call to Dublin. Some effort made, my conscious clear, my mind concentrated on getting ready for the dinner party. I knew Susanna and Jenny had found this ideal spot in the forest, which they felt would be extremely intimate with the best salsa band in Cuba, according to Susanna, playing just for our benefit. With Jenny tied up in this task and my rummaging through the bank statements of the Brisas group we don't meet at all during the day. Apart from evening cocktails, more mojitos, when we all discussed the evening's entertainment briefly, I did not see her until arriving at the restaurant. As she was in the earlier taxi to finalise the arrangements with Susanna and Rory, she was already at the table when I arrive and I was stunned to see her. Her hair coiffured up on her head exquisitely, nails and lipstick a matching delicate pink, subtle blue mascara which magnificently brought alive her soft eyes she looked just wonderful. Adorned by a long cotton evening dress, simply cut in a floral pink she shone out of the forest like a celestial light. I thought I had never seen anything as beautiful and just when my eyes were beginning to well up at my loss, she smiled and beckoned me over to sit on the seat next to her.'

'Ben, I think we'll call a halt for today. I know you are about to go to the part of your story that holds the key to your trauma and you need to be fresh. I'll prescribe a sedative now and I want you to rest before we resume. Try not to think about the party until the next session. We have to face your difficulties together. I am delighted with your progress, things are looking very good and we'll have you out of here in no time.' Aidan was upbeat but I wasn't sure it was out of his self interest he was delaying things. He looked shattered, whilst I felt alright, even if I was confused about where my relationship with Jenny was going.

Chapter 7

Aidan did not return for three days which surprised and disappointed me. If I am that important to him and I am doing really well, why wasn't he here?

The day after my long session with Aidan, Trish arrived in with news of a surprise she had for me. I was expecting her to have a copy of the News of the World so I presumed that held the secret of her surprise so I didn't pursue it. I told her of my recall of all that had happened with Aidan and she took an interest in Felix and Maria.

'I read about them in your article and I couldn't figure out what they were doing there.'

I felt as though I could explore my mind as to whom Maria and Felix were, without compromising my promise to Aidan not to delve further with the story without him. I was anxious not to lose the impetus and tried to piece together what I remembered of our new friends.

'Maria told us her history and it was fascinating. Felix turned out to be a CIA agent and had a view on virtually everything that had happened in the world for the last forty years. They had met in Mexico nearly fifteen years earlier and had kept in touch. Their meeting resulted from Maria's tragic loss of the love of her life.'

Trish interrupted with a smile on her face, this sounds as though your memory is flooding back, Ben. I'm all ears for a bit of scandal.'

I shake my head in mock disbelief, 'Well, to start at the beginning her father, Ernesto was a crusading publisher in Tijuana.

'He had been running a series of exposé's in the weekly political magazine he founded with his friend Jesus. They had been targeting corruption in politics, business leaders, the judiciary, even fellow journalists to such an extent the paper was the most widely read in Mexico. Their influence enormous, but it brought them powerful enemies.

'One day in the late eighties Ernesto noticed his automobile was being followed as he drove into work alone and he was apprehensive. This was not an unusual occurrence and he had mentioned to friends of his concerns. He watched the station wagon in his rear view mirror and failed to respond quickly enough when a black Pontiac Trans-Am shot out of a side street to blocked his path. He swerved to avoid the van he glanced off the front wing and as he ground to a halt he was still more conscious of his follower than the men who dismounted from the van. Suddenly he saw one of them was carrying a .12 rifle which, before Ernesto had time to react, he brought up to his shoulder and fired at close range killing him instantly. Both men hurriedly returned to their vehicle, nodding to the driver of the station wagon and sped off leaving Ernesto's body slumped over the horn in the centre of the road.

'The reaction to Ernesto's murder brought two immediate consequences which had wide ranging effects. Immediately there was a public outcry that such a public figure would be cut down for his crusade. The media joined forces in a concerted attack on a local businessman whose body guards were linked to the murder. Marches across Tijuana demanded that the killers be brought to justice and the elections that were in progress at the time of the murder were transformed by which candidate could promise most results in the investigation.

'Although two people were eventually convicted for the murder both claimed police brutality had forced confessions and it was evident that whilst the perpetrators of the murder may or may not have been caught, those responsible for giving the orders had got away without charge. And who was the driver of the station wagon who had supervised the whole operation?

'These questions played heavily on Maria who vowed to carry on her father's work with a fervour and passion that her father would have been proud of. She began her journalistic career as Jesus' new partner, and whilst he first harboured doubts as to her style, he never doubted her integrity, devotion and commitment as her column quickly attained the same status as her father's and even moved on the boundaries. I know this sounds as though she was arrogant but she told the whole story in a matter of fact way that I never doubted her. She was fearless. Her enemies were wary of direct intervention in silencing her with so much popular support.

'Maria's assault on officialdom was having a profound effect throughout Mexico, bribes were becoming less common, people were less afraid to speak of corruption, political debate became more open, but along side that the drug problem grew and a new scourge the smuggling of illegal immigrants into the States for huge fees meant Maria was never short of a leader story. Violence was never far away either in a poverty stricken country that saw much social injustice. The gap between rich and poor was openly flaunted in a society that craved change.

'Maria's personal life was apparently one of the casualties of her success. Whilst familiar with all the strata of Mexico's social world, most eligible young men were fearful of such a dynamic figure who had so many powerful enemies. Whilst her reputation preceded her, it did have a filtering effect on weeding out those who were just not up to the mark on moral fibre. Men who did seek her attention were men with ulterior motives, easily spotted, or those drawn to her by her passion, vitality, moral courage and her undeniable beauty. Juan Cortez was one such man.

'Juan was brought up in the playground of Tijuana's rich. Enjoying all the fruits of life that his father's hotel chain brought him, he found in his late teens that his privileged position squared badly with his social conscience. After he left university he felt the power of his father's influence and joined the family business, convincing himself he could do more from within the system than from the outside. He campaigned for better working conditions for his staff, taking up many issues of wages, housing, education and health until his father's patience could take no more and he decided that if Juan wished to pursue his crusade against the profitability of the company, he should at least do it without taking a salary from it.

'Juan found his new freedom exhilarating. Knowing from his former staff of all the deprivations of Mexican society he quickly threw himself into the sub world of the shanty towns on the outskirts of the city. Familiarising himself with local mafia, but gaining the confidence of the people, living amongst them – tending to their health problems, offering legal advice whenever injustice arose, organising worker co-operatives whereby casual labour could be acquired without the help of the self serving gangers and acting as arbitrator and even judge when disputes arose. He made enemies but many more friends who came to regard his hut in the centre of the slums as the social centre of the community. He paid no rent, earned no income but lived on the generosity of the people he helped, which was little in material terms but always enough to keep him rich in food, drink and cigarettes.

'Whenever he felt the need for more medical supplies or books for the schools, he felt no embarrassment returning home and demanding that his father supported him. He never asked for any other help and always pitched his requests at a level that he knew would not be refused so that he could return in a few weeks time. His father, for all his bluster and feigned annoyance, was proud of his wayward son even though he wished Juan would return to the fold and leave his social work to the authorities.

'Juan kept up this life style for three years but was aware of the increasing influence the people smugglers were having. With life in the slums being nothing more than hand to mouth, frequently, despite Juan's best efforts, it was no more than the survival of the fittest; life in the

States promised so much. Guarantees of a safe passage across the boarder, work freely available and accommodation in hostels sounded so good that many felt the two thousand dollar fee an attractive option. Of course none had that money unless they got into the drug trade, whereby they could save a deposit and pay the balance out of their wages in the States. This spiral into the criminal world generated endless problems for Juan who campaigned to expose the conditions those who subscribed would discover.

'The cattle trucks driving the immigrants were frequently caught by the US authorities and sent back. To save having to pay refunds the drivers didn't take the refugees home but to the mountains where they could not tell of their failures. Their deposits lost, they became drifters, many not surviving the extremities of the Sierra Madre's climate without the drugs they had become dependant on. Those lucky enough to run the gauntlet and get into Florida or Alabama found their wages amounted to little more than a few dollars after their keep and repayments to the smugglers had been deducted. Letters home were delusional, always painting the bright side but rarely accompanied with the promised few dollars to help out at home. All of which prompted more interest in the traffickers promises.'

Trish suddenly interrupted in mock annoyance 'Yeah this is all very well but I was asking about Maria and Felix not a run down of the Mexican Social Deprivation. I'm beginning to think you were better company with no memory.'

'Thanks a bunch, you never change do you? I have to give you the background to explain why Felix and Maria became friends. They weren't exactly the most obvious couple in the world. Actually I don't think I've ever met a more diametrically opposed couple as regards age, gentleness, passion and politics.'

'Go on then' she smiled through an exaggerated yawn.

I didn't hesitate. 'When Maria's column decided to show exactly what was happening to the thousands of illegals who were risking so much and being so mistreated she came across the name of a young man who had given up his birthright to work in the slums and asked if she could interview him. Maria met Juan on the 30 December 1993, both aged twenty six, both deeply scared by life, fighting the same war but from opposite ends of the battlefield.'

'How do you know the date?'

'Just listen will you. Their attraction was not instant, it was a whole day before they first made love, after a riotous night seeing in the new year in the slums. Maria could not believe the raw excitement, the anticipation of a new beginning that a new year brings even to the most deprived. The hope, the joy and the total respect that nearly everyone had in the ghetto for Juan. Both had lived several years without a true confidante, a soul mate but once they had discovered each other they spent every spare moment together. There weren't many, and the few were divided between Juan's sparse hut where Maria became a very welcome guest to all his neighbours and her sophisticated up town apartment, where Juan never saw one of hers.

'Their love was a discovery, neither having anything more than random affairs in the past. They found in each other passion, faith, anger, pain. They were each others religion. They were one.

'She really got to you didn't she?'

'Are you interested in this or not?' Trish's silence encouraged my engaging full throttle again.

'Their devotion to the same cause brought them together in the working lives as well, even if Maria was the crusader, Juan the soldier. But scarcely a day went by without interaction between them in the hectic world they chose to inhabit. Hardly an hour passed without them thinking of each other. Their social life was always invaded by someone who needed Juan's help or a lead that might expose more corruption in the dangerous world that Maria was fighting. Although their affair was all consuming, their time together on their own was rare and precious.

'It was one of those moments in Juan's room that was disturbed by a scratching at his door and a gentle but desperate whisper through the ill fitting frame.

'Juan jumped up to open the door for the young teenage son of one of his friends whom Juan had known for several years. He had seen Jose grow up from a cheeky street urchin with a smile for everyone to a troubled young man, bitter at the way life had treated his family and determined to fight his way to a better world. But Jose was not looking for trouble now, he was frightened.

'Juan was gentle but firm. He was totally committed to sorting Jose out, not thinking for a moment of his lost time with Maria. But she knew how he worked and fully supported whatever action he wanted to take.

'Jose told his story, unfortunately not too uncommon. He had set his sights on a new life in the States, where he could build a career for himself and send money home for his little brother to get the proper medical attention his asthma required. He met Rual Levisa, a lowlife who promised to get him into the States if he could sell a few joints a week. As targets were raised to meet his savings plan, failure meant he had to act as runner for heavier stuff. If he really wanted to speed up this progress he could start selling the crack himself. Then he was told how he could make it himself and was eventually churning out enough of crack to get every teenager in Tijuana high. Things all happened so quickly and before he realised how deep he had got caught up in this under world, his little garage factory was turned upside down and burnt to the ground after all the contents were removed. Jose knew who it was but couldn't say anything because he feared for not only his own life, but also his family's. He turned to Levisa for support only to find that his friend introduced him to two heavies who wanted their investment back and that if he didn't have $30,000 inside a week he could say goodbye to every visible limb he and his brother had. That was six days earlier, and Jose knew those guys would arrive early. Jose was pleading for help and appeals didn't get much more frenetic.

'Without seeking moral approval from Maria, Juan sat Jose down and spoke very seriously. Juan told Jose to go to the police and tell them all he knew. Name names of people he'd met, name places you'd been. And Juan would guarantee that his family would be safe in a new home out of Mexico.

'Jose went into hysterics claiming Juan had no idea what he was dealing with. There may be a couple of pigs who don't receive a bonus at Christmas from the Mexican Mafia, but he didn't know how you would spot them. They all looked the fuckin' same in uniform. He knew if he put one foot in the door of the police station he would be dead before the day was out. Jose stormed out of the door as Juan physically restrained him and told him of his plan B.

'Maria would drive him and his family to a safe house near the boarder for a few days while he sorted something out.

'Not much of a plan' Trish said helpfully. Before I had a chance to reply she held her hands up in mock apology. Whilst she was having a similar effect as Aidan her style couldn't have been much more different.

'A couple of hours later Juan returned with the Valdes family. The mother and father had rarely moved out of the ghetto and sought for nothing in their life other than contentment and solace for their three children. Their daughter Camilla, barely in her teens but displaying the blooming good looks of her mother and ten year old son Constante, pale and breathless, desperately looking to return to the bed he had been dragged from. All were quiet save for Constante's heavy hissing but all anxiously looking at Jose, expecting explanations as to why their life had been turned upside down in the space of sixty minutes but also knowing that they would not get one.

'Ben, I know Dr Sissons has been patient with you but that's not my style. Is there a point to all this.' Trish was never one to be slow in speaking her mind.

'Do you want this story or not, I thought you were the patient researcher, not leaving a stone unturned.'

'Just get on with it and wake me up when you get to anything interesting.' I strangely felt good that I was annoying her, it was like the old times. I was happy to give as much detail as I could.

'Juan arranged visas for all of them, don't ask how. It was only then Maria realised that Juan had not spoken to her for nearly three hours. He had assumed that she would do his bidding and she would. She took pride in the strength of their relationship that there was so much mutual understanding, belief in each other and so much could be left unsaid. She knew, maybe for the first time in her life, that she had found her mentor, her partner, her saviour, her happiness.

'Maria did as she was told and made sure as far as she could that Juan's instructions were followed precisely and that there were to be no retributions until after all this was settled. However she knew that Jose's father wanted to lay into his son, and Camilla was virtually inconsolable as she came to terms with the fact that she would never see her friends again and she was very close to a breakdown. Hour followed hour with no word from Juan in a town that had nothing to offer tourists with money to spend, never mind penniless refugees in hiding from … they had no idea what.

'On the third day of their self imposed imprisonment, Juan called Maria to say he had visas arranged and would be down the next day when all their nightmares would be over. True to his word he arrived, but not alone. A swarthy middle aged man was with him and had an air of a man who was supremely confident, outgoing and strong, both mentally and physically. Hard to assess where he was from, for although his English was perfect he didn't sound American, and his Spanish was equally fluent with perfect intonation to give the belief he could have been native Mexican. But his demeanour was authoritative, calculating and daring. He was in control, he certainly wasn't Mexican.

'Don't tell me. It was Superman.'

'Would you ever shut up.' I despaired of Trish but inwardly knew she was enjoying herself too.

'Juan introduced him as Felix and they all shook hands to mutual distrust. Jose was uneasy, he knew this is payback time. Your family are safe – now tell us what you know. Felix took Jose away whilst Juan comforted his mother with assurances that Jose would come to no harm, but he had to help Felix or face the prospect of some time in a Mexican prison, which everyone knew was not a very enticing prospect.

'Jose understood what was being asked of him and he saw what was on offer. A fresh start and a new identity for his family. He would never go back to Mexico to face whoever wanted to shaft him. There was no decision to make but he just felt the information he had was not enough to be worthy of this great prize. Rual Levista was small fry and anyone else he met he could only describe in general terms. And young Mexican hoodlums were not exactly rare. He did try; he did whatever he could out of respect to Juan, grateful that his family had secured a better life for themselves – even if they weren't aware of it right at that moment. Felix was pleased with every last detail he could extract from Jose.

'After two days Maria drove the family to their new home and life and she returned to find where exactly this had taken her and Juan.

'It wasn't long before she discovered it was to a new plane. If life had been hectic before with moments alone together rare jewels, they were now just fond memories. Juan discovered that what he had done, facing down the mafia did not meet with universal approval in the ghetto with friends of both sides of the warring factions. His work with Felix was viewed with suspicion by everyone and his base in the ghetto had eroded away.

'After months of finding a level where he felt he could make a difference, Juan began to restore his confidence levels with most of his neighbours and Maria found through stress that their relationship was indestructible, at least by their own hand. But in mid 1996, more than a year after Jose's call to them Juan was gunned down in an ally way by two young mobsters who ambushed him without even letting him know he was being hunted.

'Jesus!' Trish exploded out of her inertia. 'I was getting really fond of him. What did Maria do?'

'Maria was inconsolable, her grief intensified by Felix taking her aside and revealing that he was working for the CIA and that she was in real danger from these villains who would never stop looking for revenge. He told her he had tried to get Juan to leave the ghetto but he never would. It was too late for Juan now but it was time for both Maria and Felix to get out. His time done, his cover threadbare, it was only a matter of time before someone discovered his connections.

'Maria refused to leave Tijuana, continuing to crusade in her magazine, but was ever watchful. Her surroundings did make any intruders very conspicuous. And whilst she was circumspect she felt she owed it to Juan's memory to make life as difficult as possible for his assassins.

'She continued with the newspaper for years with exhilarating highs and depressing failures in exposing the criminal world. No one ever came close to replacing his presence and she told me a day never passed without thinking of him.

'When Felix returned to the States, she did not hear from him nor of him for several years, until in October of 2003 he arrived at her office, all smiles, a bunch of flowers and an invitation to a few days away. He was on route to Cuba and would love some company. Nothing but the best, and a guaranteed good time. Initially she rejected his offer out of hand but on reflection she needed a break, he was a wonderful story teller and she hadn't had any male company unrelated to work for years. Suddenly it all felt like fun. 'Let me finish a few things here and I will follow you over. I promise.'

'I'll make you a promise too, I'll never again ask you to tell a story, I have to go. I'll see you tomorrow.' Trish sprang out of the room before I had chance to question her further on her surprise, but I was getting tired, the effects of Aidan's sedatives were kicking in.

The next day Trish arrived in the hospital with the surprise she had promised. As she opened the door I could see someone was standing behind her. She looked at me a little sheepishly and said 'Hi Ben, I'd like you to met....' And Susanna stepped forward. I couldn't believe it.

On seeing her, my memory flooded back. I actually get the sensation of surging water booming through the tumbling walls surrounding my brain and in an uncontrollable rage I knock her over by pushing her shoulders aggressively with both hands. Trish is horrified by my reaction but stands by helplessly as I stand over Susanna screaming at her.

'You betrayed us; you lead us all into a trap and watched as four of my friends were killed. You bastard. You bastard.'

Susanna was crying, Trish was hysterical and I was defiant.

'Ben, calm down,' Trish was pulling me away and I eventually submitted to her will and fell back on my chair weeping as the whole story unfolded with ever increasing pain. The pleasantries of the ordered detail of my reminisces with Aidan were replaced by sharp images of unguarded hostilities. I felt out on my own, white water rafting to the depths of my troubled mind. It was all very vivid.

PART TWO

The Dinner Party

Chapter 8

I remembered thinking that this was Utopia, overstated perhaps but still wonderful. The conversational topic of who would be your eight favourite dinner guests was being played out for real. Not as I would have selected, as I had not known any of my companions two weeks earlier but as it turned out I could not ask for more stimulating company, even if in some cases it was irritating from time to time.

My friends who had gathered together in the middle of the Cuban hillside had collect several lifetimes of diverse experiences, but shared a common bond, a love of life, an appreciation of soul and a great respect for the wondrous gift of humour. By including myself I was perhaps being a little generous with the assessment of my own gifts. I prided myself more on the ability to dissect those of others.

Felix, a fascinating character, in his late sixties but had a treasury of experiences all the diplomatic work for the States had given him in the trouble spots of the World. And he was only too willing to share them with a wonderful philosophy on life in which materialism played no part. His slant on events that had dominated our front pages over the past three decades was illuminating, and always expressed with a different perspective to the conventional wisdom. He saw pathos in triumph, humour in defeat, sadness in homecoming, joy in treachery in a way I have never heard narrated. Yet deep down I felt this man had a darker side. A quiet man, but a character honed from life and not a sufferer of fools. Not that he was in the presence of any this night, with the exception of yours truly. I did not believe that of course but I did believe that if you continually underscore yourself, others will as well, which gives you the element of surprise when you do display your true intellect. Assuming of course you get the opportunity, otherwise it is a disastrous tactic.

Then there was Rory, Irish, in his forties but with the political passion of a first year student, could there be a better description of a pain in the ass? Extremely well read on revolution and a deep understanding of what drives people, in my case – mad. Politically he was at the opposite end of the spectrum to Felix but very similar in human responses. Like Felix he could tell a story that captivated his audience but never dominated the proceedings and always encouraged contribution from less informed participants whom he would enlighten with humour and his joie de vie. There were times when I felt this bordered on being sickeningly patronising but his quintessential cynicism, borne out of his resolute Irishness, gave him, in my eyes at least, the benefit of the doubt. If there was an opposite view, Rory would not let a topic die without expressing it, though I doubted any sincerity in most of his arguments. He was an interesting man, but troubled by demons and certainly capable of deviousness.

Anton was a Bolivian footballer coming to the end of his career but still retained his boyish charm, swarthy good looks and romantic deep South American accent that captivated the multitude of female devotees that his, admittedly short, career in Real Madrid had brought him. All Anton's talents were directly inversed to my own and it had taken me a while to warm to him but his charm disguised a rapier mind which was the perfect foil for any inconsistency, deviation or inaccuracy that Felix and Rory may fall victim to, of which I totally approved. He turned out to be good fun to be with, and despite his wealth and adoration, retained a humility that was particularly endearing. He would take up the cause of the underdog, whether or not he actually agreed with their sentiments. I suppose you wouldn't call him a deep thinker, but that would undermine his intellectual versatility. He was the antidote to anyone who was beginning to get too fond of themselves, and as I never fell into that category, I found myself agreeing with much of his sentiments.

Maria was a sophisticated Mexican woman approaching her forties. A stunningly good looking woman who had risen in the male dominated publishing business world of her homeland taking no prisoners on the way to the top. Ruthless in ambition maybe and obviously capitalist in stark contrast to Rory but still showing compassion for genuine injustice that she would sometimes express in a most disarming way. Never predictable, always interesting, she too brought much to the dinner table, however her contribution would be more circumspect and thought out. You felt she spoke with authority and would always stand her ground from the cynicism of Rory and the gentle leg pulling of Anton with deft skill. Not afraid to use her femininity but obviously possessed other personal qualities that could never be described as feminine. I think to be truthful I was in awe of Maria, which made me feel uncomfortable. She seemed formidable and whilst being a very sexy lady I could never quite imagine my ever moving her earth.

Ramon was a young Bolivian politician who had taken over the reigns from his father in the volatile political environment of his homeland. Self interest had motivated much of his decision making but was still proud of his country and would claim that his survival in the melting pot that was Bolivian politics would not only ensure equality for all but also economic prosperity. Few of us had too much belief in his ability to fulfil that laudable aim and in truth had little respect for his integrity from the short time that we had known him. However we did accept that his vision and even his practical application of it was infinitely more acceptable than most of the alternatives that were available in Bolivia. Anton particularly gave him a hard time with many stories of corruption and intrigue and would, frequently, cruelly refer to his small stature. But Ramon was well able to argue his corner without ever losing his composure no matter how hostile the questioning or cruel the personal comments. Well read and articulate, Ramon was still able to sprinkle his political arguments with witty anecdotes and his cunning and survival instincts shared common ground with me, even if he had managed to use these skills more successfully. There I go again.

Susanna was a beautiful Spanish girl that Anton had met in Madrid just before I met Jenny. She was tall, swarthy and obviously Latin but strangely freckled in a most beguiling way. Her hair was short and dyed honey blond which added to her rather unnatural but alluring look. In her late twenties with strong opinions of her own on where Cuba should be in the World and how America should be made pay for the illegal blockade of trade that they had imposed for forty years. Never overawed by our companions she leant a passion and a sparkle to all our sparings. She would be quick to pick up on anyone she disagreed with and usually ended every injection of humour by any participant with infectious laughter that raised the spirits of all of us. I really liked Susanna, but then I think we all did.

Then there was Jenny. She was probably in her early thirties, but looked very fresh faced. Her shortish brown hair tied back revealing a round face, sort of innocent and open but housing her wonderful eyes. Large and the blue contrasting with the vividness of the whites, they just melted anyone who dared to make direct contact. She was tall and slender, had gentle provocative curves and invariably wore clothes that were figure hugging, loose, chic and casual. Any contradiction in that description I feel shows a lack of imagination in the reader, a quality I must admit to not having any deficit. She showed compassion and concern for everything and everyone she came in contact with, and that had just captivated me, because, I suppose, I just couldn't understand it. But she still retained a quirky, adventurous outlook on life which she obviously loved. She had in the space of a few days become the sole object of my thoughts. I could see that my conduct could have a disconcerting effect on her as we had gone through an emotional and physical roller coaster over the past few days, still she seemed to reciprocate my feelings at the moment. Her being by my side in such stimulating company was enough.

Modesty should prevent me from saying that my own contribution was of any significance in such exalted company. But this was not the time for modesty; I felt I orchestrated the evening. I was the facilitator, the one who called time on subjects that got too involved, brought in contributions from people who hadn't said too much or curtailed those who had said the opposite. Not that my skills were required too often, but I knew without a referee the sarcasm and passion would clash from time to time with possible terminal effects on the evening. That's the way I saw it, I have little doubt that others saw my contributions as little more that inappropriate snide remarks. Maybe, but I was good at them.

Susanna and Jenny had suggested that we hold the party as a farewell to Maria who was heading home the next day. They had found this restaurant, Fiesta Campesina, twenty miles inland from the holiday resort of Valadero which was hidden away in the middle of a small wood. Easily accessible by car, but it still retained an atmosphere of being in the heart of the forest. The wooden circular building had a dried grass roof and open sides and gave the ambiance of eating al fresco largely I suppose because we were. A traditional samba band took up their positions. Consisting of two guitarists, a bass player, a man on the bongos and a very elderly man who took turns on the vocals when ever he could raise the energy, they presented a bizarre combo. The solo by this exquisitely aged musician on the claves, two short sticks knocked together to provide the samba beat, was the focal point of his performance. Whatever cynicism is implied by that comment, I cannot deny that he added style and authority to the act, even if his contribution was little more than his age. I couldn't imagine anyone attempting his performance under the age of eighty five, except perhaps nubile young ladies, but that would be a different story. They all moved as they played, not in any sort of cohesion, certainly the singer would move at half the pace of the rest of them but they all unmistakably had the same rhythm. They jammed to suit the audience and seemed to judge our mood to perfection. We encouraged them at every turn, sang when we recognised an air and clapped enthusiastically on reaching the end of every rendition. I say 'we' rather loosely, they actually got up my nose but like most occasions a few drinks broadens my musical appreciation. Undoubtedly they were enjoying themselves as much as my companions were.

They played to herald our arrival, initial drinks and during the order taking but then disappeared when we started eating the main course, which I thought was a very good idea. Although we were offered a choice of menu, the food was just placed in the centre of the table and we just helped ourselves to any thing that took our fancy. We all took equal status at the round table, in the centre of the raised floor with all the other tables empty, the restaurant catering more for the day time trade. The barmy November evening was the perfect setting for verbal jousting. None of us were excluded from the mickey taking and none feared a counter response, which was never far behind any personal comment or controversial declaration.

After the early forays into discussing the location, Cuba, our work, how we would miss each other and how we must never let this moment die, Maria suggested we say the first thing that comes to mind when she says dogs... cats...rats....coffee...the ocean... The varying answers leading to much discussion of the revealed feelings of us all when she explained they are the psychosomatic reflexes to the inner thoughts on yourself, your partner, your fears and enemies, your home life and your hopes for the future. Bullshit claimed Rory who has been exposed as hating friends and partner, living with his enemies, never went near the future whilst being prepared to live totally in the present (if that's what twenty cups of coffee a day means). I started to agree with him but feigned derision to win Jenny's approval. She saw through my duplicity and smiled a knowing 'what are you like?' smile. I try to emulate this unspoken conversation but probably failed to make any facial expression that can be translated into anything coherent.

Susanna claimed that her choices showed an unease with herself and her friends whilst wishing to destroy all her enemies. She didn't like her environment and had fears for the future, which she said was totally accurate. Hearing what she said made me review Rory's assessment, pretty accurate too with my own choices. Particularly what I said about cats. I was apprehensive of cats and felt I could never get close, I loved them but never trusted them and never felt they gave anything back. I wondered whether I was basing this subconscious assessment on Katie or Jenny. Suddenly I wanted the subject to change before I had to give any self analysis a public hearing.

Fortunately the discussion moved on to the most evocative lyric in pop music, "I'd walk a thousand miles just to shed this skin" in Springsteen's Philadelphia or Meatloaf's "And the last thing I see is my heart, still beating, still beating, breaking out of my body and flying away," took my favourite positions which was meet with universal horror of my macho grossness. Maria thought 'The first time ever I saw your face I thought the sun rose in your eyes' was just immense. Susanna started mentioning the poetry of the Smiths which we all thought was ridiculous and then Jenny suggested that Bette Midler's 'Stay with me Baby' in the Rose when she collapses on stage was the most moving piece of Cinema she had seen. Susanna wanted a second go. Lou Reed's Perfect Day over Cold Turkey in Trainspotting was so iconic yet ironic as well. Anton couldn't resist joining in with Bohemian Rhapsody in Wayne's World. Felix ignored him completely with his suggestion of Barber's Adagio for Strings playing over the wartime desolation in Platoon.

Another change of direction … if we're talking desolation what about the real life desolation in Iraq at the moment where no one was safe. Whatever evil Saddam inflicted on his people there was law and order, Maria stated. But only for those who agreed with him, Felix was quick to take up his Government defence and I suddenly took an instant dislike to him. Was he a programmed automaton? He then went onto the philosophical point that it was better to do the wrong thing for the right reasons than the right thing for the wrong reasons. The general consensus was that this argument may have some merit, not from me- the argument is horse manure, Bush's motives were devious at best and we all felt he was doing the wrong thing for the wrong reasons. I intelligently pointed out that the man was a moron, which I felt had escaped everyone's notice. I was delighted that whilst I didn't get too much vocal support for what I thought, I sensed it was almost the universal view. There followed a number of Bush jokes. I particularly liked the one where he snatched the schoolbag from a young boy thinking it was the last parachute and claiming as he jumped from a distressed plane that the world needed him.

Then who you'd most like to meet and what you would say to them. As an observer I would comment that the men wanted to save the world whilst the women wanted to change their sex life, it was here I discovered I have a female side. Probably sexist but it lead nicely on to the next topic, what was the best sex you'd ever had, where and with whom. My conclusion here was that women were more capable of recalling detail, that the occasion and tenderness were more memorable than the physical encounters. I had a feeling that the male experiences were somewhat embellished, but I'm sure Anton would deny that. My own, with two Brazilian sisters on the banks of the Amazon after saving their lives from man eating bison, was of course entirely truthful.

Who you would like to take the lead in the story of your life brought an animation to the discussion with little easy consensus even if we all eventually agreed Jack Nicholson was perfect for Felix after he had preferred Robert de Nero. I had thought Jack wouldn't be able to handle an American accent and that Felix should stick to directing, but I bowed to the general view. Anton suggested Antonio Banderas for his lead, the rest of us felt Jim Carey or even Norman Wisdom would be more appropriate, he just smiled that annoying smug 'you can't touch me' smile as he gave Susanna a hug. Susanna, herself, fancied Jennifer Lopez for her role but we disagreed, too little brain power, Kate Hudson or Natasha Kinski would give a little more piazz, to which she didn't seem to object to too much. Rory thought that a combination of Bruce Willis, Liam Neelson and Omar Sharif would give his life the certain 'je ne sais quoi' that he felt he merited but we thought Orson Wells might be more his style and he would bring a dark intrigue to the role. His disgust at this suggestion, largely because he objected with being associated with a portly, old even if extremely intelligent man, brought in the compromise of Anthony Hopkins. Ramon favoured the moody Andy Garcia and whilst we saw where he was coming from we didn't want him to feel too self satisfied and the casting committee settled on Danny de Vito to which he immediately fell into a ten minute sulk. We awarded Maria's role to Diane Keaton, after she had rather sheepishly suggested Maureen O'Hara and Jenny was given Meg Ryan following a long discussion on the merits of Mia Farrow and Goldie Hawn. Ramon came out of his self imposed exile to suggest that Woody Allen was perfect for my role, which I really didn't object to even if I had thought the hard nosed journalist, dedicated to the story would have been better suited to Dustin Hoffman or Tommy Lee Jones. As long as I got the girl and rode off into the sunset I didn't care.

Then a discussion on global warming, followed by lighter matters, the most suspenseful book we had all read. Another moral dilemma, would you grieve more if your partner decided to leave you for another or if they died. Again that went with the sexes, are we all stereotypes? The girls feeling the revenge need greater than the boys if their partner left and that satisfaction could be sought from that. Once again I felt a strong bonding with my female side. Where we all stood on sexuality and spirituality. Where was the best place in the world. Right here, right now, well actually in about two hours time if all went to plan, my alter ego working overtime.

Emotions were raised ceaselessly from joy and laughter to despair and anger as each of us eloquently expressed our hopes and desires and fears and experiences with fervour and authority. I had never felt more stimulated, never more at home, as the night passed through course to discourse. Even my cynicism was mellowing, which was probably the most surprising event of the evening until our little soiree was rather rudely interrupted.

The appearance of four armed men guarding each of the open doorways of the restaurant brought a sudden halt to proceedings. Immediately stunned and a realisation of our vulnerable state quickly dawned. Our exits were blocked and it looked as though we were trapped by these renegades. Many thoughts flashed through my mind in a micro second. The first being – this has totally fucked up my plans for later, then in a more contemplative mood I considered what motive they had for their uninvited appearance. Robbery was the most likely, but I didn't have any money. Maybe Maria or Anton had resources that could send them on their way without undue hassle. Maybe they were politically motivated and Ramon's enemies were paying a social call. They could be terrorists taking us for ransom. Whoever they were they could not be more unwelcome and my desire to express my underlying sentiments of "Fuck You" was sensibly suppressed. I managed to hold on to some discretion.

My flimsy thoughts of defiance were quickly shelved, but we could not just let it happen. We should fight, but there was no possible way we could attack them. The staff seemed to have disappeared; maybe they had gone for help. Before their appearance there was no sound of a scuffle or any commotion, they just arrived in silence waiting for us to react. Maybe they were just soldiers on patrol; they didn't look stressed and were very disciplined.

Whatever their motives and they weren't looking for directions, they were very intimidating in non matching combats, berets and each armed with a pistol locked in its holster with three of them holding rifles held diagonally across their chests. The man without a rifle was extremely self assured, tall, dark and moustachioed. I thought he bore a strong resemblance to Tom Conti but

I sensibly kept that to myself as well. He had no beret but there were epaulettes on his shoulder of a shirt that bore no resemblance to any official uniform I recognised. He walked towards us and spoke in Spanish, to which Susanna replied with a certain venom. All was not right. After searching all my life for a soul mate I could not let it go like this after just a few days. It could not end here. Jenny searched for my hand and squeezed it. Actually it was the other way around, more to console my feelings than offer too much in the way of support to her, but I did want her to know we were in this together, whatever it was.

Chapter 9

It's fairly obvious from Susanna's pitch that this wasn't a kissagram call and we followed the mimed instructions to move over into one corner in relative quiet.

The leader then addressed us all in good English, which rather surprised me after his initial instructions. 'My name is Captain Gonzales, I have been ordered to bring you to Madruga in order that you may help us in our enquiries'

'Why?'

'Who's ordered you?'

'Who are you?'

All questions in relative politeness, before they gave way to the more determined and angry 'Who the fuck do you think you are?'

Captain Gonzales smiled, I hate smugness, but smugness with guns is acceptable I suppose. 'The answer to all your immediate questions are held by my men', pointing to the rather imposing hardware on view, a rather superfluous gesture, 'but you need not fear for your safety. You will be treated with respect and will come to no harm nor discomfort during our journey so long as you don't give us any trouble. Now if you will follow me your coach awaits'

We looked at each other waiting for inspiration to dawn on us. Eventually Rory captured our collective thoughts

'Captain Gonzales, we would like to know exactly what is happening here. We do not wish any trouble and would like to return to our hotel without any causing you any difficulty. Could you suggest how we could go about this to your best advantage?' I'm not sure I like Rory's positioning as self appointed spokesperson, but now isn't the time for a bruised ego. Anyway I agree with the suggestion, we should buy our way out of this, preferably with Maria's money.

'Sir, I have no idea what you are talking about, but my orders are to kill any one of you who does not wish to accompany us. I would assure you that my men would have no difficulty in complying with any such order.'

Suddenly the reawakening to the fact that things could get considerably worse sends a chill through us all as he continued, 'Would Senors Miller, Da Silva, Santini and Ramos follow me and the rest of you go with Corporal Morentes' pointing to one of the bearded guards.

He knew our names, this was not a mistake and he was beginning to look extremely professional. Any thought of a trying to run for it, or maybe a concerted, surprise attack was quickly dismissed – these guys knew what they're about and we didn't. It was time for discretion, follow orders and see what happened. Although not another word was spoken, we know we were all thinking the same.

Outside the restaurant two army trucks with drivers were waiting. Built around thirty years ago apparently before the discovery of suspension, they conveyed us to our unknown destination through a four hour journey, never once going on a road that you couldn't touch both sides of the hedgerows that adorn the scenic route we took. It was dark, not another vehicle in sight except for the lights of the other truck following three hundred yards behind. Our drivers took full advantage of the quiet roads and drove in what in any other circumstances would have been described as dangerous. Despite fearing for our safety, comfort became an even greater concern with the state of the roads, the sudden sharp bends, the wooden bench seats with precious little to grip on to and our knees rubbing against the rigid back of the seats in front; the driving was sadistic and tortuous.

I was feeling terrible, but maybe the immediate physical discomfort took my mind off the imminent danger that we would be in when we arrived at our destination, whenever and wherever that was to be. Barely a word was spoken between us but I know that we shared the same thought that rebellion, even by four able bodied men to one guard would end in tears.

At three o clock in the morning with only one small toilet and water break in the middle of nowhere, we arrived at a series of concrete prefabs surrounded by trees bathed in darkness. Not being able to get our bearings as to how big the complex was, or how many, if any, others are barracked here, we were roughly dispatched to a room each. Mine had nothing but a bed with dirty linen, a cracked wash hand basin with only one tap and a stained toilet without a seat but at least it did flush. No window and no means of communication to any of the others I felt despair and a coldness down my spine as the door was locked by my guard. On my own, scared, confused, sore from the horrible journey I find sleep surprisingly easy, after my initial summary of the situation failed to provide any answers into why we were there and what I should do next.

Feeling a lot stronger after the four hours rest that was abruptly terminated by my captor; I turned my immediate attention to the breakfast offered. The bread, cheese and bananas which accompanied my morning call along with a little sunlight as dawn broke through the open door, were very welcome and did briefly make me feel there was a positive solution about to reveal itself. Looking through the bright doorway to try and put some markers down on my surroundings, I noticed a second armed guard who immediately settled any thoughts of rebellion. I think I was grateful that decision was made for me.

My captor didn't speak English but was quite friendly and indicated that I had to go at eight to some meeting and presumably an explanation as to why we were being held. I was guessing they were viewing Maria or Anton as ransom targets but why take the rest of us hostage, it seamed so unnecessary. Not that I would want to leave the others to their fate. As usual with my assessments, the actual truth of the situation turned out to be rather different to my predictions.

The hour went by very slowly but eventually my guard returned to march me through heavy undergrowth to another series of prefabs to which I was invited to enter the largest, and sit down on a plastic bench to be joined one by one by Maria, Anton, Felix and Ramon. We questioned each other as to our treatment, what had happened to Rory, Susanna and Jenny and what do we thought we were doing there. Our conclusions were the same, we had no idea. Curiosity turned to anger as we were left alone for nearly two hours which passed without any of the good humour that had courted all our previous discussions. We were all fearful, the offspring of a marriage of ignorance and uncertainty. Eventually Captain Gonzales and a similarly dressed soldier with a black patch over one eye made their entry.

Captain Gonzales spoke first, 'Gentlemen and Maria please allow me to introduce my colleague and good friend General Suarez, the leader of the 'Friends of Che'. He would like to enlighten you as to why you are here and how we can make your stay with us as comfortable as possible.'

Felix visibly paled at this news, however none of us were too overjoyed. My immediate thoughts were that we were being held hostage by a gang of political fanatics who probably, rather ironically, have principals but no morals. But why us.

General Suarez appeared to be pleased that the opening line has had a visible effect on us. His body language revealed a lack of confidence which seemed to be bolstered by our discomfort. I could imagine being in a one to one situation with him and his begging for mercy, however that wasn't going to happen. He was enjoying the power his henchmen give him.

Felix uttered one word, 'Bastards' before a guard, receiving a nod from Suarez, jabbed the butt of his rifle into his belly. Winded but not unduly hurt he slumped to the ground with a resigned look that depressed more than anything that had happened in the past twelve hours. I knew now that there was a reason for our being here. There was no mistake.

Chapter 10

General Suarez started to address us in excellent English and appeared to enjoy the enlightenment he was about to break on us. 'Dear people, it is such pleasure to welcome so many nationalities to Cuba, it is a shame that you will not enjoy all the wonderful features of our country, but you may take pride in what your short stay will achieve. Friends of Che is a world wide organisation based here in Cuba to fulfil the aims of Che Guevara in bringing socialist government to the whole of South America free of bestiality of the imperialistic regime of the United States of America.' I looked across at Anton who just shook his head in disbelief. What was this moronic tosser up to?

Ramon was the first to question this charade and proclaimed 'I am a senior diplomat in the Bolivian Government and if I should come to any harm you will provoke a major international incident.'

Anton also was quick to chime in 'What have you done with Susanna and Jenny... and Rory' as an after thought.

Before I could join in, the General moved forward to Ramon and sniggered quite sinisterly 'Senor Santini if I were you I would try to engage your brain just a little before you speak. Perhaps if you did, you might think a major international incident is exactly what we would like to provoke. Anyway you are a pip squeak in a corrupt government which will be overthrown by the people. If you would give me the courtesy of explaining exactly why you are here you might understand what our next steps will be.' Turning to Anton he changed his demeanour and added softly 'Senor Da Silva be assured that your colleagues are safe but what I have to say to you is of no interest to them.'

The mood had changed, not that I was ever happy at been taken hostage, I had never felt under direct threat. This bastard wasn't very pleasant and I didn't trust a single word that he uttered out of his mouth. He was a contradiction, a pathetic bully but ultimately scary. I hoped he was saying that Jenny was safe but she was not one whom he had selected for this special briefing. Before I thought of anything else, he continued to snarl. 'Senora Rodriquez, if I may start with you, you are a very successful business woman who has lived in Mexico most of your life. I congratulate you on your stunning success and on your life devoted to exposing evil and corruption. I applaud you.' Maria sneered at him but stayed quiet. 'And will you allow me the courtesy to comment that you are also very beautiful. But you will recall you have not spent all your life in Mexico. You and your family fled there in 1969 when you were just five years old. Do you know why?'

Maria looked suddenly so scared I didn't think she even heard the question. 'Why what?' she asked before she realised what he said and then added 'and don't you ever make any personal reference about me again.' I'm not quite sure how she could prevent him but her defiance impressed me.

Suarez ignored the reprimand and continued 'Why your father chose to leave Bolivia in such a hurry'

Suddenly I felt an ice pack running down my back, so Maria was originally from Bolivia, as were Anton and Ramon and my father spent time there. What was the connection other than a piece of geography? And why Felix? What did he know that the rest of didn't?

Maria's concentration became a little more focused — so was everyone else's. What was happening? 'I've no idea' Maria stated very slowly and with a cold sharpness that revealed her inner strength, a desire not to be bullied.

General Suarez smirked which provoked a total revulsion in me. I never felt as much hatred in my life but was impotent to confront him. He was enjoying this. 'Your father left Bolivia in a hurry because he feared for his life in a country that changed its political character overnight as Senor Santini will no doubt testify. He was in charge of the personal guard of General Rene Barrientos whose presidency came to an abrupt end in a helicopter crash in 1969. Being responsible for the General's safety, he realised that he had no admirers on either side of the political divide. He felt that discretion was the better part of valour. An excellent piece of judgement, as all around him people were beginning to find that assassination was a very expedient way of dealing with their problems. He made the rather astute decision I feel, to seek a new identity in Mexico with his wife and daughter.'

Maria was now transfixed, not that any of the rest of us were bored by this story. All of us acutely aware that

there was unlikely to be a happy ending. Suarez continued 'I can see now you are a little surprised by this story.
Were you not aware of your father's rather blackened
history?'

Maria appeared to be about to say 'Go fuck yourself',
but instead she changed her demeanour and defensively
began to answer Suarez. 'I never knew I wasn't born in
Mexico, my passport is Mexican and when we moved I
was always told that it was to move from the country to
the city so that my father could get work.'

'Very sensible, but your father hardly needed to seek
work as he had enough money to establish his printing business with cash he had extracted from several
sources in his rather dubious rise to the upper echelons
of the Bolivian military. The rather clever choice of career also helped him to dissolve into his new environment without any difficult questions. He was obviously
not alone at the time trying to seek his fortune in the
big city. He developed his business well and succeeded
in promoting his own social persona before his unfortu-
nate demise. All this left you a formidable forum and a
deep political conscience to launch your own publishing career after he was cruelly cut down. He was a capable and conscientious man who gave you much, but
probably his most intriguing inheritance was his secret
past. His real name, as I am sure you are most anxious to
know, was Bernardino Huanca, sergeant in the Bolivian
Rangers, the man who captured Che Guevara'.

There was a pregnant pause, I've never heard a group of
people so quiet, yet so anxious to speak. Suarez delighted
with himself at the management of this breaking news
item, I had the feeling he wanted to milk every situation.
Maria had visibly drained of colour, but Felix seemed

to know more than the rest of us. He had an air of resignation, an acceptance that his case was heard, verdict guilty by association and now just awaiting sentence.

Maria rose to her feet, and although shaky, delivered an emotional address in the face of her tormentor. 'My father was a brave and wonderful man who risked his life daily to expose corruption and drug trafficking in my country. His relentless exposés in his column brought his eventual assassination at the hands of evil men who would kill their own grandmothers for a few pesos. He was not scared of them and I am not scared of you. And I will not have his memory besmirched by a little tin pot soldier who captures and torments women with fairy tales of no relevance to any one.'

Suarez smiled smugly, 'Maria you are doubtless a brave woman and I have no desire to torment you but you are wrong to dismiss your father's past as having no relevance. His past and our future will resonate across the world in the next few days.'

The rest of us looked at each other not knowing what revelations were going discredit our past and what plans Suarez had for us. I can spot a good story and Suarez was right, this had all the hallmarks of a sensational 'Hold the Front Page' story if he handled the situation well. And if he sought to maximise the publicity the implications for our reaching maturity were extremely serious. But how could we be responsible for the sins of our fathers – and did they have any sins any way. My father was a doctor for God's sake but I had a feeling it would be a while before I would learn anything.

Suarez continued, timing perfect, but a little over anxious on delivery. Why was I marking him like a judge in a talent contest? I amazed myself in my ability to trivialise any situation. Perhaps I was just trying to keep myself together in the face of a trauma, or maybe I was just too stupid to realise what was going on. Either way I was quickly brought back to the current situation.

He turned to Ramon, 'Senor Santini you will be aware of your father's position having spent his entire career in the army and risen to the heights of General before he died. A decorated man, a true patriot who served his country loyally. It could not have been easy given the almost annual change of political masters he would have had to have served. Then he made his own move for political power, one clever enough not to have pinned his colours to one mast but strong enough to bring with him military strength and with it minimal social unrest. His support was vital for any successful power struggle, and his ability to run political office without committing to any side has been one of the marvels of the South American politics in the last thirty years. Had Machiavelli not been born I am sure your father would have given his name to be forever immortalised in his place. Not that you were a slow learner, I must congratulate you on your ability to run with the hares and hunt with the hounds. My assertion that Bolivian political life can be compared to the animal world is, if you will excuse me, very deliberate. However it is not you that we are discussing... is it?'

Once more Suarez engaged in a theatrical pause after his rhetorical question, giving us time to digest all that he was saying. We knew that we were there for some morbid charade and that we all had some connection with the events in Bolivia over thirty years ago but what motives could be strong enough to go to all this trouble. Then a sudden realisation pierced my consciousness... I have been trapped here along with everyone else by an elaborate plan to bring us all together... and Jenny must have been a part of that conspiracy. My world fell apart with a sledge hammer blow. My mind spun through all our time together, where were the warning signs. It couldn't be true, yet there was no other explanation, I felt a total hopelessness that totally disorientated me. I tried to dismiss the idea, but I couldn't. The thought crushed my mind... Jenny had betrayed me... I felt cold and light headed. I never thought a woman could have affected me this way. I was truly devastated. Suarez's words float over me without any emotion. He can no longer damage me any further.

I thought of when I first met her in Madrid, who made the first move. I reflected that I had picked her as a soul mate, not the other way round. Where were the tell tale signs to suggest a trap was looming. I don't think there were any. It was me that encouraged her to come to Cuba. Everything was so natural. It couldn't be true. I fell in love with a beautiful girl... who is twenty years my junior, my alter ego rushed to remind me. Now the initial desolation has worn off. I felt foolish, then angry then a combination of both as the helplessness of the situation sunk in.

Suarez continued his soliloquy about Ramon's father oblivious to my mental torment, 'It is the role your father played all those years ago, although for some reason he has tried to forget his role but he was the Captain in charge of the unit that brought Che to his eventual execution.' Another pregnant pause. I couldn't care less, I wanted to attack someone, to scream some sort of defiance but nothing happened, my body and brain seemed to working under different commanders. I wanted to go asleep and wake up from this nightmare. I did not want to hear any more of this sick joke, but Suarez sensing a growing discomfort amongst us all and brushing aside any questioning that my fellow hostages attempt to make, started to speed up his discourse and raised the pitch an octave. The drone that was churning through my mind became a whine that I couldn't ignore even if the words meant nothing to me.

I looked across at Anton and realised he was slowly coming to the same conclusion that I had. He was obviously picked up in the night club by Susanna nearly two weeks earlier which had brought us all to this fiasco. I felt angry, but could see Anton reacting like a bridled bear. He was looking for something to hit, but knew it would be pointless.

'Senor Miller I am sure you are wondering what significance all this is to you'. I nodded, not caring what he was going to say. 'Your father volunteered for some overseas work in the late sixties, presumably feeling that his talents as a doctor should be spread across the poorer nations of the world after he qualified before he settled down to the rather serious business of fulfilling his family commitments and making a rewarding career for himself. As to how he managed to persuade your mother that leaving her and their young son for a year was a good idea, you may be able to help us. I would hazard a guess that as a young man he felt trapped, suffered a social conscience and that his relationship with your mother was exposed to the pressures of years as a hospital junior doctor working all hours for little return. He needed a career break. I do not know why he chose Bolivia and how he got seconded to the Bolivian Rangers, but that is what happened. He was the medical backup to the troops trying to quell rebellion in the Bolivian mountains. His conscience would have an endless struggle with his Hippocratic Oath I am sure, but presumably he argued with himself that the alleviation of human suffering among poor people is laudable whatever their politics.' Dulled by the pain of Jenny's deception I could still hear Suarez's words and felt my brain screaming in defence of my father's character but my heart was left unmoved. He continued with a revelation that was so stunningly pictorial that the image would stay with me as long as I had control over the use of my mind. I was shaken visibly and the blood drained from my body leaving my feet feeling as though they were in a bucket of cold water. 'Your father cut the hands off Che, prepared their preservation in jars of formaldehyde and injected his body to prevent the degeneration of his features.'

I wanted to hit out at something and flew at Suarez with a rage I have never known in myself. Screaming an unending series of no's my attack was brought to a sudden end by his professionally applied blow across my temple with the butt of his pistol. As I struggled with my undignified position I knew there was nothing I could do. Two guards appeared in the doorway but Suarez waved them away, totally confident that he could handle anything we could throw at him and he was right. A fact which added to my dejection.

Maria came over to comfort me and I could see tears in her eyes as she helped me back to my original position, holding my hand in sympathy. We were all suffering some sort of psychological torture that Suarez enjoyed applying but it was not over. We had no defence, nothing to say, we accepted that he was telling a story that must have some basis in fact but cannot believe our fathers had a major part to play in such a momentous piece of history without ever hearing of it before. And he hadn't finished with us.

He reached for a glass of water and offered the same to us with a hand gesture which we all refused with head movements. I was dying for something but would rather suffer the thirst than take anything from him. He acknowledged our defiance with a wry smile.

Whilst lying in a pool of desolation feeling I've just had every piece of my world torn asunder. My mind lead me into another thought. This whole scenario, my trip to Cuba had been set up by Rory. He must have engineered the whole thing. The whole O'Hara scam was probably fabricated just to get me to Cuba. How could I have been so stupid. And all that rigmarole with Leonie's brother. My mind was bursting with confusion and hatred. But the charade with Suarez continued unabated.

'And now Senor Da Silva' Anton grimaced in preparation of learning the part his father had to play in this black tragedy. 'As you know your father has not had a particularly auspicious career, in fact since leaving the army in 1970 has drifted from job to job in search of some commitment that may keep him away from the joys of looking at the world through the end of a bottle. His marriage dissolved in acrimony and probably his only joy he has left is the undisputable pride he shares with all those around him when watching your donning the Bolivian shirt. He loves his football, your success has transcended to lift his world, he has friends now that he never thought possible once it dawned on him that he was the person who executed Che Guevara.'

Anton slumped to the ground. He had never felt a great bond with his father after he left the family home following the endless rows with his mother but he had always kept in touch. His father had brought presents at Christmas and had followed his career with such fervour. Anton had supported his father with a house in La Paz but had only occasionally sent him money as he knew he would only drink it. But for all his failings he never thought that his father would shoot anyone in cold blood, never mind probably the greatest political icon of the twentieth century.

Not content with reducing Anton to an emotional heap, Suarez went on to elaborate. 'Apparently your father volunteered for the task in some sort of act of retribution for a couple of his friends who had died in combat the previous day. He failed in his first attempt and then walked up and shot Che from point blank range in the throat , as he lay on the ground, tied to a chair.'

For the first time Suarez lost his composure and seeing Anton slumped to the ground, lifted him by his collar against the wall and then kneed him in the groin with a venom that appeared to have been building up for decades.

'For God's sake' Maria cried, but somehow I felt a sort of relief that this man was not an automaton, had feelings and therefore had weaknesses. I felt for Anton, but knew, like the rest of us that any physical pain he was suffering paled in front of the deluge of mental agony.

Suarez walked out of the room and immediately the two guards came in and motioned to us to huddle together, which we did without comment. A further guard came in with water, bread and bananas which we nibbled at in silence. Occasionally two of us would make eye contact, but neither could find the words to console the deep void that we all shared. Somehow there was nothing to say. Education was meant to broaden the mind; our lessons so far have shrunk them to nothing. Apart from the occasional question as to our physical well being we spent an hour and a half in silence, contemplating what we had learnt and what it meant to our immediate future. My emotional feelings seem anesthetised and I didn't spend too much time, probably for the first time in a week, on thinking about Jenny. I just wanted it all to go away.

Not knowing what was going to happen next, and watching my charismatic friends reduced to speechless zombies was totally depressing and even Suarez reappearance into the room failed to raise any feelings. I no longer cared about what he was going to say. I had nothing but contempt for him but realised I could not change what was going to happen in the next couple of hours, maybe days or even the rest of my life how ever long that was going to be.

'My friends,' Suarez spewed forth 'I apologise most profusely for my outburst this morning. I am sure you understand that this is a very trying time for all of us. But prey let us continue with our story.'

He sat down and took the patch off his eye revealing an empty socket, completely healed, smooth if just slightly veined and with a small hole about the size of ballpoint nib in the centre. If his demeanour was threatening and his actions ruthless before, he now epitomised evil. I felt mentally drained and physically impotent in the presence of this man. Living through a mixture of fear and total indifference to any more that could be said, I was somehow transfixed by this hole in his face that I had never seen before anywhere and which he used so successfully in undermining any feeling of strength that we might have felt we still had. It seemed like a spy hole into hell, daring us to look beyond.

'Felix, you alone I cannot surprise. You know why you are here and may be you will be so good as to enlighten us more on the details of the capture and execution of Che Guevara. You were of course the main reason why he was captured, you are Captain Ramos of the CIA who was working undercover in Bolivia and who personally took charge of the Rangers as they were trained and moulded into an effective anti guerrilla unit.'

I knew I said that I was no longer interested in what was going around me, but things change. We all looked in disbelieve at Felix, how can someone who has spent the last two days regaling us with his adventures of his lifetime have failed to mention that he was responsible for the capture of the greatest political rebel ever to have lived. Felix looked at us in silence, no explanations are required really and why should we feel enmity towards our friend when the other bastard in front of us could have us shot at any time. However the silence came to a crescendo and Felix stood up and walked over to stand beside Suarez.

'What General Suarez says is correct, it is the single reason why I come to Cuba rarely, and for fear that zealots like him still exist. Obviously I made a mistake in coming back to my homeland even after thirty four years. I am deeply sorry that my presence in Cuba has threatened all our lives, but I do not regret my part in the capture of Che Guevara who was beginning to destabilise the whole of Latin America. I believe the CIA acted in the best interests of America and ultimately of the Western World.'

'Enough, you capitalist scum spread your tyranny around the world and you cannot see further than your own interests. Even your own Jesus Christ was persecuted, tortured and ultimately crucified. You think, just like all Empires, to destroy what you fear or don't understand.' General Suarez rose to the situation but even in this day of surprises just threw one more in that is the daddy of them all. 'Che Guevara was the reincarnation the Orsha God of Statesmanship and you lady and Gentlemen are about to be our sacrifice to his honour.'

Stunned and speechless, we were quickly escorted back to our huts to contemplate exactly how our fate was to be enacted, without a word between us. Felix in fact moved in front of us to avoid eye contact, but I didn't have anything intelligent to say anyway. I felt betrayed for a second time in a few moments, but it was nonsense, Felix owed none of us an explanation for neither his beliefs nor his actions a generation ago. To say that my sacrifice to the temple of idiocy was of no consequence to me, showed just how far I have travelled from my self centred world of cynical Dublin journalism in less than a week.

Back in solitary confinement and given time to think about all the gruesome details we had just discovered, the consuming thought was the betrayal Jenny had visited on me. Whilst that ate away at my insides I realised that this whole trip was set up by Rory. What kind of fuck was he, – could he be the revolutionary zealot thinking this was his move for immortality or was he just a gangster setting up the whole scenario for a few tawdry dollars. Probably the whole O'Hara story was fabricated to lure me into this spider's web and I've just spent a whole week on a wild goose chase. My mind tangentially spun off to consider the cost of the trip before my alter ego rescued any exercise down that avenue to convince myself that I should not be bothered by my expense account if I was going to be shot in the next twenty four hours. And what of Susanna, I had thought her feelings for Anton were totally genuine, but her part, and what a part, was to snare him into the honey trap. I had really liked her. Whilst my feelings for Jenny were fairly strong I felt she hadn't encouraged me in any way. But Susanna and Anton were lovers in every sense. He had to be devastated.

My thoughts were interrupted by the guard entering my room, whom I ignored and remained prone on the bed staring at the ceiling. I was alerted to Jenny's presence by the soft footfall as she sat on the bed and looked me in the eye.

'I swear I didn't know this was going to happen'

'Just fuck off and leave me alone', my mouth engaged before my heart had a chance to make contact with my brain.

'Listen Ben, you have to believe me. I wanted no part in this. Susanna owed Rory some money from a drugs scam he was operating, bringing coke into Europe. She panicked and dumped $150,000 worth of cocaine down the loo when the customs in Madrid looked as though they were stopping everyone. He suggested all sorts of retribution on her unless she agreed to help him get Anton and you to Cuba as part of celebration of the anniversary of Che's capture. He told us you were both related to people involved at the time but probably didn't know you were. He was planning a major re-enactment of the capture to seek publicity for his socialist beliefs and the best way to achieve this was to include some of the original participants or as near as he could. There was no mention of sacrifice, God I am so sorry.'

'Save it, Jenny. I don't want to know,' which was close to the biggest lie I have ever told. 'Rory's interest in socialism is somewhat sullied by drug running. What do you think he was going to do with us?'

'I don't know, we weren't thinking straight. Rory said there was going to be a party or something. I don't know. But we thought it was going to be a celebration not a sacrifice, I swear. Susanna was absolutely distraught saying she would be running from him for the rest of her life if she didn't do what he said. Being the good revolutionaries we are we were interested in the whole deal about Che anyway. She begged me to help her and when your best friend begs you for help, you do what you can, don't you?'

'Not when you snare someone to their death, no you don't help them.'

'She didn't know that, I swear to God, Ben please believe me. Susanna loves Anton, truly loves him. She didn't think anything like this was going to happen. She's devastated now.'

'Yeah, and Anton's over the moon, you stupid bitches. And what of you Jenny, how do you feel about me.' I went to grab her by the shoulders to try to look her straight in the eye but just as I did a guard came in with my evening rations. A lump of cold pork and cold boiled potatoes. A little bread and polished off with a nice vintage bottle of tap water. He dropped the whole lot and raced over, threw me to the ground before hustling Jenny to the door. On his way past he kicked my tray over and sent every morsel of food across the dirty floor. My hunger wasn't really at me anyway, I couldn't have cared less if Conrad Gallagher had produced it.

I watched as Jenny walked out the door, heard the lock turn and went back to my contemplation of the ceilings cracks, waiting for the evening to pass.

The evening came and went without too many social engagements. I was alternating between thoughts of mindless revenge ... on Jenny, on Susanna, on Rory yes especially Rory, whilst my life flashed before me. Not too much to feel proud of – was I leaving anyone in Ireland who would mourn my passing in anything more than a cursory thought. More food was thrown into me and I was left to more of my own thoughts. Pretty much in turmoil at that stage. I started thinking of the irony of being in the heart of probably the greatest news story I have ever reported on without ever being able to file it. I amused myself by thinking my last request would be access to a fax machine to report into the office. That moment of frivolity was quickly drowned by the realities of the situation. I felt like crying. I never have before, but I had never felt more in sympathy with myself. Sleep was a luxury as available as the fax machine. My thoughts started to recycle. I should negotiate repeat fees. With nothing to console myself, nothing to occupy my hands or my mind, I find each minute drag endlessly as I scour for any evidence of changes in the light outside which might indicate the coming of the new day and answers to the question of what was to become of us. What seemed like a couple of hours after midnight, I heard the key in the door and Jenny came in on her own and sat on the bed. I was numbed...why had she come now, I didn't want anymore explanations. I say nothing, not knowing what I could say but the surprise of her presence jogged my mind into action. I should tackle her on the thoughts that had besieged my mind since we first met and how my life had been turned upside down with the current situation. I had been rehearsing part of this speech for so long but now I felt I was flying by the seat of my pants, I had to go for it but I had no idea what I was going to say. Strangely Jenny seemed to be aware of my difficulty and stayed quiet to let me speak.

'Can I talk to you'

'Well maybe now isn't a good time, I haven't long.'

'Yeah well this is important, can I talk to you for a few minutes without you interrupting me and you promise to hear me out'

'Go on'

I froze all over again, should I have started with how I felt for her before our kidnapping or how I felt betrayed. But she must know that, I decide to say to her what I would have said if our capture had never happened. I was filled with the dread of making a fool of myself, but I could not understand that how, in my present plight, that could be a concern.

'From the moment I met you and virtually every minute since we have been together I had felt that I've never been with anyone like you. I thought, and still do, that you are a really special person with as much love and compassion and humour and spirit as I have ever met in one person. I love being in your company.' Actually I was quite pleased with what I had said, in the event, un-rehearsed. I was direct, succinct and not lacking in passion. I couldn't bear to hear a rejection, so I was keen to make as many points as I could.

'I don't want to hear this.'

'You promised not to interrupt... but I know that we have such a little in common, as it turns out a little less than I anticipated. I am twenty years older than you and any friendship we might have had could only survive with some special nurturing. And that can only happen if we both wanted it more than anything else in the world. I really had my doubts that that was ever going to be the case. But our time together and particularly making love on the beach was the sweetest moment in my life which will live with me for ever. I just wanted to tell you that and that I don't really want you to say anything now, but what I felt for you hasn't changed. I don't know what you feel for me, but in a sense it does matter now. What does matter is that you have to realise that you are above this ... you... you could be anything you want to be. You have to escape all this baggage you have let yourself get immersed in and become the really wonderful person you could be.' I stop with a realisation that I have managed to say exactly what I wanted to say with no rancour nor reference to horrendous situation I found myself in. For once in a long time I'm proud of my motives and rather smugly, my delivery.

'Fuck you, Ben, I wasn't expecting that, I don't know what to say ....err...thank you.' I must admit that I would probably have preferred to hear 'I love you' but at least it wasn't a complete put down.

'I still feel betrayed and can't understand how the fuck you could set me up and that every feeling you had was just a means to an end, an end without much purpose as far as I can see.'

'Ben, it's not turned out as I thought, I did believe in what we were doing and I had to help Susanne but I didn't think that I would feel anything for you when we first met. Things just happened and I know I have trapped you but all the fun we had meant as much to me – it wasn't an act. Well maybe it was but it didn't require any acting ability. You're a pretty nice person.'

'Who doesn't deserve this'

'Who doesn't deserve this'

'Then do something about it'

'Well yeah,' she smiled for the first time since our capture and I remembered exactly why I felt the way I did, 'I've been thinking about it, that's why I'm here, nice of you to ask. I really do care about you.'

I started to fantasize in total confusion. Was I clutching at straws? But visions of the prenuptial lunch of My Best Friends Wedding came to mind and a chorus of 'Say a little prayer for me' sweeping up behind Jenny. It was a ridiculous scene but I couldn't think straight. She did feel something for me and wanted to help. And I did need it, but she was the one that got me into this in the first place, and some of her cronies wouldn't have had any problem knocking me off.

I tried to put some sanity into my mind by attempting to talk through my thoughts. 'Listen, this whole scenario is a disaster. Whatever your motives were the realistic ambitions of the 'Friends of Che' are none existent. They have no political aims in mind other than some pan South American revolution which is just as outdated now as it was when Che was alive. He was fighting Spanish imperialism a hundred years too late. Trying to counter the threat of American imperialism and also rid South America of all the fascist Governments that were in power at the time. It was never going to be unified in one glorious revolt. It was ill conceived then and just a nonsense now. Granted by disposing of five descendants of the assassination of Che they will get worldwide publicity and maybe raise the interest in Che all over again. Maybe you'll sell a few Tee shirts, but you won't achieve any political change of any sort. But you will be a fugitive for the rest of your life, possibly not in Cuba but you'll never be able to go freely anywhere else. And if you're caught you'll be charged with murder. Are you saying you haven't left any tracks behind you, of course you have. And even if you do get away with it, will you be happy with your part in killing five innocent people, well four anyway.' I felt guilty in implicating Felix as a full player in Che's murder, but I was slowly coming to the conclusion that he at least did have to face his conscience, though in fairness he shouldn't have to face the bastards calling themselves the Friends of Che.

I could really feel the tension; she was saying nothing, just staring into through the window adjusting her straps again. I can't understand why I felt sorry for her, I wanted to put my arms around her and say everything was OK but my alter ego was calling me fucking mad. This was the girl who trapped me and placed me in this crazy situation which could very realistically turn into a very bad moment. I couldn't stand the silence, suddenly I realised I was in love with her that there was probably nothing she could do or say that I wouldn't forgive. This was madness; I turned to face her and saw tears trickling down her cheeks which only gave a sparkle to her face and raised my feelings towards her further. Instinctively I took her in my arms but she didn't respond, looking at the floor eventually sobbing very quietly 'I'm so sorry.'

'Yeah but what are we going to do?'

I started to realise that this was the time to move, it maybe the only opportunity I was going to get to make an escape bid. What of the others? Escape first and raise help, my alter ego came to the rescue with a welcome drop of common sense.

'Do you know where we are, Jenny?'

She nodded.

'And do you know how we can get out of here without raising a manhunt'

'There is no 'we.'' This hit me like a hammer blow, I didn't want to get away. Before I had a chance to respond she continued.

'Listen, I've got to stop this. If you make a run for it and your escape isn't realised until the morning, I think I will be able to persuade the General easily enough that you will raise the alarm and all hell will break loose. So the only solution would be to let the others go if they promise to forget the whole episode before the place is swarming with troops. And the Friends of Che will just dissolve back into the mire that was their lives before this travesty was enacted and that they can rise again to honour the name of Che Guevara sometime in the future.'

'Yeah like fuck that will happen.'

'It's the only way – if we go together they'll look for us. I'll be missed immediately and we won't have a chance if they catch us. But if you go and I don't report anything wrong until the morning it'll be too late for them to come looking. Anyway I don't want to go with you, but I don't want to see you hurt.'

'They'll go crazy with you' I said before realising what she had just uttered. She didn't want to go with me. Once again my mind was in mayhem.

'No, you've got to hit me... hard. Think of the way I tricked you, Ben. You must be able to drum up some vitriol to knock me out. Then I can say that I came to see you and you went berserk and attacked me. They'll be mad at me for letting you escape but if they see my bruises they'll probably believe me.'

I saw that she was right and started acting totally on instruction with a numbness that completely restrained any aggression. I discovered anyway that woman beating wasn't that easy. Whilst seeing the virtues of her argument – probably knocking her out would save her life, I still couldn't bring myself to punch her hard. After a few rather pathetic attempts to inflict some injury we eventually agreed on a compromise that would look convincing. I hit her fairly hard twice with a two foot piece of timber which didn't do too much damage but did give some superficial scratches on her face along with a rather endearing reddened lump under her eye. I kissed it better and start to say something. She stopped me before I had a chance to put some order on my thoughts.

'Just go, Ben, you are wasting time'

'Which way?'

'We are around fifty five miles south of Havana, just head through the forest for a good while, I'd say about two to three hours and you will eventually come to the main road on the coast which heads for the city. Don't talk to anyone.'

'Jenny'

'Just go'

'That's all, just go?'

'Yeah'

I turned to go with a lump forming in my throat, realising this probably was goodbye, and moved to kiss her but she pulled away.

Whoever said parting was such sweet sorrow hadn't a fucking clue, I was choked, and she was crying too but I realised that everything had been said and I really had to move.

I walked around twenty yards down the path turned and pressed two fingers to my lips and place them over my heart. To my amazement and absolute delight she followed suit. I started my journey with a bounce I wasn't expecting.

Chapter 11

Travelling through the forest, at night, wasn't too pleasant if not to say totally non productive. I could have been going round in circles for all I knew. Whilst keeping to the path was the only sensible course, it was the way I would be followed when they realised that I had gone. I hoped Jenny managed to get away with her story. The depressing thought occurred to me that she was in real danger and there was nothing I could do to help, but I suppose I was getting used to that.

I had to make the most of my head start, it was the only way I might be able to help the others and get Jenny out of the clutches of the mad men she had around her. I quickened my pace, taking razor like cuts on my arms and legs as the leaves of the palms swiped my forward movements. It should not have taken long to travel four miles but it seemed to go on for ever, I was consoled that Cuba was fairly free of dangerous wild life but the palm leaves were giving me hell.

Without resting for a second I managed to make it through the forest to come to a series of prefabs and what looked like a school, in a clearing miles from anywhere.

Everything was pitch black but there were a number of pick ups around to suggest that they were inhabited. Moving as quietly as possible I was still aware of every twig I stepped on, every stone I disturbed. I got beyond the buildings only for a light to go on and two teenagers in vests with firm muscles glistening with sweat come outside for a cigar. I am pretty certain they were farm workers conscripted from the cities but I could not take the chance that they would not hold me if they caught wind of my presence. So as I lay perfectly still, they chatted and joked for what seemed an eternity, as I mentally told them to get the fuck out of there. Eventually they sensed my telepathy and went back indoors and I breathed a sigh of relief. I was grateful for the physical rest but it hadn't done much for my stress levels.

Thankfully I was back on a road but still not knowing which direction I was heading. I jog-walked for over an hour through winding lanes, making decisions at Tee junctions which were purely arbitrary, my sense of direction not to be trusted, not that I placed too much faith in my instinct either. I consoled myself with the thought that if anyone does come after me they were unlikely to make all the same decisions as I made and I was pretty sure they didn't have any dogs to take up the scent. I thought it must be close to three thirty, still a couple of hours before daybreak and hopefully the discovery of my escape. Eventually I reached the main road tired but exhilarated. I was still only five or six miles from the camp and if I had taken a wrong turn which was almost inevitable, I might even be closer, so there was no time for complacency. I travelled on the road until daybreak when I could hide from oncoming cars with the advance warning their lights give, but then turned into the fields and travelled the route of the road away from the attention of possible hostile vehicles. Progress was getting slower and I was tired and hungry. Every limb ached with the multiple razor cuts from the palm leaves all over my body. I needed to find some refuge to build up my reserves but nothing came to mind. It was nearly eight o'clock, hopefully fifteen miles away from my tormentors and I would be unlucky to be caught by them, but I could not trust anyone not to be a sympathiser of the Friends of Ché.

I decided to continue away from the roads and thought I would be safe enough to look for somewhere to rest for a couple of hours out of the sun, bathe my wounds in a river and find some sugar cane which should keep me going for the next few hours. After another half hour of weary travel I found all three of my objectives on a leafy river bank and recuperated in the countryside equivalent of a four poster feather bed in a five star hotel, well in relative terms. I lay down under a large banyan tree which offered full shade throughout the day, nicely away from the beaten track, and slept. The inner brain must still have been working to avoid a complete recharge of batteries, but still it was nearly three in the afternoon before I recovered my full senses, aware that it was very hot but that I had let my own needs surpass those of my fellow hostages.

Back to the main road taking less care about being the possibility of being caught as the roads were busier and there were several travellers on foot making my movements less obvious. I began to take more chances and risked raising a thumb like everyone else. A truck driver stopped and offered me a lift into the next town which was about a ten mile journey to Santa Cruz del Notre, a dormitory town with little or no facilities for tourists and nowhere for my being able to raise the alarm. I asked a young man who approached me if there was a police station before I considered the consequences. He replied that there wasn't any need for police here as there was no crime. Rather shaken by just how much the young man could be mistaken I realised that it probably was for the best. There was no knowing who could be trusted.

I knew there was nothing I could do until I got to Havana and it was too late to travel there at that stage. Several women approached me with offers of bed and breakfast, one of whom I eventually succumbed to and enjoyed a meal, shower and few drinks with immense relief. I thought I was well away from my captors and I would not be able to do anything else for my friends until the morning. After the meal I retired to my room to try to concentrate on the events of the past few days and although Jenny continued to dominate my thoughts I considered the implications of what had happen to the Chronicle. How was Paul going to react to the news that the whole story was a set up? With Paul, Kate, Jenny, Susanna, O'Hara, Che Guevara, my Dad, and Rory running through my mind like a four hundred metres final in the Olympics, I had no need to count sheep as I fell into a deep if fitful sleep.

Chapter 12

Morning came, with relief that I had not slept much beyond dawn, and I took the first available bus that wasn't jam packed with workers to Havana and arrived just before midday. Getting off the bus in the centre of the city, my heart lifted by my successful escape and the need to be effective in securing help for my friends, I saw the New York Herald Tribune banner headlines on the news stands which shattered my very being.

'Friends of Che execute hostages.'

I slumped back onto a park bench feeling so guilty. I could have done more, I should have done more. Why didn't I get a taxi to Havana? Poor Maria, Anton, Ramon and Felix they didn't deserve to die. My mood changed quickly from self pity to anger. Those bastards, I swore that if it was the last thing I would do I would find Suarez and his cohorts and make sure they paid. A nasty realisation that it was just bravado, what could I do. They had probably scattered all over the country by the time I was reading about them. Another wave of helplessness washed over me as I managed to negotiate the purchase of the newspaper and staggered back to the bench to study the report. The words seemed to pass through my brain without bothering to make connection.

'FRIENDS OF CHE ADMIT TO SLAYING HOSTAGES'

The underground revolutionary political party, the Friends of Che' today issued a press release through their commander, General Suarez which read as follows.

' Matanzas 23 November 2003.

Today the Friends of Che completed the programme of executing four prisoners who were party to those responsible for the murder of Che Guevara.

Felix Ramos was the American agent who trained and commanded an elite group of Bolivian Rangers. It was under his command that Che was captured and executed without trial.

Maria Rodriquez, a Mexican business woman, was the daughter of the Bolivian soldier who made the arrest of Che

Anton Da Silva, an international footballer, was the son of the soldier who shot Che in the heartless, illegal execution

Ramon Santini, the Bolivian Minister for Health, was the son of the Bolivian Commander in Chief of the forces at the time.

A fifth prisoner, Ben Miller has escaped, and we are making every effort to bring him to justice. The justice his father didn't give Che Guevara when he hacked off his hands with a hand saw.

The Friends of Che is a worldwide organisation devoting itself to the uniting Latin American Countries in socialist govern-

*ment expelling capitalism and all the imperial influences of the
United States of America…..'*

I could not read anymore and but contemplated my situation. I had no where to turn, I could not help my friends any more, they were gone because I chose my skin above theirs. The police could not be trusted and my face was pasted over every newspaper in Havana as an enemy of the Friends Of Che who presumably had possibly the silent majority of Havana solidly behind them. I studied the article and the background spread inside the paper in full and found no reference to Jenny or Susanna which was the one small comfort of good news I could glean from this horror movie I was starring in. Other than the press statement there was no account of the circumstances. Just reams of historical accounts of previous 'Friends of Che' atrocities and speculation on how we were captured and how we were brought together in Cuba at this time.

The more I think of it the more bizarre the whole situation was. Just who was pulling these strings that we all happened to be together. Either they were incredibly good at organising or else they got monumentally lucky.

I could not stop thinking about Maria, Anton, Ramon and Felix and felt so sad. Those bastards killed four beautiful people for what? I would have loved to get my hands on Suarez. But it was just a flight of fancy, what could I do? I felt so desperately alone.

I made myself as trampish looking as possible, which did not take to much effort, found a bar and sank as many Cuba Libras as I could. I considered what had happened to me, what had to be done and as the Havana Clubs mounted up, how I could start putting some justice on this whole crazy world.

Realising that my face had probably been circulated across every newspaper in the world, I could not risk too much exposure to anyone. I had grown a beard, which helped and was a lot scruffier than in the photos. Also I wasn't a criminal, people would not be scared of me but who could I trust? That was easy... no one. No doubt a few of the local boyos would see me as a meal ticket if I happened to be in the wrong place at the wrong time. I was being sought by ruthless men who probably felt I could identify them so I would be a priority. And 'Friends of Che' would have many sympathisers in the officials of the bureaucracy. Using my return ticket was just not possible, the realms red tape would eventually tie me down somewhere in the system.

I could think of only one solution, get into the Irish consulate as soon as possible, but after discrete enquiries I discovered there wasn't one. All representations could be referred to the Consulate in Mexico. Perfect, I could see myself explaining the delicacy of my position to a Mexican secretary over the phone. There had to be a plan B. The English Embassy, worth a try, so I headed down to Miramar. It was no surprise that the offices were closed for the weekend with no ambassador's home address obviously available, and I didn't want to ask any further questions. So I had to lay low for the day. Fortunately the goons hadn't taken my wallet and I still had a few dollars, enough to see out the weekend in some back street bed and breakfast which as it turned out, the one I chose was just fantastic.

My host was delighted to entertain me and had wonderful stories of life in Havana before the revolution which suited my present predicament. If he recognised me he did not let on, delighted in a captive audience for his story telling. He served up a dinner that would grace any hotel. I don't quite understand how he managed to serve up such a feast when meat was rationed, but he explained that if you could prove you had a guest you were able to get extra supplies which could be extended to feed the rest of your family. I was therefore a welcome visitor to the entire family.

I restricted my need to get out to just one journey downtown. After dinner, washed down with most of a bottle of golden Havana Club, when the feeling of being a prisoner just got too much for me, I sauntered into the city. I felt that I didn't want to draw too much attention to myself with my host if I stayed in doors all the time, so it was time to exercise my legs again. I wandered through the dilapidated streets of Havana chased by young men trying all sorts of schemes to relieve me of a few dollars and even younger girls who were openly trying to suggest that I should be engaging in a little more carnal pleasure. They might well be right but these girls were disturbingly young.

I trusted one bar with my custom which turned out to be a little more than I expected, four mojitos costing me thirty dollars when they were less than five dollars in a 4 star hotel. I tried to argue but there was just no point. Anyway I just wanted to melt away into the night, and it was good fun while it lasted. I realised something was happening which gratefully had nothing to do with me and I followed the crowd down the Malecon, the mile long promenade on the waterfront, as a Carnival approached. The atmosphere was electric, beer wagons on every street corner filling your own bottle of any size for two dollars. Everyone was in good form and happy to make friends but on the other side there was a darker element. I twice felt my pockets being touched. I was beginning to feel uncomfortable. To everyone around I was a tourist – a target, but in reality I was a refugee – a target. I realised I had to get out and return to my haven. Watching my back, suspicious of everyone was not the way this town should be seen. I long for my bed and the peace of untroubled sleep and wonder when I would ever enjoy that luxury again.

Monday morning arrived with bright sunshine and a throbbing head, what was I thinking of, I scolded myself. It is time to get down to the Embassy. After a very quick breakfast I explained that I might or might not return depending on circumstances and settled my eighteen dollar bill for full board which compared rather favourably with the bill for ninety minutes drinking the night before. I took the short walk across to the Embassy in the old part of the city to arrive on the door step a few minutes before the doors were due to open. Seeing one of the staff enter the building I go to follow him just as a tug on my arm turned me around.

'Good to see you Ben' Rory said.

I froze in my footsteps, you bastard. I didn't believe this. What was he doing here? The answer to that did not take too long to sink in. Maybe just maybe he wanted to explain his part in this whole shabby affair. I reasoned with myself that he would have news of Jenny sufficiently to hear him out. My thought of Jenny being the first I had of her for eight hours, perhaps I was losing my obsession. Then again they were flooding back with a vengeance. Before I got a chance to put any of my thoughts into words he roughly pushed me away from the consulate door and said 'It isn't open for another half hour, would you fancy a coffee' Given that I couldn't escape because I had to come back here and he would be waiting presumably until I did, I agreed to talk to him and followed his lead a few blocks down to the Plaza de Armas where we found a table nestling in the beautiful morning sunshine and mulled over our recent adventures like old friends catching up. But obviously from very different perspectives.

'I think you have some explaining to do, Rory you fucking bastard. You tricked all of us into a trap which eventually lead to four people being cold bloodedly murdered. And for what – some fucking ridiculous cause that benefited no one. Can you say anything that could convince me you are not some fucking moronic animal.' I decided to take the bull by the horns. I felt threatened by him and he wasn't going to help me get home but I just wanted to know why he got involved with this creepy organisation and how he could be a party to the assassination of innocent people. Friends, for Christ's sake.

'Maybe you're right Ben, and maybe I don't give a shit what you think but as it happens I didn't intend for any of this to happen. We just wanted the publicity and there was no need to shoot anyone. I am sorry but... c'est la guerre. But just for your information Jenny and Susanna knew nothing of what was to happen. As far as they were concerned we were just organising a day in the newspapers. They were a little surprised.' I wasn't absolutely certain but I think I saw a smirk which was just too much to take and stood up to punch him, but before I could land a blow he caught my hand 'Take it easy Ben, there's work for you to do.'

'What the fuck do you mean, work to do. I don't think you've staked out the Embassy just to do me a favour. You want to finish the job you were contracted to do. So I want to tell you… Fuck You. And now tell me what happened to the others. God you are the living anti Christ.'

Rory smiled 'Ok, one thing at a time. I'm here because Jenny wants to see you but she didn't know if you wanted to see her. So I'm a sort of messenger boy if you like. Why I'm doing this I've no idea.'

'Yeah, and I believe you, you twisted piece of defecation. This is just another trap and unless you want to shot me in the street I am walking back to the Embassy right now and tell them everything I know. I'm sure international pressure will turn you into fugitive for life.' I stood up and begin to move, but Rory was quick to stand in my way.

'Just five minutes I can bring her here in five minutes, then will you believe me? If you turn around now you'll never see her again.'

I didn't know if that was a threat or just stating the rather obvious fact. Either way I knew I'd never be able to live with myself if I walked away and he was right.

'On her own, I don't want to see you or anyone else, do you understand'

'OK, five minutes' I watched as hc disappeared down a side street.

I looked at my watch, to check the slow passage of the five minutes, I was both elated at the prospect of seeing Jenny again, but also absolutely distraught at the thought that I had probably just fallen for another trick and half a dozen heavies were going to appear at any minute. Seven minutes passed, and my anxiety levels were increasing. This was stupid, I had to get to the Embassy and got up to go when a soft voice behind me melted every bone in my body.

'Hi Ben, you're looking a little dishevelled'

I turned around and saw what I can only describe as the most wonderful sight I had ever seen in my life. Jenny, fresh faced and bronzed, no make up, smiling in a pink and green tee shirt, a pink, short skirt and leather sandals. Her hair was full of curls and she looked just perfect, with the exception of a slight bruise under her right eye, I felt relieved that I did know my own strength and it wasn't very inspiring. Any thoughts I had that I still hadn't forgiven her disappeared in a second. 'You look just stunning, I never thought I would see you again.'

'Yeah, I know, but this isn't a social call.'

'What do you mean, Rory said you wanted to see me' I managed to blurt out, my emotions getting tangled by every second that passed.

'Listen Ben, Rory is seriously bad news and I hope after all that has gone on you'll believe me. For some reason he wants to talk to you in private away from Havana. I don't think he has anything to do now with the 'Friends of Che', they've gone underground anyway. They got their day in the spotlight and will disappear for a few years before some one else comes up with another hair brained scheme. He wants to put the record straight before you head back to Ireland, and all that may or may not be believable except he told me that if I didn't get you meet him he would kill Susanna.'

'He what...., the fuck.... he what, what's going on...... what's he playing at...where does he want me to go?'

Not for the first time my ability to think coherently had gone awol.

'You really don't have to go Ben, I think you may be in real danger. But I am going to try and save Susanna if I can. I will be really pleased if you can come too but I guess I'll understand if you don't want to.'

I didn't have to think twice; at last the time for my indecision had come to an end. 'I think I'm nuts about you, Jenny. Every time I'm with you I don't want the moment to end and every time I'm away from you I think of nothing else but getting back to you' which I suppose hadn't been quite the truth over the last few hours but it was close enough. 'And the thought of being with you for a few hours more is just wonderful, and whilst we're about it we can try and save Susanna's life. Sounds good to me.'

She threw her arms around me and gave me the longest kiss I have ever had in public. I was lost in oblivion as several tourists stood beside us and applauded as we emerged from our embrace, just slightly embarrassed but deliriously happy.

She smiled at me in one of those special moments that I knew will last longer in my memory than any photograph. 'He has a house in Matanzas, about three hours away, which is where he has Susanna. He will be there at five this evening and expects us to be there, or else'

'Ok, let's go. But you have to tell me what happen to the others.'

She took my hand and began to tell the story of the assassination. 'Yeah, I owe you that. After your escape Suarez questioned me for about an hour trying to get some information as to where you would have gone. I think he believed me that you had hit me. I suppose he understood your motive. Anyway I stated the obvious, that you would have gone to Havana to raise the alarm. I tried to tell him to let every one go, that it was over but he became frenzied and looked as though he was losing any sense of reality. Actually he looked like a rabid dog. I think he was more concerned with saving his skin than worrying about mine. He left me on my own but heard him bark out his orders that Felix, Maria, Anton and Ramon should be brought out immediately. I still hadn't realised what was happening until I heard the soldiers clutch their rifles. I ran outside and before anyone had a chance to realise the enormity of what was going on Suarez gave the order to fire. It was terrible. They just stood there, not really believing what was happening to them. I didn't either. I know this sounds stupid but there comes a time when you are not shocked any more and you just feel as though you're in a movie. You know you're a voyeur witnessing another piece of fantasy. Anyway you convince yourself it's only a joke and everything will be alright. Then the soldiers raised their rifles and fired a volley of shots. I saw them, Ben, just falling to their knees in slow motion and then collapsing together just like kids playing cowboys and indians. No blindfolds, no last requests, it was all over in seconds. After the gun fire subsided, and that seemed to go on for hours with smoke lingering to make the scene look like a still black and white photograph, they were riddled with bullets... it was horrible...' Jenny stopped for a couple of minutes in tears and struggled to continue.

'... there was a deafening silence. Rory and Susanna didn't see what happened but ran out of their huts when they heard the shooting and froze on the spot. No one moved, not Suarez, Rory, or any members of the firing squad. It was as though they had been playing at soldiers, following orders like robots and suddenly their collective consciousness woke up. You could see they knew that they shouldn't have done it and just looked at each other, frozen as though their actions had brought a divine retribution.'

'Susanna was the first to move, breaking free from Rory's grip she ran over to Anton's body wailing in a devilish scream. She just held him in her arms, sobbing with her eyes and mouth wide open. It was the worst thing I have ever seen... I just wanted to run over to her and console her but I knew she was beyond any calming and I just stayed still as she looked at Suarez, Rory and the firing squad with blacks eyes that just spat out hatred.'

'I don't think the arrival of a helicopter crammed with an armed battalion of paratroopers could not have had more of an effect. The soldiers were literally petrified. She started to wail, it was awful and she went on and on. Physically you just couldn't do what she did, but things take over. Still screaming she picked Anton up in her arms and started to walk towards the soldiers. I can't explain how but she looked bigger, like giant a Amazon woman seeking revenge. She was truly awesome. She sent all the soldiers into a panic, and they just disappeared. I swear it was the strangest thing, they dropped their guns, ran for the trucks and left. Suarez, did the same, but obviously didn't share the conscience of the others as he must have been the one to issue the press release, but he just disappeared. It left me and Rory to comfort Susanna and try to give some dignity to the bodies. After helping to bring them in doors and place them on beds in some appearance of rest, he left to raise the alarm whilst Susanna and I washed them down as best we could.'

'Rory returned in a small jeep, after about an hour, saying that he had told an agricultural school about what had happened and that they had rung the police who would be up here in around fifteen minutes. He suggested that we should leave more or less immediately as he didn't trust the police to look any further than the three of us for suspects. I tended to agree with him, but Susanna said she wanted to stay with Anton. Without any warning he struck Susanna across the forehead with the butt of a handgun he suddenly revealed. It knocked her out cold and I looked at him aghast. He told me to get her into the jeep or he would shot her there and then. So I did and we drove into Matanzas where he has a house.'

'That's where she is now, under the guard of some heavy called Jose and that's why I'm here. He said he had to talk to you and that Susanna would die if I didn't do what he asked.'

The fact that my escape had been the catalyst to the murder squad was something I was trying not to think of, but it was unavoidable now. Jenny had the same soul searching as well… if she hadn't come to my room two nights ago… if… if… if… I looked at her, defenceless, innocent, beseeching me with those huge eyes to help. I held her hand trying hard to offer comfort but more seeking it myself. I had nothing to say.

After a few moments of contemplating Jenny's story, I tried to lift our spirits with the matters in hand 'We have no time to lose, come on, we have to find Susanna.'

Chapter 13

We discovered a bus that took us back to Matanzas, not caring this time about the possibility that we may have been followed. Travelling with Jenny anyway added more anonymity, but I had the feeling that the Friends of Che would have gone to ground, literally I hoped. Arriving in Matanzas around four hours early there really was nothing we could productively do. Whilst our minds were racing with what was ahead of us we still managed to put all the horrors of the immediate past behind us and pretend to be carefree lovers walking through the streets of a poor but very friendly town. We found ourselves recreating the time we had in Trinidad walking hand in hand, smiling at the locals and their giggling at our outward show of affection. And it was only brilliant with another group of unique settings to photograph, men fishing from rubber tyres, teenagers cavorting a la 'Dirty Dancing', a child's birthday party, a sports museum with just old photographs and a couple of plastic trophies, the fresh fruit and meat market, a brothel, the queue for the chemist, the magnificent statue of Jose Martine freeing Liberty from her chains. If only I had my camera! It is funny how the mind operates at times, given all that was going on I could not see how my missing the shots was important, but it was. Despite that I had another great day letting myself be drawn into situations that I had promised myself I would not happen by trusting people, do I ever learn. But I would imagine it would have been better, if the sword of Damocles had not been hanging over us.

Five'o'clock approached too quickly without our arranging a game plan of any significance. After we find the only hotel in the town where Rory had arranged to meet us, we considered our options. 'I think I will just go in and demand Susanna's release in exchange for my capture and see what happens'

'Not too inspiring, what if he says no and then he has both of you' Jenny calculated, 'you have to have some lever over him.'

'Look, he's not going to get away with this, trust me.'

The words sounded hollow, Rory was probably armed and I wasn't. Jenny tried to let me down gently. 'He's not going to just hand her over. I'll call him to say that we all meet in public and Susanna and I will leave you two to discuss whatever. But the reason he wants you in Matanzas is because he can do something here he couldn't have done in Havana, which I presume is not going to be too pleasant.'

Facing tricky situations has suddenly become commonplace and did not hold the fear in me it would have done a couple of weeks earlier. However there was no point in being stupid. I had tried that for too long. At that point a rather friendly Cuban leant over us and suggested we might like to follow him and without a seconds warning wrapped a muscular leg around mine catching his toe behind my calf. With a simultaneous movement he took an arm as I was thrown off balance and lifted it up behind my shoulder blade. I had this panicky feeling that both joints were going to pop and I was helpless. 'Shall we go and see Senor Megan?' he asked almost politely to which I nodded in the affirmative. Jenny followed us without a word. The best laid plans of mice and men etcetera... well at least we didn't waste any time thinking up any.

Rory was waiting for us in his house and welcomed us warmly 'Jenny thank you very much. It's so good to see you again Ben welcome to my humble house.'

Actually it was anything but humble, from the outside you would be forgiven if you thought that building was condemned but inside with tall, spacious, colonial rooms decorated and furnished with an artistic flair, and in the main drawing room a huge fan was playing with the flies overhead. The large leaded window was adorned with bright blue glass at the top which gave a soft light to part of the room whilst the rest was bathed in the bright evening sun. The entire house was spotlessly clean with clinical white walls and tiled flooring. Jenny was not concerned with the décor. 'Where's Susanna you slime ball?' she asked with some delicacy. Well none actually.

'Really Jenny, I am surprised at you, Susanna is in the Hotel bar as we speak waiting for you. Perhaps Jose will take you downtown to show you.'

'I'm going nowhere without Ben' she said defiantly but Jose had different ideas and threw her across the room without seeming to move. I jumped over to him only to be meet by a swinging right hand that knocked me off my feet and left me dazed, bleeding and impotent as Jose marched Jenny out of the room. She turned with her huge forlorn eyes that seem to cry 'Goodbye' and places two fingers to her lips and down to her heart. I didn't respond, my body and spirit broken, as I watched her disappear behind the door. It was my last sight of her, though I was unaware of that at the time, but my eyes followed her as she struggled against the immovable Jose. Proud and strong, young and beautiful, tender and my love. She gave me strength.

Rory shattered this vision with a diatribe that lost all the pleasantries that any conversation I may have had with him before. Maybe it was time to be honest and I should have been grateful for that. But my heart was low, I felt nothing but contempt for this man who was now keeping me from being with Jenny.

'Perhaps I should start from the beginning.'

'All I want you to do is release Jenny, Susanna and me and hand yourself over to the police to stand trial for the murder of my friends.' I recognised the rather unlikely outcome that I was suggesting but it did boost my air of defiance that I wanted to show.

'I think a few things have to be explained. First of all you are in no position to dictate to me what you want and second if you think I am interested in your rather childish calls for justice you are naively misguided. However I would like to tell you exactly why you are here. I think it would be fun.'

' Listen I don't give a shit about your idea of fun, let me out of here' I stood up and go to pushed Rory out of the way, but with surprising force he landed a punch straight into my solar plexus. Winded I looked at him, feeling rather helpless as he sat down and began his monologue without looking at me.

'As I said, I shall start from the beginning. About four months ago I met Denis O'Hara who was over in Havana to shag a few young ladies who delightfully don't recognise an old man when they see one. Being able to arrange such things we met several times in the course of his three week stay. During that time we built up a strong relationship on mutual needs, his for young pussy, mine for good old Yankee dollars and a few bottles of Jameson, which we both could feed ourselves in virtually unlimited quantities.

'During one particularly long session after both our appetites had been satiated he told me of the trouble a certain hardball journalist was giving him in Ireland. Like a dog with a bone he wouldn't let go and he was getting closer every day to uncovering something of the truth. And if he was allowed to go too much further he would have enough evidence for the police to press charges. A long trial with a possible jail sentence was not how he planned to spend the next five years so he thought it time to take pre emptive action. That journalist, as you have probably guessed by now was you.' He turned and smiled at my still prone body.

Like a steam roller nothing was going to stop him relaying this little story. I know I keep saying this, but I thought I had heard so many surprises this week that nothing could catch me off guard again. I was wrong. This really was coming out of no where. To say I didn't see it coming was the understatement of the century. He obviously sensed my surprise and noticeably relaxed. He was enjoyed ridiculing me, but I was too interested in what he was going to say next to make any comment. 'I see I have your attention now,' he smiled and continued, 'We discussed many things, not too much about what he was trying to keep out of the papers, not too surprisingly I suppose, but why I was in Cuba, how I made a living and what benefits Cuban life had'

'I was sort of wondering that myself' I heard myself saying before I remembered I wanted no part of this conversation, I just had to hear what O'Hara had to do with this and then wait for my moment to make a move and get to Jenny's side.

'I arrived in Cuba full of the virtues of real socialism in action, no private ownership of property, no private enterprise except for the essential one man businesses like farming that cannot work without motivation, free education and health service and everyone earns the same. The result is what you see a happy people not eaten away by envy. I quickly learnt that being in the right place at the right time and possessing one personal quality that few of my hosts possess, ambition, it was quite easy to make a lot of money providing tourists with what they want.'

'You're a pimp, you bastard. And kids for Christ sake, you make me sick.'

'Your moral judgements are of little interest to me, but I am certain any information I can give you on Denis O'Hara will be music to your journalistic ears. So if you will allow me the courtesy of continuing without your pompous interruptions.' He paused only momentarily before continuing 'I am in the happy position to be of service to a lot of rich influential men, of whom Dennis O'Hara is most definitely one. During the course of one of our discussions I discover that his distaste for your activities has reached the point that he felt that action had to be taken.

'Obviously you did not appear to be a man that could be easily bought showing no proof that the finer things in life held any attraction to you. Also your home life was in such turmoil that even if we could get something that might be embarrassing on you, there was little indication that you could give a shit if we exposed you or not. You'll be pleased to know that your lifestyle makes you unlikely to be a target of blackmailers. You don't have anything worth protecting. A rather dubious quality don't you think?'

For the first time I thought about what he was saying in agreement, yes he was right, my life was a mess, well up to when I met Jenny. Thank God O'Hara doesn't realise how he could have put pressure on me now. I nodded as a broken man in agreement as he continued. I thought he thought he was in confession. Good for the soul and all that. But I was still curious at the tone the conversation had taken. I took it that he meant the question to be rhetorical as he resumed with only the briefest of pauses.

'Further employing hit men was too dangerous now as the Veronica Guerin murderers discovered, with the full weight of the Criminal Assets Bureau turned against them and all that meant in turning up media interest. So after much thought we decided that the best option was to somehow get somebody else interested in disposing of you, deflecting any suspicion and ultimately interest away from Mr O'Hara.'

Not for the first time in the last few days I was completely floored. Mixed feelings of fear that I was dealing with an amoral psychopath and anger that everything that had happened to me and my friends had been a complete charade, I leant against the wall to pull myself upright and to buy a little time to collect my thoughts before launching into a strong a tirade as I can muster.

'What are you saying you evil bastard, this whole 'Friends of Che' fiasco was a complete hoax just to get me off O'Hara's back. And four people died for absolutely nothing of their own making just so some screwball Irish cunt can avoid answering some embarrassing questions over who lined his pockets.'

'Not exactly Ben, though you do appear to be getting most of the picture quite quickly. 'Friends of Che' do exist and General Suarez is very keen to exact as much revenge as possible on any one involved with the assassination of Che. Obviously getting the actual people involved is quite difficult now though they did manage to knock off a rather senior major who was the commander in chief of armed forces at the time, in Paris in 1998. And Felix and Anton have been long targets of the association. When I met General Suarez in the summer he did take to the idea of a multiple assassination being a glorious way to give their organisation as much publicity as Al Qaeda got for blowing the Twin Towers. And I think he probably now is quite happy with the results, with the added benefit that he is unlikely to be sought by any other than the Cuban security forces as the Americans will hardly make too much of an incident which actually only affects one of their citizens. Castro has already made all the right noises that no stone will go unturned until these assassins are brought to justice. We all know how long that will take.'

'And why Maria and Ramon, did they have anything to do with it?'

'Ramon's father is who he is, we were lucky that you ran into him in Bolivia and that he took such a shine to you. Being a fan of Anton's and with Susanna encouraging him it wasn't hard to get him on board. Maria's involvement was largely irrelevant.'

'Hardly for her.'

'Yes, well that's as maybe, but we knew nothing about her until she joined Felix and fell for his rather unique style. When we discovered that she wanted to follow Felix and he was only too delighted to have her around we did some digging on her and learnt she had arrived in Mexico City at an early age when her father started up his print business. He was successful and we could find nothing of his past before he started on crusading. Of course he is dead now so not in a position to refute anything and Maria would probably know nothing of her years before the move to the city. It isn't difficult to persuade someone that their parents have a secret past, most of us would be only too delighted to learn they come from some intrigue and mystery. As far as the world press go they accepted the press release issued by the 'Friends of Che' as gospel to make sure they get the story out as soon as possible. If any of them do doubt it and put in some undercover work, it only prolongs the day in the sun for Suarez and his gang.'

'And my father' I asked with some incredulity wanting to believe he could not have sawn off a dead man's hands but also not wishing to believe that I could have been such a fool to have fallen for it. And it crossed my mind that I am asking questions which are only going to delay my seeing Jenny again, but I could not help myself.

'Your father was in Bolivia, but we have no record of what his involvement was. He may well have been attached to the military, they generally don't take no for an answer but it is more likely he spent all his time in La Paz involved in WHO immunisation programmes, trying as they were then to eradicate small pox in the world.'

'And what now?' I ask with a little indifference, feeling numb and stupid about the lies I have swallowed and the murderous farce I have been involved in.

'I now have to shoot you and let the 'Friends of Che' have their final victim, and rather more importantly that I can collect my hundred thousand dollars. You may think that I have settled rather cheaply for your removal, but remember O'Hara is my second paymaster. I take some pride in being paid by two people to do the same job. I think you should feel quite proud in how unwanted you are!'

Chapter 14

Facing Rory with a gun in his hand, having declared his intention to shoot me left me fairly well focused. I had always fantasised that if ever I was in a situation where the odds were stacked against me I should be able to use a superior intellect to overcome an opponent. Of course that did make the assumption that I had a superior intellect, and Rory had up to now displayed no evidence that I could trample all over him in the mensa stakes. However it was worth a try, he probably hadn't shot too many people and probably none who he knew personally. He would certainly have some reservations. Against that he had incriminated himself in his involvement of a hit job (mine), drug trafficking, procurement, not to mention a mass murder. He did have plenty of reasons for holding his resolve.

I watched him from my prone position, saying nothing. I thought he expected me to react to his final revelation. Anger or humiliation maybe, but I had to do the unexpected, putting him off guard, making him nervous. I sat still for as long as possible trying not to show any emotion. Let him break the tension, he was not going to just shoot me without some sort of declaration, that wouldn't make sense. Why did he make his confession, he wanted me to wallow in self pity or he wanted to test himself against a caged animal. He had no reason to hate me so I thought this whole episode was based on his feeling superior. He was feeling untouchable. The idea sprang into my mind that he may be right, though my alter ego came to my rescue-- don't think like that, this is his weakness, killing me before he plans to would be admitting he had to resort to non personal strengths. He would avoid that, I had to keep this situation running away from his plan whatever that was. The silence became deafening and I could see he was getting a little uncomfortable that I still had not reacted to what he assumed would be devastating news. He finally broke the tension.

'The time has come, we have to go now to meet General Suarez, you will appreciate that Jenny and Susanna are still in Jose's very capable hands, so don't try anything stupid.'

I saw a crack of light, first he was not going to shoot me — that was just bravado talking, he was going to leave the dirty work to his henchmen. And second he thought by his holding Jenny and Susanna he had a lever over me. The problem was that he was right, but I did not have to let him see that.

Still not moving as Rory edged slowly towards me, I considered exactly what I was going to say. This had to be good, I prayed for inspiration.

'Rory, let me explain something to you. Given that I am facing certain death why should I make this easy for you. Kill me now if you wish, but presumably Suarez won't be too pleased with you and you will have to explain the gun shot, not to mention the difficulty of removing my body from your house. And if you do decide to shot me, what do you do to Jenny and Susanna, whilst it would be a shame, it won't really make too much difference to me, I will be dead. I don't believe there is any more mental pain you can inflict on me that could persuade me to do anything you wished. And I also believe that my mind is strong enough to endure physical pain. In other words and I would like to make this as plain as possible so that you understand exactly where I am coming from, go and fuck yourself, preferably with a diseased sugar cane.'

I thought I saw his anger rising, but he doesn't change his movement towards me, as he grabbed me by my shirt to lift me upright, his warm breathe invading my face that I instinctively spit straight in his eyes. I had never done that before and felt elated. Now he was really mad, my superior intellect coming up trumps I proudly congratulate myself. My plan was working, he was shaping to beat me up. Why was I so happy about this, my alter ego once again failing to appreciate the finer points of my well reasoned, if not well researched, theory. Rory punched me in the stomach with such force that my head came down on his shoulder knocking him momentarily off balance. The instant that happened the rising storm that had been building up for sometime without either of us really noticing blew the window shutters back, clattering into the room and hitting Rory in the small of the back. Still bent double, I saw an opportunity to rush at him with every bit of strength I could muster. The rain started pouring in the window which seemed to lift my spirits, maybe this was God giving me a sign that he was on my side. I did not care what I did as I was beyond any physical feeling. I knew Rory was not happy as I rammed into him, my shoulder into the pit of his stomach, and into the wall next to the window. The gun jumped out of his hand as though it had suddenly turned red hot. As he slumped to the ground I saw his face looking up at me and give it the hardest kick I could, throwing his head backwards as blood spurted out of his mouth. His eyes closed and I relaxed my aggression only to feel a hand grabbing my kicking foot, pulling me off the ground and banging my head on a chair leg. Both of us stayed semi dazed for a second before he slowly got to his knees, blood still rolling out the corner of his mouth. We both spotted the gun together, neither being able to reach it, but Rory was nearer to being on his feet. Just as he began to lift himself from his knees he turned as we heard an ungodly groan followed by a crashing noise that seemed to surround us. A large tree toppled over from the garden into the house showering roof tiles everywhere and spewing plaster and brickwork into the room. A long branch speared through the window catching Rory straight in the face, as he turned to see what was happening. He was knocked over and lay motionless, pinned to the floor as broken glass and plaster were sprinkled over him like a cake dusting. The sugar cane has come to fuck you. Thank you God, was my last thought as I felt consciousness slipping away.

I woke after a few moments or days for all I knew, with the wind and rain still flooding through the hole where the window was, forming muddy rivulets on the floor with the plaster that shattered off the walls with the impact. One of the shutters banged endlessly against the wall as darkness pervaded the whole eerie scene. I saw Rory's body spread eagled on the floor with one of the smaller branches piercing his throat. I go over to check his pulse knowing from his eyes there hasn't been one for some time. He was dead and a wave of satisfaction came over me. Whilst the final blow was not down to me, I felt some pride in engineering the situation which had lead to his downfall. I tried hard to reconcile these thoughts with my inability even to destroy the life of a spider at home but consoled myself with the evil that Rory had enacted on me and my friends. Devine retribution and it was beautiful.

The storm would keep everyone minding their own business for some time and I could not see Suarez bothering to do too much travelling in during the storm even if Rory failed to make an appointment. My only worries were about other people in the house trying to see the extent of the damage but I heard no voices or movement so I didn't feel any immediate need to move out into the driving rain. Any thoughts of looking for Jenny and Susanna were also dismissed until there was some let up, they would have to wait until the storm died down. Given that Rory was killed by an Act of God (however vengeful) there was no need to fear being discovered. So I thought I should find some food and prepare for a long night searching for the girls once the storm had died down.

An hour passed as I sat in a chair drinking a can of beer I found and eating some cheese and dry bread, listening to the rain, looking at Rory's body, feeling shamelessly smug. This self indulgence was brought to an abrupt end with a crazed beating on the door, followed by a gun shot through the door lock as the door burst wide open. Momentary fear passed as Susanna's silhouette appeared at the door way looking straight at Rory's prone body. She raised her gun at arms length and fired four shots in rapid succession into his chest which leapt limply with each strike.

She slowly lowered her arm and I rushed over to her embrace her whispering softly, 'He's dead, Susanna. He's dead.'

She turned to me with a distant look as though she saw straight through me. Her hair was flattened by the rain flowing down her face, which dripped from her chin down her cleavage exposed by the dirty torn low cut and now virtually see through tee shirt. Her hips carried her skirt provocatively as rain continued its fall to ground from the jagged ends. The body language was all aggression and her face so intent that when I looked at her straight in the eye I thought I had never seen anyone as potently sexy in all my life. She would doubtlessly refute it later and possibly I would concede that it was a totally inappropriate observation but she looked magnificent.

I was still hugging her as she drops the gun to the floor and sobbed uncontrollably for several minutes before I got her to sit down, brushing her hair out of her eyes with my fingers. I knelt beside her holding her hand whispering 'It's Ok let it all out, Susanna it's all over now.'

She looked at me with doleful eyes full of tears, lifted me up to sit beside her and started the sentence that would haunt me for the rest of my life. 'Ben, I'm so sorry, Jenny's dead, she…..' I heard nothing else. Every remaining piece of life left in my emotionally and physically battered body just drained out of me and I lay back as Susanna continued '……..was thrown through the windscreen of the pick up. Jose was driving like a mad man…'

'I tried to save her…I did everything I could to make her comfortable in the back of the truck and drove her back into town for help…But it was too late. I'm so sorry

Ben. She's still there. I just came to seek out Rory and kill him.

Her turn now to take me in her arms and both of us wept together, no more explanations required, both our lives beautifully recreated and savagely destroyed in the space of a few days, as the wind slowly blew itself out timed by the pendulum beat of the window shutters getting longer and longer between their clattering against the wall, slowly beating a hypnotic rhythm inviting total submission.

Chapter 15

I woke up as the sun rose with Susanna in my arms. The room was drying out with a damp stench of stale debris. It was still a complete mess and flies were beginning to hover around Rory's body, which had begun to lose any look of humanity as his colour has totally drained from his face, replaced by a waxy jaundiced glaze, which had contorted as his muscles tighten. He looked as though his whole body has shrunken by his soul taking leave with his life. I woke Susanna and she too was repulsed by the sight and thought we should get out as quickly as possible. No argument, but I had to see Jenny.

'We can't Ben. Look I'm really sorry, but we've got three dead bodies in the town with the authorities trying to find some explanations. With Jose's gun shots in Rory, Jenny's body in Jose's pick up and Jose's body twenty minutes out of town even the Cuban police are going to think that natural causes aren't the only explanation. And it won't take them forever to connect us to everything. As soon as the morning comes there are going to be thousands of troops in the area to clean up the mess. That's how it works. They may even be there now at the truck. We're going to have to leave her for the authorities to deal with. We have to get out of this country and quickly.'

I could see her logic, but there were still things that had to be done. 'OK but I have to go down to the Waterfront first, I have to say my goodbyes. I'll meet you over the bridge in twenty minutes. I promise I'll be careful'

She knew she would be wasting her time to argue so she reluctantly agreed and we left the hell hole that was Rory's house to pick our way through the debris the storm had strewn over the streets to follow our different routes. Although early there were still plenty of people around, all helping each other and there was a great feeling of camaraderie shared by everyone embraced by an unseemly good humour. I wasn't in the mood to reciprocate, but still couldn't help being moved by the willingness of these people to help others when their own meagre possessions had probably been lost forever. It contrasted so poignantly with our own self centred world but none of that was my concern at the moment. There were no troops nor police around so I felt at ease as I headed down to where Susanna had said the truck was. I found it straight away but it was surrounded by dozens of people chaotically attempting to do the right thing. With no one in charge, no evidence as to who owned the truck and no identification of the beautiful young westerner in the back, I pinned for someone to take control.

I scrambled through the group to see Jenny there and said a prayer for the second time in a few hours but for vastly different reasons. 'You will always be with me' I whispered and bit my lip as tears formed in my eyes. This was heathen. I could not trust these people to do the right thing, but then what could I do if I was arrested. Susanna's right, I had to go 'God bless you, Jenny and thank you for giving me a reason for living. I promise I will always honour your memory.' I hesitated to absorb as much as I could of her. I knew this was the last time I would see her.

I joined Susanna as agreed and we started walking down the Havana road for a couple of hours hitching but no one was travelling in our direction. Several trucks filled with troops streamed into Matanzas confirming that we had made the right decision. I promised myself that I would come back one day and honour Jenny properly. Eventually an empty truck does stop and took us into Santa Cruz del Notre and I felt a certain déjà vu as we board the bus for Havana from the same spot as I had just three days earlier. Three days that I had felt both the ecstasy of meeting Jenny again and the agony of her death.

The bus was oppressively full, which meant we were standing, crushed against the crowded wooden seats and feeling every bump in the road. Consequently it was very sweaty and humid and both of us were feeling mentally and physically weak after the exertions of the last few hours. Susanna went through the whole story of Jose's driving and I explained how Rory had managed to fall victim to the storm. I decided not to tell her that Anton had died because O'Hara wanted me dead, nor did she mention how Jenny had died. Instinctively we both felt we both needed each other too much at the moment to complicate our relationship with blame. After we had exhausted all the details we were prepared to give, we continued in silence. Nothing more was said, our physical discomfort of being dirty, hungry and crushed in a packed bus seeming inconsequential to what we had both lived through the last few days. We knew there was more to say but I just wasn't ready to listen.

As we approached Havana I turned to Susanna and said that we needed to talk, that there was too much unsaid and we had to decide what to do. She replied that we needed to clean up first and should check into the first hotel we could find that wouldn't raise an eyebrow at our dishevelled appearance.

There was little difficulty in achieving that and we found a room with the exquisite luxury of a bathroom.

After our showers I rang down for a couple of drinks and sat Susanna down in front of me. 'Now tell me what happened and don't miss out one detail.' I said very dispassionately.

'Yeah, Ben I will. It's just that there is just so much I don't want to talk about, if you know what I mean.' I did and smiled ruefully, trying to encourage her, it probably worked but I felt guilty as she started to cry as she sat down preparing to tell her story.

The bell boy arrived with the drinks before she started and looked at us curiously but left without saying anything clutching the five dollar tip a little too avariciously.

Susanna began very hesitantly at first but then she appeared to be easing her conscience as she moved into the story. 'After Jenny brought you to Matanzas, Rory wanted to talk to you alone so Jenny was dragged away with Jose to find me. I was a prisoner in an old tobacco warehouse which, like most buildings in Matanzas was open to all who wanted to investigate... except for my room. That was up a spiral staircase, windowless and with nothing but tea chests, newspapers strewn over the floor, dirty coffee cups, plates and cigarette butts. I probably didn't make the place look any tidier. When Jenny arrived I was so pleased to see her. I can't explain the feeling, the emptiness I was suffering after Anton was murdered, and I remember thinking that after Rory took us that I would never go home again. And I didn't care. But seeing Jenny again was such a boost, I just jumped up from one of the tea chests when I saw her and gave her a hug that nearly killed her. I remember saying 'God bless you' which I hadn't said for years and we both just held each other in mutual relief. Jose was a pig, pushing both of us down the stairs with a pistol he had extracted from his jacket. Jenny objected 'Rory said we could go free if I brought Ben to him,' but Jose just laughed saying that he only had to kill one of us to spoil both our days if we caused any trouble. I don't know if you've been threatened by a laughing man – but it was really scary. Anyway he spat at us disdainfully, pushed us down the stairs and forced us into a pick up that was parked beside the river.

'He started the engine the same time as rain formed the first droplets on his windscreen. As we drove away from the town, down a long street with nothing but telegraph poles on either side, visibility was getting more restricted as the rain started to belt relentlessly against all the windows. The wind was building up to gale force as the vehicle started to toss with the elements. It seemed to come out of nowhere, with no warning and as if to announce that we had arrived in hell nightfall fell instantly. Jose seemed to be unaware that driving conditions were getting any worse and drove like a demented cowboy at a reckless speed, just concerned to get his task, whatever it was, over with as soon as possible.

'We looked at each other apprehensively, both think-ing that neither Jose nor his driving held out too much hope for our collecting our old age pensions and instinc-tively that something had to be done. The elements took matters out of our hands though. As we approached a bad right hand turn in the road, the pick up lost its back wheels and skidded in the mud down an embank-ment and into a tree at the rear wheel driver's side. It turned through 180 degrees, heading down hill off the road, towards several trees at fifty miles an hour, appar-ently getting faster rather than slowing down. The first blow threw us all forward into the windscreen and as the truck turned again, it moved downwards broadside into the next tree rolling from the resulting impact sev-eral times before coming to rest on its side, in a clearing covered with ferns and loose shale.

'I looked around as I shook myself back to full conscious-ness to see Jose's body slumped to the right of the steer-ing wheel, blood trickling from his right temple and his lips a very dark unnatural colour. His shirt was open to the waist and I noticed heavy bruising to his chest and guessed if he was alive, he was in no position to con-tinue his imprisonment of us. There was no sign of Jenny and I struggled to find a foot hold to exert enough pres-sure to clamber through the broken windscreen, aware of avoiding the millions of pieces of shattered glass. I was delighted to discover all my body parts appeared to be functioning OK and welcomed the lash of the warm rain on my face as clambered out of the cab. The relief of my own well being was quickly laid aside as I saw Jenny's body stretched out, motionless twenty yards up the clearing.

'I ran over, knelt beside her prone body and took her head in my arms as Jenny opened her eyes, dazed but focused. 'We've got to get back to Ben, Susanna he's in big trouble' she whispered before closing her eyes again with the rain sweeping across her face, washing her hair flat against her eyes and cheeks.

'I whispered 'Yeah course we will, just rest Jenny for a couple of minutes.' It was terrible, both Jose and Jenny needed medical attention quickly but we were in the middle of nowhere in the middle of a rainstorm a dog wouldn't venture out in. I had to get help and realised Jose's gun might be more than useful in getting transport of some kind and clambered back up the loose stones up to the pick up. Climbing up to the drivers door and pulling it open, required a lot more strength than I had anticipated and I was exhausted. Then the pick up gently rocked and I fell on top of Jose, screaming when I discovered that he was cold and an arm fell limply across the gear stick.

'I searched his pockets and discovered the handgun, which I stuffed into my jeans and jumped out of the pick up, again rocking it as it teetered on falling back onto its wheels as I scrambled out of the way before it crashed down, throwing Jose body half out of the windscreen.

'An idea crossed my mind, perhaps the main functions of the truck were still working and I tried the ignition. It kicked first time, it was brilliant, hopefully the axel and gearbox were OK too. Dislodging Jose out of the drivers seat was more difficult than I thought it would be, his dead weight lodging in every crevice of the twisted vehicle, but I eventually managed to pull him clear of it. Jumping into the driver's seat, I tried moving the pick up forwards, inching slowly forward my heart leapt, it was working. I kept the motor running, not trusting the truck to start up again and went to help Jenny climb aboard.

Mercifully the rain had died down, but the wind was still howling like a mad dog.

'Jenny thought I had gone but I told her we had to get to a doctor and that I would never leave her, and I meant it, she was all I had left in the world. I will always remember what turned out to be her last words, 'Don't worry about me, get to Ben, Susanna please. Rory has him behind the hotel on the second floor of 28, Parque de la Libertad.' She closed her eyes again as I lifted her onto her feet, wrapping my arm round her waist and pulling her arm behind my shoulders. Holding on to her wrist and taking her weight evenly across my body we inched over towards the truck. Leaning her against the end of the pick up I took one side panel down and slide Jenny's body into the floor. Taking off her jacket as a head rest I made her as comfortable as possible and jumped in the driver's seat and noticed the engine had stalled. I prayed it would restart and it did on the third attempt but it was slipping all over the place as we edged back up to the road.

'The relief of getting to the road was shattered by our not being able to get out of first gear, and so we were slowly grinding our way back up road to Matanzas fearing at any moment that the engine would explode. I suppose the rain for kept the temperature down.

'After travelling for two hours never above ten miles an hour with the engine grinding the whole time, over a journey that took less than twenty minutes going out, we got back into the river bank in the city and I jumped out and caressed Jenny. I took her head in her hands and screamed 'No, Jenny, nooooo' as I discovered her motionless in the back. I hugged her to me as close as I could rocking backwards and forwards sobbing gently at first before a raging passion burnt in me consuming every thought. My only true friend and my only true love killed because of that bastard. As I jumped from the truck, I took the gun and went in search of Rory, determined for revenge. I guess you know the rest. I'm sorry Ben, it wasn't a glorious end, just a stupid waste of a wonderful, beautiful person.'

I couldn't think what to say. I felt anger, mostly at Susanna, but I knew she was suffering every bit as much as I was. We were victims of a cruel, pointless gesture that had savagely torn our different worlds apart. And yet we survived, physically unscathed, when Anton and Jenny were brutally torn from life. Not to mention Maria, Ramon, Felix and even Rory – they were all part of a wonderful couple of days followed by a few in purgatory. I looked at the drinks, still untouched and finally said to Susanna 'I don't know where this will lead, but I have to look after the memory of Jenny. It is the only thing that matters to me. I am going back to Matanzas. Thanks Susanna for trying to help her,' and I took her in my arms and kissed her forehead.

She smiled through her tears and pulled her head to look me in the eye 'I'm coming with you, if that's Ok.'

'Course, but we need to find a change. You smell!'

'I've just showered you bastard' and released herself from my embrace with a push that sent me tumbling over drinks table, sending everything flying. I looked up at from the ground and saw she was laughing for the first time I can remember.

'Come on, let's go.'

I didn't mention to Susanna that I had another agenda; I wanted to get home as quickly as possible after Matanzas to get my hands on O'Hara. Now it wasn't bravado any more. I knew if I got him I would kill him and I was looking forward to it.

I stepped out of the hotel, more positive than I had thought possible when we arrived. I had things to do and I knew I was going to do them.

We ventured downtown to pick up a few tee shirts, a couple of pairs of jeans and fresh underwear down the market stalls when we heard a voice behind us at the top of his voice 'Susanna, you look beautiful. I love you so much.' We turned around in fear, to see probably the only face in Havana that was genuinely pleased to see us. Geronimo was there laughing his head off and ran over to embrace us, kissing both of us on both cheeks.

I could not think of anyone I'd rather see at that moment, it felt as though the clock had moved back a week and we were in Madrid again. That all that had happened has been a nightmare from which we were emerging. I knew this was not true but still felt my spirits raised as I knew Geronimo could and would help us. He lived for himself, answerable to no one and a free spirit. Whilst I knew my judgement had rather been called into question recently I felt confident that Geronimo was to be trusted and would take pleasure in helping us beat the authorities. And he would be bound to have contacts in every bureaucratic corner in Havana. Both judgements proved to be correct as we briefed him on most of what had gone on since we last met. He'd only returned from tour the previous day and knew nothing of the whole Friends of Che saga and was amazed of our involvement in such dramatic events. He went on to reassure us that most

Cubans wouldn't share their ideals. They were more interested in just getting through their daily lives and partying as much as possible. Talking of which, he reverted to type and suggested that maybe now was the right time for Susanna to join his collection of European conquests. Geronimo was being outrageous, totally inappropriate and insensitive but after going through so much in the last twenty four hours, we needed some light relief and Susanna saw it as just that and burst once more into her gorgeous laughter which proved so infectious.

'I'm being serious' Geronimo pleaded hurtfully. We all laughed as he went through all the advantages of joining his very exclusive but inclusive membership as he looked at me 'I kick both ways, Ben, so don't get complacent, you are European so you qualify.'

'Any chance you might have had just died ten seconds ago' Susanna smiled, 'but you never know…now if you were able to help us get out of the country…'

Suddenly Geronimo got totally serious. 'Yes, of course, I will do anything to help. I used to work in the airport and know the system fairly well. First of all you'll have no problem with the airline. Who are you flying with?'

'Iberia'

'Lucky you' Geronimo said sarcastically 'but at least you'll get on board the plane without any trouble. Before that you have to pay your airport taxes and get your exit visa stamped. If I met you in the airport, give me your passports, tickets and three hundred dollars and I will get all the paperwork organised without any delays for you at the departure gates.'

Susanna and I look at each other, I trusted Geronimo but felt disappointed and know Susanna was the same. By his own admission in Madrid, he had said tourists were fair game, he was against stealing but taking money willingly offered wasn't the same in his eyes. He saw our scepticism and grinned 'I won't scab you guys, but I do have to ease you through the red tape with a little oiling of greasy palms and anyway you have no choice, give me a break. Tell me where you are staying and I'll let you know how I get on later. By the way don't change the subject. Susanna I think you are the most beautiful person I have ever seen...'

'Forget it, Geronimo, see you later,' Susanna looks at me and we agree telepathically – this guy is incorrigible, but he does have style.

After exchanging details Susanna and I leave Geronimo to wander round the restored squares of Havana, neither saying too much, the horror of the evening coming back to us. I contemplated how we were going to get back to Matanzas before Geronimo arranged our flights. I knew we hadn't much time and thought maybe my getting Susanna out of Cuba should be my priority when Susanna realised she didn't have her passport, Jose had taken it from her. We had to get a car and cover the ground and hope his body hadn't been discovered.. I telephoned Geronimo and told him we were going to hire a car and would be back around nine all being well. Maybe we could meet him for dinner in the hotel. He told us to wait twenty minutes and he would have someone round with a car, but it would cost thirty dollars. No problem, I smiled to myself and wondered if there wasn't anything he couldn't arrange.

True to his word a car and driver arrived spot on the twenty minutes and we made the two and a half hour journey straight to the isolated spot where Susanna felt they crashed. All the track marks had been washed away by the rain, leaving no evidence of there being an accident as the truck had travelled out of sight of the road. As we scrambled down the embankment we were relieved to see Jose's body crumpled up in the heap just as Susanna had left it. It was not pretty with flies buzzing around all his orifices but we were very glad to see the body.

During the course of our journey Pablo, our driver had explained that he was Geronimo's brother and had given us his life story. He spoke of his little brother with great affection and how he had rescued him out of many scrapes with the authorities not to mention various Mafia style gangs he upset from time to time. But he virtually won everyone over with his esprit de Coeur. Once again we felt helpless in assessing whether Pablo could be trusted or not. We just had to hope for the best and take him on face value. He seemed sound enough, but who were we to judge given our track record?

Everything was going well so far, the passport along with Jenny's were in Jose's back pocket as well as eighty dollars and two hundred pesos which Pablo had no problem taking. We headed back into town to see if we could find out anything about what had happened to Jenny's body.

Pablo made all the enquiries and discovered there had been twelve deaths in the storms with some buildings still not extensively searched after they had collapsed. Three of those bodies were still unidentified in the morgue behind the hospital and we went over with the help of some of Jose's dollars to see all the bodies of all the storm victims. Pablo enquired what was to become of the bodies and was told that they would be buried in two days in unmarked graves in the cemetery out of town. I went to Pablo and told him to give all Jose's money to the morgue attendant to ask him to put a cross on Jenny's grave with her name on it. Pablo looked at me as though I was completely mad but did as I requested and the attendant swore he would totally comply with our wishes. I prayed again that he wouldn't let us down, but at least felt I had done all I could for Jenny for now. I promised to myself that I would return and do something more appropriate as soon as it was possible.

The return journey was made with a little more hope succeeding in both our quests, even if Pablo was bitching at losing his windfall. And we made our dinner date with Geronimo with an hour to spare. We invited Pablo to join us which he graciously accepted, even if we did have a little difficulty in persuading the hotel management that both Pablo and Geronimo were business associates, so that they could break the self imposed Cuban apartheid and join us.

Geronimo had nothing but good news. He had booked us on the twelve o clock morning flight which required our being at the airport by ten. He would pick us up and pay the airport taxes, get the passport stamped so that we could enter the VIP lounge which would be free of junior policemen trying to make a name for themselves and out of the gaze of any alert passenger who might recognise my photograph. We thanked him profusely, which only encouraged him into one final attempt 'I suppose a fuck is out of the question Susanna'

'Ten out of ten for persistence, thanks but no thanks' she smiled as I thought to myself with no disrespect to Susanna that she might have given his subtle advances a little more consideration if I hadn't been there. He was really good fun to be with, and his smile with huge white teeth was so contagious. He was exceptionally good looking as well and I wondered if his dancing work required his dressing in the multi sequinned frocks and tall headdresses that Tropicana was famous for. Possibly, but I didn't dare ask.

Susanna and I adjourn to our room happy that at last the immediate nightmare might be coming to an end, and dived into our twin beds to instant sleep which was only broken by our early morning call, with Pablo and Geronimo waiting in reception.

Everything worked like clockwork as we both feel guilty at ever doubting Geronimo. We bade our farewells with genuine sadness but promised to return soon, which I was certain I would keep to attend to the proper memory of Jenny.

Boarding the plane we enjoyed the flight in anticipation of what was to come. I realised during the course of the flight that I was drawn to Susanna and was worried what was going to happen to her. I knew I should despise her for her role in all of this but she was so innocent despite everything that had happened to us. Her charm was disarming and irrepressible and her intentions I was certain were never malicious. Did she have friends to go back to in Spain with Jenny and even Rory's work contacts now gone. Added to that the emotional turmoil she now had to live with in the wake of winning and losing Anton. There would be media pressure, something I was sure she would abhor. Perhaps she might like to come over to

Ireland for a few weeks to chill out. I was sure I could get her some part time work in the office to tide her over. To my surprise she didn't even think about it for a minute.

'Yeah, I'd love to' my pleasure at her immediate reaction was delayed for a while as I spent much of the rest of the flight thinking of what I was going to do with O'Hara.

Arriving at Madrid Airport, we said our goodbyes as she promised to fly to Dublin in a couple of days as she gets her things together and settled her affairs. I doubted whether I'd see her again but hoped so as I boarded the Aer Lingus morning flight home after a six hour wait in the small hours of the morning.

With time on my own, I questioned my sanity in bringing Susanna to Dublin. The one person, for whatever unintentional reasons, who was responsible for my nightmare.

PART 3

Susanna's Story

Chapter 16

I looked across at Susanna, my mind exhausted and her looking fragile and hurt. She wanted to leave and Trish was disgusted with my aggression and was apologetic to Susanna for bringing her to see me. I don't know how long it had been since I attacked her, my memory recall inducing some sort of blackout. But it couldn't have been long Trish still had a horrified look on her face.

'I can't believe you're like this, Ben. I have being searching for weeks for Susanna and when I find her she said you wouldn't want to see her, but I persuaded her that you were in trouble and needed help. She is here to help you and you attacked her, what is wrong with you?' I thought that was self evident, but realised that it wasn't the time to discuss the merits of my illness, a certain serenity passed over me.

'I think I know now, Susanna perhaps you might like to explain why I don't like you.'

'Actually Ben, I think you know what I did and you know why I did it. You did forgive me once. We both shared the same loss, remember?'

Trish was confused, 'Is anyone going to tell me what is going on?'

'Sorry, Trish I shouldn't have come so soon, but now I'm here I'd better tell you my story and I suppose I'll start at the beginning.'

I wasn't really interested in listening to Susanna, but knew Trish was embarrassed by my actions and in deference to her I offered no objection to Susanna's explanation. In fairness to her she was anxious to set the record straight, I really didn't know why.

Susanna looked at me, waiting for an objection but I nodded at her. It was as close as I was going to get to giving an apology and she acknowledged the gesture and prepared herself with a very audible sigh.

'Well here goes, as they say from the top. I was born in San Lorenzo de El Escorial, a beautiful village situated thirty miles outside Madrid housing a magnificent Abbey and an exclusive private boy's school, catering for the elite of Madrid's society young guns. The local economy is totally supported by the wealth that the school's residents, during the school year and tourists during the summer, brought. The village was situated in the mountains overlooking acres of well farmed and manicured land and endless pine trees. It is the perfect hide away for the rich to farm out their off spring during their most troublesome years. The Brothers, entrusted with the task of educating and disciplining the cream of the over indulged and arrogant youth of Madrid rise manfully to the task, taking no deviation from the hard line that the school had imposed on its pupils for generations. However times were changing.

'I loved the place and never really thought I would leave but there was a conflict of the modern affluence and our heritage affecting all of us. Probably even more so with the boys who had so much freedom at home and the strict discipline of the Brothers at school which many pupils found hard to reconcile. Many of the lads had cars, some the latest sports model. They all had computers linked to the internet and all the knowledge of the outside world and all that brought. They all dressed in their uniform during school hours but changed immediately afterwards to the latest designer gear and lauded around the narrow cobbled streets as though they owned them. They were despised by the local residents who benefited little, with the exception of the bar owners, from their spending power. The bars were in theory out of bounds to the boys, but a tolerance of moderate drinking by all the authorities kept a lid on potential trouble with the local lads.

'There was one sector of the neighbourhood that viewed their presence in a different light. We teenage girls of San Lorenzo had the choice of boyfriends in the ratio of six to one, and most of us took full use of this advantage to tease our affluent young suitors and I suppose you could say that I was just the same as all the others girls. I had lived in San Lorenzo with my parents all my life and we lived the typical Spanish rural life. Dad struggled financially but he coped as well as he could to bring their only daughter up to respect others and to love God. I suppose they idolised me and hoped I would escape the drudgery of rural life to follow a professional career in Madrid. And to a certain extent I was following their dream, loving my academic calling, friends with everyone in the village, young or old and worked in my father's bakery without a care in the world. I knew they were so proud of me and I did my best to be the perfect daughter. I know that sounds girly and frivolous but I really didn't have a nasty thought about anyone and tried to help whenever I could.

Looking back now with the cynicism that life has taught me, I can see that when I was sweet sixteen I probably was a prime target for all those spoilt over privileged school boys. Hardly a day would pass that some boy would share a joke or offer a night out. I knew I was the topic of group discussions in the locker rooms and to be honest I loved it. I didn't think I was a tease but I knew that I made the day of many a young lad who would sometimes be too shy to talk to me first. However there was one of them who stood out. Daniel Cordoso was eighteen, the son and heir of the Cordoso family banking fortune and drop dead gorgeous. Black hair smoothed back, soft brown eyes, flashing white teeth and the body of Adonis. He was genuinely friendly and unlike most of his fellow pupils had a grace about him that endeared him to his peers, tutors and most unusually the locals alike. When he asked me to share a coffee he expected and got a positive response.

'Our courtship lasted the entire Spring of 1990 during which we dined in the most expensive restaurants, went to opening nights on plays and concerts in Madrid and toured the countryside in his exquisite BMW soft top. His powers of personal charm and his father's rather large subvention to the school ensured that no questions were asked by the Brothers on his freedom. He met and charmed my parents, who, concerned that their daughter was getting involved with a young man a little earlier than they had wanted, could see Dan's allure and that his prospects were without equal.

'I had a wonderful final term of my penultimate year in school and supported Dan's study programme to pass the final exams before his entry into Madrid university. Not that his work needed much help, academic learning, like everything else, came easy to him.

'The first Saturday after his final exam he suggested that we went on a picnic in the hills opposite the Abbey, and he arranged all the hamper details. I knew this was going to be a special day, he was going back to Madrid, back to his family and to University. But I also knew that I loved him with all my heart and that nothing would keep us apart. His home in Madrid was only forty five minutes away, but this was to be our last day together in San Lorenzo.

'How young and naïve, it was terrible. I knew the picnic would be bitter sweet, a certain sadness but a new future beckoned and it was a beautiful day. When Dan arrived to pick me up with the top down and a hamper that would attract excess baggage charges on a flight, I was thrilled. He had everything for the perfect day, champagne with the flute glasses, smoked salmon with warm brown bread, fresh prawns, oysters, caviar, pate, fresh strawberries and cream. He had a table with two chairs, a table cloth, napkins, bone china and silver cutlery. Even flowers for the table. I was so delighted that he had been so thoughtful.

'After driving for around thirty minutes we found a delightful dell beside a running stream with the sun sparkling off the tops of the stones as the water splashes against them. Streams of sunlight shone through the leaves lighting their chosen spot for setting the table in dancing beams. It was perfect as we laughed through the canapés and champagne, delicate meats dressed with salad and exquisite desserts and more champagne. When the meal was over, we lay together for the first time in total harmony. I knew this was my defining moment, nothing would ever surpass this time and I gave myself for the first time with passion and tenderness that Dan fully reciprocated. I felt a profound being sweeping over me. I was so happy, satiated in every way, full of love even if my mind was swimming in the disorientation that perhaps too much champagne had brought.

'After laying together for a several minutes, Dan rose to support himself on his elbow and whispered 'Do you love me?'

'I did and told him so. Then I pushed him over and started to tickle him. He started laughing and asked 'Would you do anything for me.'

'Without pausing for a second I replied 'I would die for you'

'Just wait there for two minutes and I'll be back,' as Dan hastily dressed and ran out of sight back towards where he had parked the car.

'I was curious, what could he have in mind? On a day so perfect the thought crossed my mind that maybe he was going to propose. I was totally bewildered, I could think of nothing better, but I still had a year left in school, he was starting college life. We were too young... but ... but... it was the perfect end to the perfect day.

'Before I had chance to day dream any further Dan reappeared with his acned friend Miguel a pace behind him. I hurriedly grabbed my Tee shirt and jeans to cover myself up, but I just couldn't understand what he was doing there. Miguel was everything Dan wasn't, over weight, arrogant, flashed his money to compensate for total lack of any personal qualities, but was in total awe of Dan and would do his bidding without question. In return for Miguel's loyalty Dan gave him a comradeship which he enjoyed from no one else. It was Dan's friendship that gave Miguel a status in the school that I could not understand. He was, in my opinion, and in the opinion of all of my friends, a slime ball. Because he was Dan's friend I was pleasant to him and I knew I was safe in his company as Miguel would never do anything against Dan's wishes. His appearance always depressed me but today, on this perfect day, it was damming. I could not understand if he had followed us how he could have known, I didn't even know where we were going. It looked as if Dan had fetched him from a prearranged meeting place.

'I asked Miguel what he was doing and turned to Dan for answers to the same question without the need for words.

'Dan answered 'Yeah, well you know you were saying you would do anything for me....' It was pathetic, the man I loved reduced to lowest form of scumbag in just a few seconds. I closed my eyes, thinking this was not happening. I started to go dizzy and tried to get up, only to fall back as I heard Dan drone on.

'...well Miguel was saying how beautiful he thought you were and wouldn't it be something else if we could all do it together. You know my best friend and my girl friend...together'

'I beseeched him; God knows why 'No, Dan, I love you. It's precious, not to be given away. What are you thinking of. I love YOU. No one else.' I couldn't understand why he was doing this. Nothing made sense. Except I saw Miguel fumbling with his trousers.

'Before I had time to say anything else Miguel forced himself on top of me and started pushing his mouth on to mine. I turned my head away only for him to use more pressure and I felt his trying to remove his jeans by sliding his feet down the leg. I felt hot, desperate and could see myself passing out with his overbearing weight pinning me to the ground. I knew I had to keep fighting and called out to Dan but nothing came and struggled in vain as he thrust himself towards me with a crude fumbling of a bully who was out of control. Everything I had felt about Miguel was becoming horrifically true as I writhed beneath him. I started thumping him with both hands but it had little effect as often they slid off his sweaty tee shirt without making any impression on his movements which were becoming more and more frenzied. I looked over at Dan imploring him with my eyes to intervene but was struck motionless when I saw what he was doing. The lowlife was masturbating as I was being raped! All sense and reason left me as that image was indelibly imprinted on my mind. I can see it now; you have no idea how repulsed you can be by one apparently harmless action. I gave up, but the instant I stopped fighting Miguel prematurely ejaculated before he had penetrated and he rolled back, pathetic in every way. I couldn't have more contempt for any living thing. If I could, I would have stamped all the life out of him like an infected slug. His failure, whilst ultimately some comfort, added further tribute to his meaningless life. I stood up and kicked him defiantly but with little reaction and ran into the stream and washed every part of my body in the cold, fresh water, sobbing and wishing I could have washed away the past few minutes from my mind for ever.

'I dressed as quickly as I could without drying myself and looked up to see both Dan and Miguel coming towards me. I held my hand up to stop them. I was in control now, they were powerless to stop me 'Stay away from me. Don't move. I'm going home.'

'Dan looked at me sheepishly and sort of apologised saying he thought I'd be up for a bit of fun. I know the fun I wanted now and picked up a two foot branch telling them to stay away forcefully enough to convince both of them and myself that I meant it. I was going home on my terms, on my own and with dignity. I looked Dan straight in the eye and saw nothing. I would have died for you I thought, now it wouldn't bother me if I killed you.

'Dan pleaded with me not to say anything to anyone, it was the ultimate ending. He was no better than Miguel, self interest his only motivation. He was pathetic. But depressingly I knew he was safe. I couldn't face all the questions, all the recriminations about being fooled by the spoilt little rich boy if I told the police or even my friends. And how could I say anything to my parents? Dad thought the world of the perfect suitor for his only daughter. I knew he would kill Dan if the shock didn't kill him first. No, I wasn't going to say anything to anyone. People would think our relationship would have just died naturally when Dan went back home at the end of term and no one would know of how my world had been destroyed in the space of a few minutes.

'You know Susanna, this is all very well and I'm sure quite upsetting for you but I really don't ...'

I was about to say give a fuck which I suppose would have been a little insensitive in the circumstances but before I got the chance Trish hit me across the face with the hardest blow from a flat hand I have ever had. 'Just shut your fucking mouth and don't say another word you bastard. I've spent the last three weeks holding your hand and listening to your problems. Susanna is helping you, you idiot. And by doing that she is torturing herself for you. Are you OK, Susanna?'

Actually I think she was as stunned as I was, but she wanted to please Trish I think. I really didn't know what was happening here. I thought I was the patient but we seam to be involved in group therapy for anyone who wants to drop in. Anyway Susanna still wanted to unburden her soul and I wasn't going to take on Trish again.

Susanna took a deep breath and restarted her story as though my intervention hadn't happened.

'I spent the next few weeks helping in my father's small bakery but everything was different. I became morose, not going out with my friends and barely being polite to my father's customers. My parents put this down to being away from Dan and hadn't worried too much about the change in my outlook, but I suppose they secretly feared that he had ditched me as of course there was no word from Madrid even after the four week holiday he was have supposed to have gone on after his exams were over.

'When I decided in July that I wanted to get away for a while and was going to look around Madrid for a few weeks, they accepted that I needed to get Dan out of my system before the next school year and they found me accommodation in a reputable hostel. What they didn't know that immediately I arrived in Madrid I applied for a job in El Cortez Inglais in the perfume department, found a little flat off Calle de Velasquez and vowed never to go back to San Lorenzo again.

'Despite constant petitions from home to return to school and to get back to study for a university career, I began to insulate myself from the outside world. My daily routine never varied on work days, up at six, do all my household chores, walk the mile into work whatever the weather, finished at six, walk home and spend an hour or two watching TV before retiring early. My weekends would be spent on the one indulgence I allowed myself, visiting my uncle outside Toledo who had a small farm where I cared for the horses, chickens, cats and dogs. Mum and Dad would visit occasionally when it became clear I was not going to visit them. They were aware that my life was sad, but didn't pry as they knew I was not a threat to myself and as month followed month I think I did show some outward signs of becoming more outgoing. I also began to speak of my colleagues in work as though they were my friends. I think my parents lived for they day when I would announce that I was going back to school, but it was never going to come.

'I suppose my life was a concern to them, a strict ritual life week in, week out for nearly five years. During that time I did amass a healthy bank account even after sending money home every week. Money they never wanted and swore to save it for my special day. I knew they were living false dreams, but I didn't want to shatter them. In five years I hardly spoke to a man unless it was absolutely necessary. I swore to myself back on the tenth of May 1990 that I would never ever let a man take advantage of me again. I know I was the subject of idle gossip in work, but little was malicious, most of my colleagues respected my privacy and I was never anything less than polite and affable to everyone.

'I began slowly to rediscover that not all was wrong with the world. My best friend in work, Maria encouraged me to join a political group and I went with her to meetings of the socialist party which explored the social injustice prevalent throughout Spain and the merits of public ownership. The deeper I delved into these topics the greater my passion was awoken. The subject fascinated me and I sought books and videos on socialism and communism across the world. Looking back I can see I was seeking leadership, a focus in my life whom I could rely on. An idealism that wouldn't let me down and a cause that I could dedicate my life to the way I would have done to Dan if he had let me. I know what happened to me was more traumatic than physical and that I had completely recovered from the anguish of that fateful day but the physiological scars would remain forever.

'I began to worship Che Guevara, a man whose socialist motives were beyond reproach and his death at the hands of the imperialist Americans ensured that he could never let me down. And I felt America stood for everything that was wrong in the world, putting self interest ahead of any moral considerations in dealing with world affairs. Their trade embargo on Cuba was indefensible after forty years, when the Cuban's only crime was to rid their own country of a crippling economic stranglehold that America and the Miami based Mafia imposed. That embargo forced millions of people to live without the basic requirements of a modern life yet despite that Cuba had one of the best health services and educational systems in the world and it was free to all.

'Maria and I found ourselves immersed in philosophical debate and culture which spread into our every moment. Leaflet drops, organising rallies, helping the homeless we were in the vanguard of socialist Madrid. Suddenly after years of reclusiveness I found myself with a full social diary and a mundane career that seemed ever more obviously contrary to my political beliefs. When the party leader suggested that the secretary cum fund raiser position they were creating in their back street headquarters might be the ideal outlet for my talents I jumped at the opportunity. It meant a cut in pay and little job security if the fund raising wasn't fairly quickly successful but on considering my options and knowing that my frugal lifestyle would not be adversely affected I let my heart rule my head and went for it. I was never more excited.

'In August 1997 I became the National Secretary of the Socialist Workers Party and threw myself wholeheartedly into my new career. Whilst our fund raising activities were never particularly remunerative, I raised enough to keep the party solvent and it raised my profile in the organisation as being indispensable, which I just loved. Looking back again I suppose I wanted to be loved, but if I was rejecting that, second best was to be needed. And I was that! Whenever party funds could not cover my wages, I would happily forego them, my savings being well able to cope with an occasional raid. I was dedicated, willing to tackle any task, always in good humour and brought a serenity to the office which Sebastian Gonzalez, our party leader, could never have managed on his own. He was a charismatic man who led by example. He had a huge appetite for work and was ambitious for both himself and the party and constantly enthused over my role in where we were going. I revelled in the acclaim my work brought, not only throughout Spain but also internationally as the party spread its reputation to other left wing organisations across Europe. My confidence was now fully restored, but I still felt my judgement in dealing with men was a little suspect, but then I never really put it to the test.

'Sebastian was the only exception I allowed. He was tall, cultured and extremely knowledgeable I became in awe of him. He was in his mid forties and never once suggested that our close relationship was anything but professional, but I knew I had at last found a man I could respect.

'I still kept in contact with Maria and began to enjoy a social life I had deprived myself of for many years. Our coffee bar room discussions were often adjured to hostelries and when the mood took us, onto night clubs. Whilst I never became involved in any special relationship I did enjoy the company of young men again, and suppose I was flattered by their attention. I began to flirt shamelessly and loved it. It was at this time that I met Jenny, whom I found shared the same enthusiasm and sense of fun that I thought I had lost. After work and Jenny had finished her shifts in her bar, we would spend every minute together, sharing our distrust of men but loved good company. We had similar tastes in music and the arts and even if our politics clashed we never let our heated discussions affect our friendship. It was funny really because I was totally at ease with Jenny but I never told her of the reason I took little interest in men. Nor did she tell me. I think we both respected our past was exactly that. Best forgotten. As neither of us had family in Madrid, we relied on each other to help share our current problems but obviously neither of us feeling confident enough to unburden ourselves in soul searching.

The longer I stayed in the job, the more disillusioned I became. Things were not going the way I had expected them to. The party appeared to be losing members rather than gaining them. And some of the new recruits would be too revolutionary often voicing violent disorder as legitimate protest, which I was not happy with. Sebastian was totally against this and we shared a dream, a new vision for re-launching the party. Free from revolutionaries, but totally committed to defending the weak in society. He said we should publish a manifesto highlighting our aims. A society free from oppression, the oppression of poverty, the oppression of bad housing, the oppression of privileged education, the oppression of a two tier health system, the oppression of a bigoted police force, the oppression of the capitalist banks who were orchestrating the movement of funds away from the people to the commercial developers and stock traders. Whilst it didn't occur to me at the time, I was not too sorry if another motive was to hurt the world that Dan belonged to.

We would make sure every household in Spain had it, Sebastian mused. I was thrilled over the idealism of what he was saying and starting a major fund raising campaign to finance the project. Sebastian worked day and night to put the party's philosophy together and convinced me that our day was about to come. I went without wages for three months to avoid depleting the funds and by early Spring 2002 we had over two hundred thousand euro in the parties coffers. Sebastian arranged publication of the full colour manifesto and said he would subsidise the balance of the printing bill. After emptying out the entire party account and handing it over to Sebastian, I never saw him again.

'For the second time in my life I had been taken for a fool by a totally convincing man. Only this time there was more fallout. I was left being the only responsible member of a crumbling party with no assets, rent to find on the office and no credible mouthpiece. I considered going to the police but for what, my career was over and I would probably be implicated in the scam. I knew nothing of Sebastian's private life, and would have no idea where he would have gone. For three weeks I went through the motions of going to the office every day, not telling anyone what had happened, not even Jenny – I just couldn't face the humiliation all over again. The bills began to mount, on top of the rent, the electricity, the phone, insurance, solicitors fees for a libel action taken again Sebastian by one of the mainstream parties and finally, the greatest irony of all, a delivery of four million full colour leaflets proudly proclaiming a 'New Age for a Better Spain' under Sebastian's photograph. I felt like getting them over printed with 'Wanted for grand larceny.' Not only that the bloody delivery took up half the office and of course it was accompanied by an invoice for two hundred and seventy five thousand euro, less the twenty thousand deposit he had graciously paid.

Finally Susanna stopped and looked at Trish and myself. 'Listen Susanna you don't have to say any more, you don't have to do this' Trish was fairly accurately echoing my own sentiments but I would guess from a different stand point. Having said that I did feel for her and knew she was a troubled girl. I suppose that realisation, that I might not be the only victim, was in some way a step towards my recovery. With all of Susanna's story and my own newly found recollections my head was spinning. I had heard enough, but Susanna was in full flow.

'You know Trish, I haven't felt as good as this for a long time. I've never told anyone my story and I feel better. Do you mind if I tell you how I meet Rory which brought me to Anton and Ben. It is important he knows why I did what I did.' Susanna looked over at me with a look

I didn't recognise but I nodded in response. Trish added the totally predictable 'Susanna take whatever time you need.'

'Thanks Trish, when I realised the position I was in I panicked. I knew that the printer's bill would wind up the party but also I had, in my total belief of Sebastian, gone guarantor on many of the agreements the party had entered into. Certainly the office, electricity and phone and God knows what else. Even those three current bills amounted to over four thousand euro and still counting. I decided to close the door on the office never to return. Let them find me, I thought, but I knew they would and if I wasn't ready for them with some money I would end up in jail before the end of the year. I had to do something and fast.

'It was then I had a brainwave, I remembered one of the guest speakers from another European Socialist Party who had spoken to me after a meeting. Rory Meagan was Irish, a smooth talker and very fond of himself. My first impressions were that he was a creep after he came on to me during an excessive plundering of the reception champagne. He was so unsubtle and crude that he confirmed all that I felt about men. But, in his enthusiasm to impress me, he had suggested that I could make a lot of money if I went to work for him. Actually as it turned out my first impressions were deadly accurate, but I wasn't to discover that until much later. At first I thought he was a pimp and told him so as pitifully as I could. He totally denied that there was anything like that, he ran a reputable business. He gave me his card and told me to give him a ring when I changed my mind. I don't know why I kept it, but I did and I felt that I really had no choice but to ring him. I couldn't believe that I had sunk so far but desperate times call for desperate measures.

'I was very apprehensive and it took some time to work up the courage to ring, but when I did Rory was most accommodating, even gentlemanly. It was such a relief that apparently his bad behaviour was down to just a little over indulgence and said he was sorry to hear that I had run into a bit of trouble. Of course his offer stood and that he had a perfect role for me. Because of the pressures of work he couldn't get over to Madrid but suggested quite enthusiastically that I should fly over to meet him in his offices in Chatham, promising that he would be able to give me some quick money and that it would be all above board.

'I thought that perhaps being out of the country wasn't such a bad idea, not only was I escaping the immediate creditors before they forced legal proceedings but I was giving myself some breathing space. Time to reflect on what to do, who to pay, who to avoid without fearing every knock on the door. I made all the necessary arrangements without asking Jenny's help or advice on where to stay in London. I was not ready to face Jenny and the inevitable questioning of the stupidity of the situation I had got myself into. I know that's what friends are for, but maybe I'd forgotten that.

'Rory's offices were little more than a mini warehouse with a few desks in every corner, in a rundown part of a rundown suburb. It was quiet but any noise emanating from the birds on the roof or passing trunks echoed across the vacant building. Not very inspiring, but I hadn't expected too much from a man who expounded socialist views. After all they were not any worse, if perhaps larger and less homely, than the offices I had been manning for the last six years. A colleague of Rory's, Will, offered me coffee which I gratefully accepted, and spent the time trying to illicit information from him and deduce from the surroundings what business I had let myself in for. To be honest neither avenue was very productive but they did increase my curiosity levels and I was pleased to see Rory when he eventually arrived to put me out of my misery.

'My first impressions of him as I said were all negative when we met in Madrid, feeling he was sleazy in coming on to me and offering me an undefined job, but I now found him to be elegant, charming, genuinely concerned to be helpful and horrified at my tale of Sebastian's betrayal. I told him that I desperately needed to get some money together quickly or face never being able to go back to Madrid, which I just refused to contemplate.

'He leant back in his chair and told his story. How he lived in Cuba and found that the increased tourism in the country had brought a specialised import/export agency work for products that took an age to get through the normal channels. There were many European companies in Cuba now with ex-pats managing them and they needed goods which weren't available in Havana. And of course they were willing to pay. All transport was channelled through Madrid and he needed an acceptable face of respectability to be a trouble shooter, be available to respond to crisis and smooth over inevitable problems with officialdom. Also he explained that he needed someone who was able at the drop of a hat to go anywhere in Europe to pick up more sensitive or delicate items and possibly deliver them by hand to Cuba. The money was nearly double what I was earning before and there was free travel and bonuses for any particularly difficult consignments. If I agreed to take on the job, Rory would pay three months in advance to enable me to settle my affairs with the creditors and I could start immediately.

'I could hardly believe my ears, nothing dodgy, good pay, freedom to organise my own life and all my past affairs taken care of. I don't know why my experiences of the previous few years hadn't set a warning bell off in my head. But to be fair to myself it did represent an immediate solution and I couldn't wait to accept with a rather embarrassing display of gratitude. Rory gracefully put all that aside and suggested that I should head immediately back to Madrid armed with enough money to settle all my pressing debts, set up a business address, phone and fax lines, computer links and all the other day to day requirements that a busy young executive would require. And it wasn't long before the jobs rolled in, could I collect an oil painting in Germany and deliver it by hand to Havana, arrange the shipment of a piano, accompany a young child from boarding school during the holidays. There was always something to do and always someone willing to pay… and pay well. I also found that the gratuities from grateful benefactors often exceeded my salary. I honestly enjoyed the work, felt that I was genuinely helping people and was paid exceptionally well. My pendulum was once again on an upward curve.

'Every time I went to Havana I would meet Rory and he would arrange some thing for the return journey. Nothing too onerous, usually documents in a brief case with specific instructions as to where they should go. I did have my suspicions on one occasion when I wasn't told what the contents were, but accepted that it wasn't my business and I did feel a little obligation to Rory for sorting out my affairs without once suggesting anything in return. Although I felt grateful to Rory and I loved the job, even if there was a lot of repetitive travelling, I was beginning to feel that not everything was right. I suppose

I was being fatalistic, feeling that this just could not last – it never did.

'My suspicions were confirmed on returning to Madrid one time when I discovered the case I was given was unlocked. I know I shouldn't have but curiosity got the better of me and I felt the urge to examine the contents. My worst fears were realised when I found that it contained a kilo of cocaine. When I was interrupted in the toilet making this discovery, I panicked and flushed the entire contents of the package down the cistern.

'Rory's reaction to this news was totally predictable, berating my stupidity. I had destroyed his credibility and making a complete idiot of him. Did I not feel any loyalty towards him for all that he had done for me. I wasn't exactly over the moon at being used in a criminal activity that I knew nothing about, but he totally ignored that and demanded that I had to make amends to recover his lost assets. A wave a déjà vu swept over me. Another man had betrayed my trust, but Rory was different to Dan and Sebastian – he didn't hide nor was he repentant. He was blaming me for what he saw was his misfortune, and he continually bullied me into feeling guilty. He had saved me from the courts chasing me for Sebastian's debts and given me the opportunity to see the world. I wanted to get out of this situation without Rory hounding me but I couldn't see how. But I knew one thing I definitely wasn't doing any more drug runs.

'After two weeks of taking verbal abuse on the phone and deciding that I'd had enough, let him do his worst, Rory arrived on my doorstep unannounced and in a conciliatory mood.

'He said he knew that I had gone through hell in the past few weeks and he hadn't understood the moral dilemma that he had put me through. On the other hand, I had to realise what makes the world go round. There were good guys and there were bad guys, but there are an awful lot more who are neither. People doing good work in difficult circumstances, who ask him to arrange things for them and who don't accept the rules that are sometimes imposed by pompous bureaucrats and self righteous politicians. If they ask him to do something, he just did it. He couldn't say yes to one job and no to another, it didn't work like that. He was their Mr Fixit and providing he was not hurting anybody he was going to do it.

'Any objections I had were not entertained. There were no counter arguments he was prepared to countenance.

'He laid it on the line. I owed him. He had given me everything I had wanted and I let him down. It was now time for me to help him and what he had in mind was within my moral code, maybe even interesting and hopefully we can forget all this sorry episode for once and for all.

'I was delighted about Rory's change in mood and did begin to feel that maybe I had over reacted. Although I knew that my understanding of right and wrong had no grey areas, I also knew that I did not have any copyright on principles, that Rory was entitled to his moral code just as I had mine. It was not my right to be judgemental. He certainly raised my interest and I would be delighted to be able to put the whole drugs episode behind me.

'He told me of a socialist group in Cuba who wanted to raise their profile with an enactment of the capture of Che Guevara and they thought it would evoke world wide press coverage if they could get some of the children of those involved back in 1969 to take part in it.

'I really doubted that it was possible but he insisted that maybe they would not consciously agree, but what if they were caught up in some sort of party that involved half a dozen people. And they discovered during the course of the evening that they were all connected by one of the most notorious events of the twentieth century and were now in the spotlight of the world. A sort of group 'This is your life' a generation late. Wouldn't you think it would be fun.'

'I wasn't convinced but then he mentioned Anton's name and I nearly dropped dead. He said you, Ben were coming to Madrid to investigate political corruption in Cuba and both your and Anton's father were both present at Che's capture. It will be my job to ensure you meet, get on like a house on fire and that Anton accompanied Ben to Cuba, without either of you knowing anything about the little party they had arranged in their honour.

'I looked at him incredulously, how the hell could I manage that, two days to get a complete stranger to go to Cuba for no reason at all. It was madness. I told Rory he was crazy. I couldn't do it. It wasn't that I didn't want to, let's face it, Anton was gorgeous.

She stopped and looked over at me, 'Sorry Ben, you aren't bad looking but you know what I mean. No I fancied the job but it was just that it wasn't possible.

'Rory poured scorn on my lack of confidence saying I underestimated myself, and anyway I haven't just got two days. Anton frequented the night life of Madrid and if I played my cards right I could meet him that night, work my magic on him and in a week he would probably do anything I asked him to do. He suggested that I was a very captivating young lady and I should think that my life to date had been dominated by men who have abused my trust, wasn't it time to take control. Not forgetting that this was an all expenses paid holiday in Cuba for as long as I wanted, with a very handsome single, rich and engaging young man. Plus, of course, there was the little matter of the €150,000 he said I owed him. Wouldn't it be nice to wipe the slate clean?

'As I said Rory could be charming and very persuasive. Add to that forceful and devious. But it did represent a chink of light at the end of another long tunnel. I asked him to confirm that if I managed to get Anton to Cuba without him suspecting any ulterior motive, he will forget the whole incident of my flushing a kilo of his cocaine literally down the toilet. Absolutely, plus a bonus of €20,000 if everything went to plan.

'I know it was stupid but I went for it and Rory then told me that Anton would be in the Arenal night club later on. Nothing like getting started straight away.

'So that's it. I think you know the rest. That's how we arrived in Cuba. It all went like clockwork except I fell head over heels in love with Anton. I had no idea what was going to happen.' Susanna finally broke down and wept.

Trish went over to her, whispering I've no idea what, but then she pulled me over for a communal hug and we stayed like that until it got embarrassing. I pulled away and said I didn't feel too good and would they mind if we left it at that for today. Maybe we could meet up again soon. Both Trish and Susanna said they would like to and left together.

PART 4

My Journey to Desolation

Chapter 17

The next day I began to review my history like a Homicide Detective in true American Pulp Fiction style. With the help of Aidan, Trish and to be fair Susanna, I had pieced together a large chunk of what was bothering me. I knew now I had loved and lost Jenny. Been a victim of a hideous plot to recreate the capture of Che Guevara and through that had taken centre stage in a mass murder which had evoked the interest of the World's press. After listening to Susanna's story I bore her no ill will towards her part in getting me involved. Rory was the bad guy in all this and he was dead. But then there was O'Hara's role and of course Paul. What did I do about that? There were still so many questions I could not answer, which still left a cloud hanging over me. What happened after I left Susanna in Madrid. It was still a blank. I still had this feeling that my subconscious mind was hiding something from me.

Next day, with still no word from Aidan, *had I annoyed him?* – I couldn't see how unless he had been working with Trish to bring Susanna to me. Maybe he thought a bit of shock therapy would awaken the senses. If he did plan it, he was pretty good. Anyway when Trish arrived in later I accused her of just that.

'Hold your horses Ben, this isn't entirely about you. I suppose you have the idea that attacking Susanna was part of a strategy on our part. Well let me tell you it wasn't. And your conduct was disgraceful, no fucking excuses about it. You've lost your memory not your fucking marbles.

I think I had upset her. 'I'm sorry Trish, but I am feeling pretty stressed. It doesn't take much to spark a reaction. And let's face it seeing Susanna was a shock. And for all my contemptible actions something did click into place. Anyway thanks for bringing her. Is she OK?'

'Actually she's fine and would like to come in again if that's OK. Oh … and apology accepted, you prick'.

I looked across at her to see her beaming at me. I felt pretty humble that she had taken such an interest in me.

'Lets find a few more pieces of the puzzle first. I don't want any encores. Now did you bring in the News of the World?'

She threw it across the table and the banner headline rode across the front page 'World Exclusive. Ben Millers first hand account of the Che Guevara slayings'

They couldn't even get the headline factual, but it was staring at me, forcing me to remember how I came to tell the story.

I had arrived home from leaving Susanna in Madrid to a posse of photographers and reporters wanting for the inside story of my kidnapping and all the events surrounding the Friends of Che. I should have realised this was in store for me after such a widely publicised adventure but

I was taken completely by surprise. It was the last thing I wanted, anonymity was what I had in mind. I don't know how they got wind of my arrival, presumably some Aer Lingus official in Madrid managed to make a few euros. The reporters must have guessed that I wouldn't be talking to any of them, obviously saving my story for the Chronicle. However I hadn't allowed for the persistence of the TV and radio crews. There were countless microphones in front of me, only RTE, TV3 and Sky Ireland had managed to get a full camera crews there but every radio station under the sun seemed to be fighting each other rather than trying to speak to me. Looking for a way out, I saw a girl with a very knowing smile who shouted over to me 'Mr Miller you car is waiting.' The offer seemed too good to miss and I ducked the flash bulbs and microphones to join her presuming Paul had laid this on for me.

I followed her outside and a limo with the windows blacked out drove up to the arrivals door. We climbed in and the car took off, turning North on the motorway. Realising this wasn't Paul's doing I looked at my companion, fearing I was in the mire all over again. I thought this had something to do with O'Hara and I didn't want a meeting on his terms. She put my mind at rest by introducing herself. 'My name is Victoria Althorpe and I work for the News of the World. We would like you to consider working with us for a few days for which you will be well recompensed.'

I was relieved I suppose, but annoyed that I had been duped into this situation without the option to refuse. I have to learn to be more forceful. And where was Paul?

I explained to Victoria that I had to go home first and wanted to arrange some business affairs before talking to anyone.

She put her hand on my bare arm and gently stroked it, which I thought was a little forward. 'Call me Vicky please. We have spoken to Paul and he agrees that if you come to an agreement with us he has no difficulty in sharing exclusivity with us. He appreciates that we have a lot more to offer than the Chronicle could ever do. He was at pains to point out that whatever the outcome of our discussions your job will still be open to you on your return. You may ring him if you wish, but I have written confirmation of all that I have said, signed by him in the presence of the Chronicle's solicitors. We have also been in contact with your wife who expressed her desire to speak to you as soon as possible but understood the time pressures we are working under and that we need as much time together in the next two days to make a decent story for Sunday. She appreciates what the financial benefits are in this story and that they do diminish with every day that passes. We all understand the value of yesterday's news.'

I smiled in agreement, not so much at her assessment of the value of quality journalism but more at Katie's lack of concern at not seeing me after nearly three weeks away. I saw that there was a good pay off and considered that what I had to do with O'Hara might be more easily attained if I had some financial resources behind me. But I needed to deal with that quickly because he would be looking for me with the same eagerness that I was for him. I wondered if he knew Rory was dead and that I knew of his scheme. Probably not, because Rory's death might have been reported as accidental as a post mortem would have revealed the bullets entered his body after he died. If they ever did one and the fact that I had arrived fairly quickly after my first escape, only five days after all, he will probably assume that Rory didn't manage to find me.

Vicky continued, she was obviously enjoying this, wheeling and dealing. I wondered who she was and what authority she had to make me an offer. 'As we appreciate time is of the essence and that you will want to make the best deal possible for yourself. To save a lot of time we are going to the Ballymascanlon Hotel, in Dundalk to discuss terms which would be suitable to all of us. In order that your interests are protected we have arranged that your solicitor be present. But I would stress to you that we will make you an offer which we believe to be the best you will get from any newspaper in the world, however we will make it only once and if agreement is not reached at the end of the meeting, our offer will be removed from the table and we will withdraw from all negotiations. If you agree to hear our offer we will continue up to the hotel, if not we will drop you back to Dublin and let you make any arrangements you wish. Perhaps you should call your wife.' She offered me her mobile.

I admired her style and thought she had covered most of the angles. As an investigative journalist I knew the feeling of not being able to think of a sensible question only too well, the sensation returned. But I liked the idea of getting this over with once and for all, and then still having my story on O'Hara if I wanted to continue to do an expose. I smiled at her and said 'Let's go' took the phone and went through all the motions with Katie, which were not as difficult as I had anticipated. She seemed warm and genuinely concerned that I had survived my ordeal with as little trauma as possible. I didn't really want to mention that actually everything emotionally was much worse than it appeared. I would save that pleasure for another day, how I was dreading it.

The hour's drive passed quickly as Vicky and I shared travel reminisces that included much in common. However she could not compete with my adventures of the past two weeks, but we barely touch on those as both of us were aware that business has to be done first. I could not understand how comfortable I was feeling, I suppose I had no emotional energy left and was living in a trance. Arriving at the hotel I realised it was twenty four hours since we had left Havana and I needed some time to recover. I suggested we meet after I cleaned up. She appreciated what I am saying and suggested a four o'clock meeting in the board room.

Still in the jeans I bought in Havana but with a fresh Tee shirt I arrived down to my meeting ten minutes early suitably cleansed and rested after a three hour siesta. We went through all the formal introductions, Jimmy Cashman, the deputy editor, Marvin Silksmith, the solicitor, Dave Byrne my solicitor, Vicky and myself as we settle into what I felt was going to be protracted negotiations.

Vicky opened the proceedings, 'Ben, Marvin has prepared an exclusivity agreement with Dave which meets all his misgivings and gives us six one hour interviews with you over the next two days to be taken at time intervals which suit us both. During which you will supply us with all the details you can recall during the period of time from when you left Dublin to yesterday'

Dave nodded, I was happy so far knowing I could keep anything that Rory told me about O'Hara for my own personal use at as later date. If that was breaching the agreement they would not find out until well after I had been paid and they had their exclusive. I felt confident with the way things were going.

Vicky continued, she seemed to be in charge of this whole operation and was totally undaunted by chairing a meeting comprised entirely of men, all of whom were at least ten years older than she was. I wondered rather devilishly what her sex life was like. Pretty formidable, I would guess. Straight down to the matter in hand she continued, 'The only detail to fill in is the fee we hope to agree and may I suggest that two hundred and fifty thousand euro be a reasonable figure to recompense you for your story.'

I was about to fall of my seat and started to stutter that 'I am happy...' but before I could say anything else Dave interrupted, '...happy to do business with you but obviously the figure was somewhat under what would be regarded as the market value for such an exclusive on a story of worldwide interest. Perhaps five hundred thousand might be more appropriate.'

'Agreed'

'Sterling'

'I think you may not quite understand the mechanics of newspaper publishing...'

Dave turned to me and motioned for us both to leave. I was gob smacked, but before he had time to move his chair back, Victoria said 'Wait a minute, Dave' then turned to Jimmy who quietly nodded, 'You have a deal,' and without pausing she looked at me smiling broadly 'Are you happy now, Ben.'

I nodded to the best of my ability looking like a stuffed puppy in a rear car window, as we all shook hands and made the necessary signatures. The whole process from start to finish took less that five minutes and I'm nearly €750,000 richer less what ever Dave will take in commission. I had a feeling that it might be fairly substantial, but fair enough he did a great job.

After going through all the essential documentation, we wasted no time in arranging to go straight into my first interview and all six were completed within twenty four hours. Both parties were happy with the end result. Even if our satisfaction is different, the paper was delighted with a new insight into a World figure never really deeply explored along with an adventure story which could have come straight from Boy's Own, I knew I was revealing my age by that analogy. But my satisfaction was more personal. I did feel better having put some order on to the events, even if I had condensed both O'Hara and Jenny into peripheral events. I knew now that there was a record of my story which was going to be read world wide. It was a humbling thought.

After fulfilling my contractual obligations and taking full advantage of the facilities of the hotel, mainly the Leisure Centre, I had thought about a round of golf but thought I wasn't ready for the physical exertion, I began to feel rested. However there was so much to do with my work, my home life and my mental well being. I had put it off long enough. Time to head home to face Paul and then Katie and the unwanted homecoming. I was grateful for the hospitality of the News of the World's limo to make the logistics easier.

After taking in all the events of the past few days my mind started to reverse into a siding. I was mentally exhausted and desperately wanted to sleep. I knew Trish was ready to call it a day, we had hardly spoken for a while and she was in effect just baby sitting me.

Chapter 18

Next day Aidan called into see me unannounced and I wasn't quite sure if Trish and he were part of a conspiratorial double act. Whatever was going on, I was making progress and I was pleased to see him, even if he had taken his time.

I decided to assume that he knew nothing of Susanna's visit, or of the News of the World story which had sparked so much recall. I briefly brought him up to date on events and he was delighted that I was beginning to piece things together. 'Don't beat your self up too much over your attack on Susanna. It was a genuine reaction to a surge of information. Like a computer overload, but it is very unlikely to happen again. As long as Susanna is all right and doesn't hold any grudges against you, it probably released some stress in your body.'

I marvelled at his ability to see the bright side of virtually every situation. I suppose it is one of the requirements of a psychiatrist's character, I couldn't see a manic depressive having much a career in counselling.

Without any further discussion he suggested we got back into our analysis. 'Lets see now Ben, after you did your deal with the News of the World' Aidan gestured to the paper on the table, 'did you go home – you had a lot to talk about.'

'Yes, you would have thought so, but I knew I had to check in with Paul first and give him all I knew on O'Hara. It wasn't quite what he was anticipating of course but the implication in an assassination attempt would be quite a story. I knew he would want me to give something different to the News of the World story, they had exclusivity of course but there would be some human interest angle that I could give Paul, especially as it was their correspondent who was involved in the whole saga.

'But then I was really looking forward to tackling O'Hara. He would have heard that I was back but may not have been aware that I knew that the whole Friends of Che fiasco was a smokescreen. I had to act quickly and make use of this knowledge before he turned it around. I thought that maybe Paul might have known of his whereabouts and his movements.

'Then I had to see Katie. I had found and lost someone else who had meant the world to me. I wasn't really sure how she would take all that, presumably pretty badly. I could exactly see how I was going to find the right moment. I consoled myself with the fact that there probably wasn't one and maybe I shouldn't say anything.

'Finally I had to do something about paying proper respects to Jenny. Well at least I had the resources to do something fitting. But that could wait, O'Hara was the first priority and I headed straight away for the Chronicle to be debriefed by Paul and get as much information as I could from him.

'I'm not quite sure I agree with your priorities, but carry on' Aidan looked at me as though he was being told a pub story, but I had no difficulty talking the way I was. I was very comfortable with his company, and very pleased that the events did keep unfolding in a chronological way.

'Ok, I went straight in to Paul's office, which seemed so strange after so long. The welcome I got was very warm but different to his usual form. There was no slagging, all very businesslike, with a muted concern for my welfare. It was unnatural, surreal even; I felt he was going to talk about the weather at any minute. He mentioned nothing about the developments of the past three weeks, which I found unnerving. Maybe he was allowing me tell the story at my own pace, then my cynicism returned to me. Maybe he thought I had an action against the paper and wanted to react to my story rather than disturb a raw nerve. This theory was laid to rest after he had exhausted all the trivial banalities he could think of and he finally arrived at his first serious question.

'I was wondering if you could get the money through to us in the next couple of days.' He asked, now I have to admit I hadn't seen that one coming.

'Sorry I'm not quite with you.' I thought—you bastard what are you talking about. He was quick to tell me.

'I don't think I'm quite with you either' Aidan emerged from a long silence.

'Will you let me continue without interruption, please'

'Sorry' Aidan held his hands up in mock apology and I felt a little pompous, but was happy he was fully engaged in the story.

'Paul meant the News of the World money. He said 'I believe Dave accepted a cheque yesterday. No point in letting it fester in his account for too long, you know what solicitors are like.'

I said 'I'm not with you, Paul that's my money. It was my story based on my experiences. The story you sent me to Cuba was about O'Hara and that story I still have. The News of the World were only interested in the Che Guevara angle and the assassinations.'

'He was quick to reply smugly 'Not according to the contract Dave drew up which you readily signed. The money is to be divided three ways, Dave, yourself and ourselves and in view of the employment contract we have with you regarding exclusivity I think we have been very generous.'

'I know I keep saying that I fall for the sucker punch, but this one really was out of the blue. Was there any end to my disappointments? I had expected some commission, but after tax I would have been lucky if I was going to clear fifteen percent of what I thought I had agreed. I should have known Dave would look after himself, but I hadn't expected Paul to muscle in as well. I felt like I had just got the last question wrong in 'Who wants to be a Millionaire.' I was in no mood to discuss anything else with Paul, and decided to tackle O'Hara without his help. I know I should have stood up for my rights but I didn't have the energy. I told Paul I would get him his money with as much contempt as I could muster and that I was going to take a couple of days off to get myself together. He nodded his acceptance as I stormed out of his office, not looking back to see his smirk.

'I jumped into a taxi heading downtown and thought about exactly what I had to do. I had to see O'Hara quickly and decided on a course of action. He had paid to see me off and he was dangerous but not that that worried me too much anymore. I certainly had the stomach for it. He was a corrupt sleaze ball who had been getting away with it for years and I had to get under his skin. My lack of fear was my greatest asset – if it wasn't a complete bluff, my self doubt began to resurface after a few days rest. I thought about what I did have on him that hadn't already hit the head lines. I knew I had enough to put him away for a long time if I hit the right spots. I was missing hard evidence but what I knew to be fact must scare him the living daylights out of him. The Cuban adventure was just a plot to get me over there; he was involved in some prostitution in Cuba, probably not illegal but massively unacceptable P.R. for an Irish politician; he may have even got himself entangled with paedophilia, I was sure he never asked to see birth certificates. And of course he paid Rory to dispose of me. He didn't know that conversation wasn't taped and if he knows Rory was dead he would have known that I had to be taken seriously. This was probably my best plan, shake him up with a story of witnesses I have, following my investigations in Havana. Then threaten this exposure with all the ensuing media disgust. Harp on the total devastation of his family life, the humiliation of his public life and the ignominy of a criminal investigation. I intended to give him until the weekend before going to press with the whole story, to do the honourable thing. I was not going to kill him, I couldn't see how I could have got away with murdering such a public figure even if I did find the resolve to do it. My only hope would be that he either threw himself off the top of Liberty Hall or that he runs, which will add a lot of credibility to my expose.

'Armed with these positive thoughts I set out to pay O'Hara the call he would have been expecting since I returned.

'He had offices near the Dail in Molesworth Street which I called on the Monday asking for an appointment saying I was a constituent with a problem with joy riders around the streets at night keeping us awake and frightening the children. Not much of a response to that, his secretary suggesting I attended his constituency clinic on Saturdays, but she did mention that he was tied up in meetings all Tuesday morning in his offices and wouldn't be available anyway. Brilliant, that was the nearest I was going to get to an audience and it was all I need.

'I arrived exactly on ten o clock and walked straight into his office leaving his secretary in my wake apologising profusely to O'Hara for allowing me in. O'Hara was in the middle of some skulduggery with some cohorts but dismissed her with a sweep of his hand saying it was Ok. So I sat down in front of him, face to face for the first time with the man I had been investigating for years.

'I told him I thought that he might wish to reschedule the rest of your morning as I stared very confident at O'Hara's companions mentally dismissing them. They looked dumbfounded at my presence but I could feel an outrage beginning to build up at my impertinent interruption.

'O'Hara told them to ask his secretary to hold all calls and to rearrange their meeting for the next day stating he did not wish to be disturbed for an hour; adding that Mr Miller and he had some pretty urgent business to attend to. I took some satisfaction that he was taking me seriously. They got up warily, looking at me with some distain as one of them, Jim I think he said, started to protest. O'Hara raised his open palm with a gesture of total contempt, shaking his head and saying, 'Not now'.

'After Jim closed the door behind him and he was sure they were out of earshot, O'Hara launched into an effusive diatribe. 'Ben, delighted to see you, I wonder how I can be of assistance to you, I am always pleased to talk to the press. You want to write an article on the new accessible housing scheme we have planned for Lucan with all the facilities of a Dublin four development no doubt. Do you want coffee?' The complete wanker, I could not wait to burst his bubble.

'With a little self indulgence, I told him I wasn't there to feed his publicity machine, which must have come as a huge surprise to him. More that I had something else on my mind which I was sure was of great interest to him. Perhaps even the coffee can wait. I don't think I've ever said a few sentences slower in my life. I was feeling good so far, conscious that as in every dramatic production. Timing was essential for maximum effect and I was confident my next sentence would have exactly that. I remember precisely saying 'I was wondering if you could advise me of your dealings with a Mr Rory Meagan, a wheeler dealer character who ekes out a living in Havana?'

'I'm sorry but I don't think I know anyone of that name' he replied with some confidence but revealed his hand immediately by further asking 'I trust that you are not using a tape to record this conversation.'

'I stood up, arms raised. 'You have my assurance, now would you like me to repeat the question?' I told him. 'I have spent most of the last two weeks in Cuba which you will obviously have been aware and have signed statements from four girls procured to have sex with you by Mr Meagan. One of those girls was aged thirteen, though in your defence I had to see the birth certificate to believe it myself.'

'He was still totally dismissive but obviously very rattled, 'I have nothing further to say, any further discussions can be made through my solicitor. Now good day Mr Miller.' Not just yet I thought, I told him that the Chronicle was going ahead with the story on the next Sunday, not only did we have the statements from the girls taken with their parents present but also from hotel staff who were on duty when you entertained the girls. Not everyone approves of the sex tourism industry in Havana. We also have photographs of the girls interviewed, one rather appealing one of the thirteen year old in her school uniform taken by myself just the week before.

'O'Hara was visibly weakening, time to go for the jugular. 'I also have a tape of a conversation I had with Mr Meagan in which he outlines the whole scenario whereby the entire 'Friends of Che' soap opera which I am sure you will have read about was a cover for his rather involved scam to arrange my assassination. His interest in achieving this rather incredulous operation was to collect the hundred thousand euro you had generously put on my head. Mr Meagan has unfortunately come to an untimely demise to make it difficult for him to deny all this, but as further proof of this extremely clever plot I do have his diary which notes various meetings he had with you and General Suarez. You probably haven't had the pleasure of meeting the General but I would assure you he is a most illuminating character, very intimidating if somewhat gullible, as events have subsequently proved. I would like to assure you that I have been very thorough with this. It's not every day you get the opportunity to expose a man who hires people to kill you, is it?

'You may take some pride if you wish in the fact that I have dedicated so much of my life to seeing you pay for your greed and callous use of political office for personal gain. In fact your name is the first one I see every morning. I feel myself that the work was totally justified and that has been enormously satisfying. I would suggest that perhaps you might prefer to talk now without your solicitor and first consider the implications of what this story will have on your home life and your professional reputation,' I allowed myself a little malicious satisfaction.

'O'Hara leant back in his chair and pondered on what I'd said. I was not too worried by his seemingly unconcerned demeanour, I knew I had got to him, but he had been in Public Office for many years and would be used to being under pressure. Maybe not like this though and I knew he would be squirming for a response. I also knew that he has to say the first word, every second that passed would set his mind into further turmoil, but I had no idea what he was going to say. I wallow in his silence until he finally made his response.

'Mr Miller,' I was all ears, 'I think you are losing your mind resulting from some post traumatic stress no doubt after all you have experienced recently. I do not know anything of what you are talking about. But even if there was any truth in one word of what you have just outlined, I still would not be of the opinion that the Chronicle would print it. Firstly I would of course sue for every penny the paper has, which I'm sure isn't too much, but it would also open up a hornets nest which I'm sure is being destroyed as we speak.'

'A little annoyed that he was showing no contrition, I tackled the cryptic language he was engaging in 'What are you talking about, we go to press on Sunday with a story that will blow your personal and political life to smithereens, whatever you say.'

'Ben, I'm sorry to be the one that has to tell you this, but I think we have to put a different perspective on this.' I wasn't ready for a counter attack.

'He continued to be quite relaxed, possibly noting some of my body language revealing unease, 'Alright, I will admit, off the record, to having been to Cuba, meeting Mr Meagan and I'm sorry to hear of his premature demise, perhaps you could enlighten me later as to the circumstances. But my meeting with Rory was not of my making.'

'What are you talking about' I was getting angry now, realising I'd lost the initiative in the argument, which made me even worse.

'I will explain Ben', back to the informal and I had a bad feeling. 'Rory was contracted to turn out your lights, you are quite right. But not by me. I have nothing to fear from you other than a persistent annoyance. You'll never get anything on me that I won't be able to quash. Your ludicrous claims of testimony about my entertaining' –he raised his forefingers to indicate quotation marks – I wanted to hit him – 'underage girls could easily be obtained against Cliff Richard in Havana. For a few dollars

I could get sworn affidavits that the Pope was an Islamic Fundamentalist. I agree though that I would be grateful to get rid of the running sore that you have become, but not grateful enough though to get my fingers dirty. No, Ben Miller, you have other enemies.'

'Now I was totally confused and thinking fuck you, you bastard — what was coming next. This wasn't how I'd planned it. 'I'm sorry?' God why did I say that.

'Yes, I'm sure you will be,' he smiled smugly that sent shivers down my spine. I'd lost control and he knew it, as he lowered his tone. 'I admit that I did approach Paul with a proposition to transfer you away from your rather schoolboy crusade against me. But he came up with a counter proposal which I thought was an excellent idea.'

'I was putty in his hands now, in despair and desolation I whispered under my breath, 'Go on.'

'Paul felt that your, shall we say... removal, from the scene would be an adequate compensation for the Chronicle to drop any further investigations on any of my dealings.'

'Why would he want me removed?' I asked in total innocence totally unprepared for the next revelation.

'Because, you half wit, Paul and your delightful wife are having an affair. One which has developed to the stage that loose ends have to be tied up. And that is exactly what you are — a loose end.'

I could not believe what I had just heard, and slumped back in the chair. I didn't believe the lying bastard, he'd say anything to wriggle of the hook. But he had sown seeds of doubt. Yes it did make sense at some level. Paul had been overly sympathetic to giving me time off whenever I wanted time alone. Katie had always been fond of Paul and envied his bachelor life style. But I had never linked them together, not that I had ever given any of Katie's social life a thought. Roosting chickens started to invade my thinking. But why would they want me out of the way, I would have disappeared voluntarily had I known what was going on. I couldn't face any more of this and I needed to face Katie and demand some answers. I just got up and walked out of the office without a word. But I did think I heard O'Hara mutter 'Sucker', but didn't have the resolve to challenge him, thinking maybe he read my mind just a few minutes ago when I thought he was just that.

'Emma, Jim and Sean were still in the office chatting over coffee and stared at me with rather pious smiles as I walked past without uttering a word'.

'Do you want a break, Ben, you've been talking non stop for about forty minutes.' Aidan enquired, but I was anxious to keep going. I was on a voyage of discovery myself. I wasn't learning of my marriage break up but I was short on detail and I wanted to remember as much as I could even if it did hurt. I knew if I stopped I may never be able to get back.

'No I'd like to go on, if you're OK with it.'

'No problem. So after I had a couple of beers in town it began to make sense. I couldn't believe that Katie would go to such lengths but she had hardly said two words to me in the previous four months. Not that I would have been much better, burying my head in the sand, delighted when she wasn't in so that I wouldn't have to explain where I was and where I was going. I should have been interested in what she was doing but I didn't care. What will the kids think? At least they were old enough to get on with their lives. But I couldn't tell them their mother had tried to kill me. God, how could she have thought about it; surely I wasn't that bad. But it was time to face her, tell her she could have her precious Paul, but I had to assess this; maybe O'Hara was just trying to twist my mind. If he was, he made a pretty good job of it.

'I arrived home around seven fairly steamed but well aware of what I had to say. Katie was in the kitchen and surprisingly friendly, I wondered if she had word that I knew all about her affair with Paul, but she couldn't have.

'Welcome home Ben,' she kissed me on the cheek, 'do you want anything to eat before you tell me exactly what's been going on. I thought you were chasing a football story.' God, she sounded defensive, why couldn't anyone say what they were thinking any more.

'No..., listen Katie, we have to talk about us and I mean right now.'

'Yeah, OK, what's on your mind?' I got a puzzled look, but she may just have been mirroring mine.

'She followed me into the lounge and she sat down to where I gestured. I remained standing feeling ludicrously like a school master with an errant child, 'Katie, are you having an affair with Paul?' I rather surprised myself with the directness, possibly a bit of my work practice seeping into my personal life. But I was pleased, if I'd thought about it too long I would have fudged it.

'She didn't rush her reply but was very measured. I had the feeling she had prepared this speech for some time now. 'Yes Ben, and I'm sorry you've found out. I wanted to tell you myself and give you my reasons. But I could never find the right time to break it to you.'

'Yeah sure, you'd rather have me killed in Cuba,' as soon as I said it I realised I should have let her talk more first. Possibly I was flushed with the self praise over my initial candour. But it did change Katie's demeanour immediately, from being remorseful to aggressive. I knew I wasn't going to get the intimate details now, but I never wanted them anyway.

'What the fuck are you talking about?' I seemed to have said or heard that question about twenty times that day but I gave her a full account of my meeting with O'Hara. She sat through it genuinely amazed, I didn't know if I was being fooled again but it really was of no consequence. I just got up to leave. 'I'm going now and I'll have somewhere to move to in the next few days when I'll collect my stuff. I think we should sell the house and buy an apartment in town and a house in the country. You can have which ever you want on the proviso that it's left to the kids in your will. See you.' Katie angrily tried to convince me of her innocence or at least to persuade me to hear what she had to say, but I wasn't interested. The admitted affair with my boss and good friend was just as devastating. I knew after failing to impose my will on my earlier meetings in the day, I was not going to show any weakness in this one and left without uttering another word.

'I spent the night in Bewley's getting slowly plastered. During the course of the evening Susanna texted me to say she was arriving in Dublin at noon and could I meet her. I turned the phone off and added a chaser to my order.

'I woke up on my hotel bed having no idea how I got there, but apart from my head feeling as though it's stuffed with newspaper I was surprisingly sprightly. I could not wait to get down to see Paul again armed with O'Hara's accusations and Katie's confession.

'After just an orange juice, I headed down to the Quays. I waltzed straight into his office and give him everything. He knew what was coming and even failed to put up much of a defence on O'Hara's story. I told him I didn't care whether the stories were true or not, he was welcome to Katie, they deserved each other and then I got stuck into him. 'Oh yes, your job, you can stuff that up right your hole as well.' I turned around before he had the time to say anything. I really didn't want to hear a word. 'There's one more thing' I had thought about getting physical but had dismissed it as childish but the thought suddenly became overwhelming as I turned round and planted the sweetest punch I had ever landed in my life straight on his cheek bone, following through to hear the faintest of cracks as my fist hit his nose. I felt something give and saw blood spurting down into his open mouth as he staggered across his desk. The feeling of satisfaction was just immense. In the space of a few days I had loved and lost a soul mate, twice been threaten by a serious gun totting maniac, had four good friends murdered, been cheated out of a fortune and now lost my wife, my home, my best friend and my job. But strangely I felt great; the human spirit is a wonderful thing.'

Aidan couldn't contain a smile. 'You know they say violence never solves anything, but you've no idea how many times I have to prevent myself from suggesting to patients how much stress can be released by the wonderful surge you can get from beating the shit out of someone. Excuse my unprofessionalism, I really did not say that.'

Aidan had again managed to complete a bonding exercise and I thought either he was really good at his job or he could be a very good friend. I was now totally relaxed and anxious to get as far as I could.

'I went off to the airport to pick up Susanna. I had really so much to tell her and I was looking forward to seeing her again.

'When I met her she looked great, we shared a coffee in the airport and I relayed my sorry tale. I had no home to offer, nor a job but I did have a small fortune and suggested that we let our hair down for a few days.

'She was all on for it but felt that it might be appropriate first to go back to Cuba to make sure everything was done properly for Jenny. I was brought back down to earth but I agreed and said 'Of course, I could do with a break from all this shite. You know when I came back from Cuba, I was mentally and physically drained, and in the space of four days since I got back, I feel as though I've been through a wringer and squeezed dry. I'll go down to the travel agents tomorrow, but first I'll get you a room in Bewley's and show you that the salsa dancing in Dublin is as good as Havana.'

'Yeah, right' she replied sounding more Irish than I did.

'Our return trip to Cuba came and went without too much incident. We managed to get a proper headstone for Jenny in beautiful inlaid marble which I knew would become a pilgrimage for me during the coming years. It was simple and understated but showed she was someone special. I think she would have liked it. Susanna and I spend about ten days together just seeing through the process of getting our lives back on track in beautiful sunshine with no desire to do anything but gently get through the days without the stress we had been through. She considered going over to Bolivia to see Anton's mother, but I didn't think it was a good idea. Not particularly surprisingly she totally ignored my advice and went anyway and leaving me on my own for a couple of days. She had other reasons of course, which on contemplation I agreed with. She needed to honour Anton's grave as I had Jenny's. His body had been flown back to Bolivia to almost a state funeral which obviously Susanna had not attended and wanted to spend time at his side.

'Time on my own in a country I thought I loved proved to be a little unsettling. I could not think of anything to do except retrace the last few days of Jenny's life. I hired a motor bike and I found the restaurant in the hills, talked to the staff who would rather not remember anything of our fateful evening and I didn't press them. I tried to follow our route to the prefab village where we were held captive, which I find surprisingly easily, less than an hour from the restaurant. Either Suarez' men got lost, or they deliberately drove around to confuse us. Then my escape, which I didn't follow too accurately but it still brought back the feelings of tension and physical pain. Finally I drove to Matanzas and seek out Rory's house. It was exactly in the state I left it with the tree still piercing through the window and the shutters gently tapping against the wall. Rory's body has been removed of course, probably buried in an unmarked grave near to where Jenny was, but I wasn't that curious. I stayed some time in the room, thinking mostly of the last time I saw her alive, but also of my fight with Rory and also of Susanna's magnificent entrance. It was a room which I know will fall into decay quickly, but in the space of a few hours created so many images that it will never die in me, even if I have had so much trouble remembering them.

'On Susanna's return she was more morose, but was happy she went. Anton's mother really appreciated the gesture and made her very welcome, though I doubt she told her the full story. I think we have both learnt more of ourselves in these few days, about priorities and perspectives than we had in our lifetime before we met in Madrid those few weeks earlier, but it was time to move on. We had more or less decided independently that it was time to go home, but of course neither of us knew where that was. We both had to find somewhere to live and a job. After much discussion, I didn't encourage her, she felt she would like to try and settle in Ireland. On our return and all the festivities of Christmas, which of course were somewhat muted, we both found our own niches. I did some freelance work mainly for satirical magazines in the UK and enjoyed a little run as a minor celebrity appearing on breakfast chat shows whenever any topic came up that had anything to do with Central or South America.

'Our house found a buyer quickly, though the closing date is set well into the New Year to enable Kate to find somewhere else to live. The apartment I eventually acquired out of the anticipated proceeds of the house was totally functional. Estate Agent speak for very small but situated in the heart of town in Parnell Street. It was very noisy and encouraged me to spend as much time out of it as I could. I wished Kate had let me have the country house, which she bought in Carrick on Shannon, however that was pretty small as well.

'Susanna quickly got a job as a Montessori child minder in a school in Clonskea and loved the work and found a small bedsit in Rathgar. We didn't keep in regular contact once we settled down, some how our meetings seemed to encourage morbid memories which both of us were trying to forget. I suppose that's a little ironic now.'

Aidan nodded approval and I am totally impressed by his ability to stay interested for so long.

'Although the process of getting back to daily routine was quite difficult I did not spend too much time thinking of Jenny. I regretted never having said to her how much she meant to me though I did manage to garble something once about Cuba being the most exciting experience of my life and she always seemed to be there at the best and worst moments. The subtly of the conclusion that I was drawing that this wasn't a coincidence was probably a little too obscure but she smiled, probably at the effort made at the attempted compliment rather than the sentiments themselves.

'A couple of months later I found myself alone at the bar in Nostromo, a restaurant in Leeson Street when I ran into Susanna by accident and joined her company. Eventually the group she was with left to go home and we progressed to Buck Whaley's discussing everything that had gone on in our lives. It was a bitter sweet meeting for both of us but during the course of the evening I got more and more fond of the idea of telling Susanna every single feeling I had for Jenny. She had guessed most of it from previous conversations but this was different. A real confessional. She was about the same age as Jenny, attractive and was still traumatised by how she had laid a trap for Anton who she eventually came to adore and was devastated by her part in his murder.

Not to mention the trauma surrounding Jenny's death. I talked to her about my feelings and cynically realise now this is a wonderful technique as a chat up line to lay all your emotions bare. We talked, leaning on each other spiritually as we discussed our mutual problems and drank more and more.

'I got on really well with Susanna in a different way to before. We had up to now been thrown together by fate, I know not really, but as far as our time together it had seemed that way. Both of us were in relationships albeit of different intensities. Now we were both free aimless spirits with a lot of baggage. On leaving she invited me to her apartment to give me the benefit of her advice. I got occasional regrets about ever opening my mouth but I'm fairly well jarred, geared up to a good heart to heart and Susanna was a good listener.

'I went through where I was in my mind, I thought Jenny and myself couldn't have had any sort of relationship when there was twenty years between us, but I didn't say anything to her and will never know how she felt. My fear, that I didn't want her to think that I was crowding her in any way or that I felt attracted to her sexually, was probably the overriding consideration. The contradiction in that was that I was but apart from one beautiful moment on the beach in Havana which was more down to circumstances rather than mutual feelings, it never happened because I never faced her with the truth.

'I suddenly become conscious of the fact that all of this is probably less than flattering to Susanna, it couldn't be that easy to listen to someone rattling on about how wonderful someone else was. But to her credit she stuck to the task manfully and concluded that she knew that Jenny, like any woman, would have been flattered by my high regard and would not be freaked out by any genuine expressions of affection. And letting a negative thought surpass all positive ones can never be a good thing.

'That said over the course of three hours in a single girls flat as dawn approached gave me a good feeling, not least that Susanna would trust me enough and be interested enough in my story to forgo a night's sleep.

'I realise that her loss has been equal to mine, maybe heavier losing both Anton and Jenny and as though we are both thinking the same thing we took each other in our arms gently, letting so much to say unsaid.

'I visualised Susanna in the doorway in Matanzas, gun in hand, wonderfully strident and tell her exactly how I felt at the time. She smiled at me obviously coyly but not ashamed of being called sexy and leant over to kiss me. Instinctively I react very positively. It probably wasn't right but it did feel good.

'She got up reaching for my hands, pulled me up and guided me into her bedroom without a word spoken. Whilst I could see how lovely Susanna was I still had never thought of her in physical terms but that was changing rapidly as we lay together making slow, gentle and caring love for longer than I have ever had before.

'Looking back on our brief affair, if that's what it was, I can say honestly that it wasn't love, nor lust that attracted us to each other that night, just a mutual compassion, a desire to mend the emotional wounds that both of us had cruelly suffered. Perhaps she wanted to show me something about age, but I don't think so. There was no element that wasn't spontaneous. It gave us the opportunity to move on with the rest of our lives with hope whilst still keeping the memories of beautiful relationships we had shared. I have never felt guilty nor felt that I was unfaithful to the memory of Jenny. It was part of the healing process and I am sure Susanna felt the same.

'I saw Susanna occasionally afterwards, probably having the friendship with her that I once had envisaged having with Jenny when we first met. It was really strong and she had settled so well in Ireland, dating a doctor who I actually approved of, even if I did squirm at the paternal role I was adopting. But then sharing two weeks together that changed both our lives forever and so dramatically means that I felt as though our relationship was special and that we did have a mutual concern for each other that would never be broken, or so I thought at the time. I had totally forgiven her for her part in setting up the operation which only makes me feel more embarrassed about what I did to her when she came in with Trish.

'Don't worry Ben, Susanna understands. Your mind has still blotted out some memories and also some thought processes. It is not unnatural. But I think that's enough for today.

Chapter 19

Aidan didn't make another appointment so I was surprised to see him the next day. He was anxious not to lose the momentum. To the relief of both of us I was still in fine form and keen to continue where we had left off.

Aidan started 'From where I stand, Ben, you look as though you are coming to terms with your personal life but have not put any closure on anything. Your marriage, your job, nor your conflict with O'Hara. And still I feel you have not let everything go. What I'm curious about is why you went back to Cuba a third time – You had paid your respects to Jenny, hadn't you?'

'Emm.., I'm not sure myself. I know I felt the depression setting in. I know it had started much earlier but I was on too much of a roller coaster ride to realise. Time was passing.' I looked across at Aidan wondering how he saw a clinically depressed man explain how he was once REALLY depressed. I think if I were him I would start to wonder where I was going, and he sensed my embarrassment.

'I know this is difficult, Ben, you are about to explain why you had a breakdown. This is not a weakness. God – you had been through so much I'm amazed you psyche stood up as long as it did. Take it easy – this is the hardest part. You are doing really well. If you can get through this you will be making huge strides towards a full recovery and getting out of here.'

I acknowledged his encouragement, but somehow getting out of hospital wasn't an incentive right now. I wanted to know why, when I had remembered so much, I still wasn't happy that I knew the whole story. 'Shall I go on'

Aidan nodded to say yeah, yeah, of course.

I eased back in my chair and began to philosophise. 'Time was supposed to heal everything according to legend but as my fifteen minutes of fame began to fade, my desire to submit copy to various editors for them to accept, reject or even worse alter at a whim, waned and my apartment was looking more and more like an Iraqi holiday home. I began to search for reasons as to why my life was not developing the way I wanted.

'Lethargy and indifference put me off tackling O'Hara, he should have been my first priority but I knew it was going to call for a lot of ground work which I was just not interested in at the time. He definitely wasn't the soft option, but then I thought Dave Byrne was. I wondered why I hadn't chased him before, he took me for a fool and laughed all the way to the bank. It didn't take long for me to persuade myself that I should pay him a visit.

'His offices in Fitzwilliam Square were immaculate, with a reception area looking like a private art gallery. The beautifully manicured secretary ushered me into the conference room which was also magnificent, twelve large backed walnut chairs round a matching table polished to be able to see a reflection. The summer sun streaming through the four Georgian windows casting noughts and crosses play boards on the table.

'Dave doesn't normally see people without an appointment but I'll let him know you're here' his secretary informed me.

'I'll wait' was my curt reply.

'And so I did. Apart from Miss Ireland popping her head round the door to say that Dave would be able to see me in about twenty minutes I was left on my own for nearly an hour and a half. I was not bothered, he would be repentant for keeping me waiting and it did give me a chance to run through exactly what I was going to say to him. He abused his position of trust in making an agreement with such commission arrangements favourable to himself. I was going to report him to the Law Society unless he repaired this huge injustice. I would accept a reasonable commission of ten percent without quibble, but taking a third was tantamount to theft. I started to work yet again on my delivery, controlled anger would probably be the most prudent approach, but maybe animal rage might be more fun. Scare the bollocks off him. I smiled to myself, it was a little out of character but that might make it all the more effective. I kept mussing over the variety of scenes and his responses when he entered the room with my back turned.

'Ben, good to see you, sorry to keep you waiting' he held his hand out as I turn to approach him and added 'God, you look a mess, are you OK?'

'Taken aback by this observation which I must admit I wasn't aware of, I did think that his appearance was anything but. His navy Armani suit pressed to perfection and blood red tie contrasting sharply with the brightness of his white, starched shirt. His highly polished black shoes had the effect of making mine grey, his hair slinked back and his face almost buffed gave the overall impression of authority. I was not to be overawed.

'I started 'Listen Dave I know I've let the grass grow under my feet but I've had a lot on my mind recently. I'm very unhappy about the terms of the agreement you made with the News of the World. I don't think you were acting in my best interests and that you took advantage of my undoubted tiredness. It was made immediately after I got off a plane after travelling nearly twenty four hours. Not to mention the fact that I was returning from two weeks of mind numbing activity. The commission you arranged for yourself was obscene, and I was obliged to sign the agreement under undue duress. You encouraged me to sign without reading all the document and I want to renegotiate the terms now. And what do you mean I look a mess?'

'I wasn't really happy with the performance, he didn't seem to be too concerned and I sensed I wasn't anyway near angry enough.

'He replied without pausing 'Ben, I didn't mean to offend you, I just thought that you look as though you've been through the mill a bit, and I know you have. I'm sorry about you and Kate and I hope things work out OK. Would you fancy a night out soon I have tickets to the Santana concert in the Point, we could take in a club afterwards.'

'Now I knew I wasn't angry enough, he was completely ignoring me I thundered 'Are you listening to me, you slime ball. I want the two hundred and fifty thousand euro you stole from me, or I'll go to the Bar Council.' I managed to raise my voice enough that Miss Perfect popped her head around the door and asked if everything is OK. Dave nodded to her nonchalantly.

'He was really cool. 'Sorry Ben, I'm not with you. I most certainly did not encourage you to sign anything without fully understanding what you doing. If my memory serves me correctly you grabbed the hand off me in your anxiety to sign the document. You will recall that you were about to agree to accepting a total of a quarter of a million before I interjected on your behalf, which I have no doubt Victoria Althorpe will confirm. I would further point out that you had an exclusivity agreement with the Chronicle before you met the News of the World that would have negated any agreement had I not acted on your behalf before hand. Rather than screaming blue murder I would have thought you might have been a little more gracious but I understand you've been through a lot. Let's let bygones be bygones I really think Santana is a good idea. No hard feelings?' He held his hand out to me, I couldn't believe I'm not getting to him at all.

'You condescending fart' I fell into the vernacular to attempt to break the façade, 'you're a thief and I want my money.'

'He never blinked 'Ben, before we go any further I would advise you that this conversation is being taped and there are other people in the building who can probably hear you. What you are suggesting is slanderous and I would ask you to desist from making these obviously fallacious statements. You have no grounds for complaint and I would warn you that by taking this further you would lead yourself open to a counter action of defamation of character which I would doubtless win. Now if you'll excuse me I have work to do.' He turned to leave the room before I had a chance to say anything. I chased him into reception but he carried on walking into his offices which were protected by a security lock. I looked at Miss Spotless saying nothing but her mixed look of distain and trepidation made me feel very small. She began to suggest that I might be well advised to leave now, but it was a conclusion I had already reached. Walking out of that office was about the most belittling experience I have ever had. I felt defeated and humiliated. I kicked the front door on the way out but somehow that didn't make me feel any better. I questioned myself again, was I going to let this guy away with it. Well maybe for the moment. I must bide my time waiting for an opportunity to get even, which would surely come sometime.

'I headed into Kennedy's on the Quays to think about what I was going to do. During the course of downing a few pints I ran over the events of the afternoon and what I could do about getting my life back into order. I decided I should see Katie and see if she would have me back. She must have tired of Paul, he was insincere and shallow. And she must have been totally unaware of what he tried to do to me. I would tell her that I forgave her and understood what lead her to look elsewhere. I reviewed the advantages and possible outcome of such an approach as I go from a state of depression to drink induced euphoria. During the six hours I hardly spoke to anyone except to give my drink order. Watching Sky News on the TV followed by one of the football matches from the European Championship I drifted into a fog that didn't clear even when the barman swept the premises and I staggered the quarter mile to my apartment. I didn't even make it upstairs and slept on the couch in my clothes. Morning came early with a filthy mouth but a clear if aching mind. Dave was right I was a mess. There was no point going to Katie like this. There was probably no point going at all.

Chapter 20

'A few days later by a strange twist of fate I met Caroline, Katie's younger sister on O'Connell Street after my rather extended breakfast in Bewley's. She was a lovely girl and was sort of in awe of Katie and myself when we first got married and was an angel with her nephews and niece when they came along. She was very upset by our marriage breaking down and was pleased to run into me to have the opportunity to have a heart to heart.

'I was pleased to see her as well as friendly faces were scarce at the moment and welcomed any news that she may have on Katie. I suggested a coffee in the Gresham which of course meant an early pint. The hair of the dog and all that. She was a little surprised at my drinking but avoided the temptation to comment on it as she sat down to her coffee.

'How are you getting on, Ben?' It is funny how a simple question like that brings everything home. I was still in the clothes I had slept in, I hadn't shaved, I hadn't brushed my teeth. My breathe probably smelt vile, I cringed at the thought. And now I was drinking at eleven in the morning. And my sister in law is concerned for me, I wanted to run as far away as possible.

'Not very well actually.' I said, a few words which had a surprising effect. I actually felt a little better. It's not that I was coming out of denial, I had never really thought about it before. It was an acceptance that things could be better. Funny isn't it.

Aidan agreed, 'The human instinct is for self preservation, and whilst that more commonly is attributed to the physical state there's no reason to thing that the psychic world doesn't have a similar defence mechanism. An interesting observation. Carry on Ben.'

'Caroline asked if I wanted to talk about it and she was a good listener, but whether I wanted to burden her with all my problems was a question that I would need a little bit more time with. But I would talk about Katie.

'I'm sorry, Caroline. I look a mess I know. I had a bad night last night, you needn't worry about me. Have you heard from Katie recently?' I needed to know.

'Yeah, she's staying down in the house in Carrick more or less permanently now. It's lovely, overlooking the river, very peaceful. I think she needs that after what she's been through, I mean what you've both been through. I think Paul goes down at the weekends, but I don't think she wants to live with him permanently, it's like falling from the frying pan into the fire, if you'll excuse me saying. Anyway I don't like him. They were both deceitful to you, that can't be right.' I thought to myself if she only knew the whole truth she would go berserk.

'Is she happy?' I asked pining for a negative response.

'I don't know to be honest, but do I sense that you want to give it another try. I think it may be a bit too early, but you could go and see her if you want, I don't think she'd run you. But don't think she'll fall back into your arms with a few promises, because it just won't happen. If you are going down you need to get yourself straightened up, you really have let yourself go.' I smiled in acknowledgement of her accurate perception and her less than compassionate concern for my feelings.

'A few more enquiries about her kids, do I hear from mine and why not — they're a great stabiliser you know and we parted with a kiss on the cheek. I hoped I had no body odour.

'I was left with time to do a stock check on my life. My shirts were all stretched at the buttons; I wore jeans all the time with black formal shoes. They looked ridiculous. I did usually keep myself fairly clean but have reduced my showers to every other day and when I didn't shower I didn't shave. My flat needed a whirlwind through it. I hadn't ironed a single garment since I started living on my own. I realised that not one person has visited me since I moved in, and that thought depressed me so much. My hair hadn't been cut since I came back, not that much of a problem as growth is fairly slow these days. I was drinking at least six pints a day, talking to anyone who dropped into Kennedy's. They rarely came back for a second helping of my philosophy. I hadn't contacted anyone of my friends since Christmas and apart from that wonderful meeting with Susanna hadn't had any contact with the opposite sex. Hardly surprising I suppose. That was just a summery of my physical state, I'd rather not think of my financial position and I'd forget about the psychological well being altogether. I could not remember when I had a positive thought towards anything that was happening around me. Even Spring time annoyed me, talk about 'Taking the time to smell the roses' I didn't even notice them and think I'm allergic to them anyway.

'I woke up from this inward soul searching to discover another pint in front of me. This was not the solution, and for the first time in my life left an unfinished drink behind.

'I had to go and see Katie, show her that my life was together and hopefully let her see that we could have a future. The only problem with all that was that I was in bits.

'I spent the next few days on the dry, visiting a gym for the first time in twenty years, tidying my apartment and buying a whole new wardrobe. With every positive action I get a superior feeling and I felt sharper all round. The fact that I might be deluding myself about the reception I was going to get did not enter my head.

I couldn't wait to get down to see Katie and rang the kids to tell them of what I intended to do. None were over enthusiastic but that didn't dampen my ardour. At least I was going to get one thing back on track.

'I arrived in Carrick on a beautiful Tuesday afternoon. I felt I should go unannounced but I was sure our daughter will have let Katie know that something was a foot so she wouldn't be too surprised. I spent a little time to take in all the surroundings for a while. The white cottage glistened in the sun with the half barrels of geraniums and fuchsia was quite magnificent. Beyond the well kept lawn the Shannon meandered its way through rushes that appear to form traffic lanes in the river. Trees growing on baby islands scattered through the waterway and a cruiser slowly disappeared out of view with the sun glowing on its bows. It was quite idyllic and so peaceful. I felt at home. I knew I had got a few mountains to climb but I had a good gut feeling.

'I was about to knock on the door when a sudden wave of apprehension took over. Was this the right thing to do? Was I being fair to Katie? My alter ego sprang back into action, fair to Katie for fuck's sake! And I used the knocker with purposeful force. Katie answered the door, quickly and didn't seem too surprised. She was friendly but a little distant.

'Hi, Lynda told me you were planning to drop by, come in.' We went through the pleasantries, comment on how well we both looked, though she had lost weight and really did sparkle, I sensed that my recent improvement had not probably regained the ground lost since we parted, over six months ago now.

'She invited me in, went through all the pleasantries. 'Good to see you looking in good shape,' (I suspected Caroline's mid term report hadn't been too complimentary), 'would you like a cup of tea? Have a look around the place while I fix something.'

'I did as she bade and was impressed with her interior design skills. It really was a lovely place to live, with all the rustic charm that she had tried to decorate our home with before I had derided her simple tastes. Katie called me with the tea, which was accompanied by a huge plate of delicately prepared sandwiches. Despite my earlier protestations I dug into them with nervous energy.

'Katie,' I felt there was no time as good as the present to strike, 'I was thinking... I'd like to give us another shot. I mean I really miss you. I know we've had some rough times recently but I've come to realise over the last few months that there really is only one person in my life and you mean everything to me. I won't make the same mistakes again, I promise. No more drinking and we'll start doing things together again, like we used to. Remember?' Not enough passion I'm thinking so I add 'I really love you with all my heart.' I knew it sounded gutless.

'She looked at me for a long while without saying anything, a half smile on her face and then took my hands in hers and rested them on her lap. My heart was racing, I felt like a fourteen year old on a first date as I make full eye contact. 'Ben, I'm really sorry, it's over. It's not just you, I've moved on. We don't live in the same world. It's nothing to do with Paul. Whatever he and I had died the moment he did his deal with O'Hara, which I swear to you I knew nothing about. But you and I are just not compatible any more, maybe we never were. I hope we can stay friends and you are welcome anytime to come up here but you have to understand there is no relationship between us other than being parents to the same kids.' Sensing that she may have been a little too forthright she adds 'Would you like to go for a stroll around the river. It really is quite beautiful at this time of the year and maybe you can come and visit me for a few days and I can show you the virtues of country life.'

'She seemed so explicit and happy in her response that I couldn't think of anything to say. Offering a defence for my suggestion felt ludicrously out of place. I tried to be as civilised as possible, showing her that I could take the damning end to our relationship without tears but I was welling up. I had to get out of there. I made some pretty weak excuse. 'Of course we'll keep in touch and I'd love to come for a few days but I have to get back to Dublin before nine to see a friend of mine'. She kissed me on the cheek; 'Take care' and I sensed that she was tearful too. I could not look at her now and I wriggled away losing all sense of dignity hardly murmuring a goodbye.

'I climbed back into the car and sped off without looking back. I had gone from eternal hope to desolation and despair in twenty five minutes and drove to the Dublin side of Carrick, park in a lay by overlooking the river and sob unrelentingly for nearly two hours.

'The next day I spent entirely in bed, there didn't seem to be much point getting up. I was not really depressed, just numb. I had done all I want to do about getting my life on track, there just wasn't too much point to anything. I started to think about O'Hara again and that I would have to do something to upset him but I just could not raise the energy to think of what I could do to get under his skin. He thought he was untouchable and I was beginning to agree with him.

'However Paul was another kettle of fried calamari. I had really let him off Scot free. He had tried to have me killed, stole my wife, screwed €250,000 of me unethically and happily accepted my resignation. Just one punch on the jaw was not enough to settle the score no matter how satisfying it was.

'But I knew I just couldn't face him either, my record of showdowns to date hadn't been too impressive and if he were to get the better of me I just couldn't live with myself.

'I was given a good talking to by my alter ego, 'Are you a man or a mouse, for God's sake? Just face him down and punch his lights out properly this time.' If only it was that easy. I knew I was not going to do anything about him either and felt so pathetic. I rolled over and pray for sleep which never came.

'Images revolved around my brain, Jenny, Rory, Katie, Paul, Susanna, O'Hara mixed with love and hate. Then the time in La Paz, the midnight Jacuzzi in Valadero, our night in Toledo, the night the Friends of Che surrounded us, the storm that killed Jenny and Rory, the negotiations with the News Of the World, discovering O'Hara's backhander was a fabricated story, seeing Jenny for the first time and seeing Katie for the last time. And probably most consuming, the thoughts of the sacrifice of my friends in the name of Santeria. My mind felt as though it had been pulled through a mincing machine. I could not focus on anything and yet everything was going through at ninety miles per hour.

'I didn't eat, sleep, wash or change my clothes for three days which seemed to go on for ever. I ignored the phone, left the television on all the time without paying any attention. When I did manage to put two thoughts together I eventually came to the conclusion that I was a weak, pathetic excuse for a human being and no one would miss me if I just disappeared.

'I managed to catch a glimpse of myself in the mirror which only disgusted me and confirmed everything I thought about myself. I started to get hungry but couldn't face going outside. And I had no visitors until Caroline broke the door down and her eyes just cried out in despair.

'What are you doing to yourself?'

'Leave me alone Caroline. I'll be OK.'

'Yeah right' she said with such derision I shrank from her gaze. Unbelievably she then spent the next twenty four hours with me, bullying and hassling me until I finally arrived at something like humanity, well fed, rested, and showered with an accompanying pep talk that would stimulate an amoeba. I didn't know why she was so concerned. Maybe a family guilt over the way my marriage had gone, but looking back she was only fantastic. Much better than any psycho analysis I have ever had or heard of, with all due respects Aidan this was before I met you.

He just smile and rolled his hand.

'I started not feeling quite so sorry for myself, I even made one or two grabs for Caroline which she easily managed to fend off. She left me feeling, as she had earlier in the week, that there was some reason for going on and that I had to get some sort of focus into my life that was forward looking. Before she left I eventually burdened her with some of my story and she made me realise that I was the only one hurting from the festering wounds that Paul and O'Hara had inflicted. I couldn't understand how she managed to twist my mood round so easily but I feared that if I stayed on my own in Dublin for very much longer I was going to fall straight back into the abyss I had created for myself.

'I just knew at that stage that nothing was going right for me. I had some money but no job. Any friends I had disappeared and I'd lost touch with Susanna. I think I felt I had to get away and be with Jenny. Does that sound stupid?'

'Nothing sounds stupid, Ben. You did what you did because you felt it was right. I know this is a little unfair, but you were so low I wonder if you ever contemplated suicide.'

I was a little taken aback by the stark suggestion, but answered honestly, 'No, I don't think so. I wanted to be beside Jenny, but I don't think I considered joining her. I think I might have tossed around the idea if I'd thought about it but I think I was thinking in very narrow lanes. Probably just as well.'

Aidan smiled 'Probably.'

'It didn't take too long to make up my mind. There was nothing to keep me in Dublin. And there was no one to tell me it was a bad idea. I thought about why I went to see Katie, was I really only trying to replace the love I never had with Jenny with the love I had lost many years ago with Katie. It was selfish and totally unrealistic. I needed to find peace of mind and I felt I could only do that by being close to Jenny. Spend time at her side and tell her everything I wanted to before she was so cruelly taken away. Honour her spirit the way I never was able to honour her body. The more I thought of what I should do the more obvious it became, I had to go to Cuba and every minute brought a new reason why I should go with more anticipated excitement.'

'I made my arrangements without telling anyone. Caroline called everyday and I persuaded her that I was back to feeling fine and she accepted that I wanted to do my own thing and that I had to get away for a while. She gave me her blessing along with good wishes from Katie on the strict understanding that I phone from wherever I was going. I felt guilty that I couldn't trust her with my actual destination but I knew she would probably try and stop me, if she knew, thinking it was a backward step.

'I was happy in myself that it wasn't and for the third time in nine months made the long haul to Havana via Madrid.

'I had some difficulty getting through immigration this time having to explain my three trips in some detail. Eventually one of the Airport police recognised me from the press coverage I had received and accepted that I had to look for some reasons for what had happen to me to enable me to put things back into perspective. I was not sure if I made any sense or he just gave up on me as being another crazy tourist, but I didn't care.

'He replied in perfect English that there was no better place in the world for doing just that and once again a wave of euphoria swept over me. I had done the right thing. I could lay a few ghosts to rest and get back to living a proper life. I found private lodgings in Calle Brasil in the heart of old Havana which was comfortable, affordable and very friendly. It lent itself perfectly for my planning the rest of my life. It gave me once again the opportunity to explore this wonderful city of contrasts which I did with the help of my landlord, Ricardo. I found the same spirit in him that Geronimo had, delightfully playing the system in his battle for survival. He showed me all the places to shop, drink, eat and party, not that I was too interested in any of that, but I found his outlook refreshing. After a couple of days rediscovering the city as a resident instead of a voyeur or refugee, I decided that I had to get back to Matanzas. I felt as though I was ready to talk to Jenny. I was not despondent, I was full of anticipation of what I believed would be a spiritual homecoming.

Aidan interrupted me for the first time in nearly an hour. I had this feeling that I was talking to myself, that he wasn't listening and that I was just reliving my trip in my own mind. He must have sensed some of that as he was concerned that I was over exerting myself.

'I don't know if you realise this, Ben, but the tension in here is electric. I don't want you to hamper your efforts in recalling your adventures, but we are on dangerous ground here. I sense you are coming to the climax in your story. To the point of your breakdown. And I want you to be aware of the possible consequences of facing the same situation in your mind. I don't know what your reaction will be. This may be very hard on you, are you sure you are ready for this.'

I acknowledged the change of mood and Aidan's concern and paused for a minute to collect my thoughts.

'I don't know either, but I have to go on. If I blank this now I may never be able to recall what it was that lead to my crash and I will never be able to come to terms with it. I need to know and I need you with me Aidan.'

'There's no problem, Ben. I'm not going anywhere.

I smiled and braced myself for the last trip on the roller coaster.

Chapter 21

July 19 2004

Havana and Matanzas

'I visited Jenny's grave every day for a week after hiring a car and making the six hour return journey to a strict routine. Whilst it wasn't particularly sensible to stay in Havana I discovered it was a good way of getting through the day and I enjoyed going back to Ricardo's house and telling him of my adventures. Not that he understood why I was doing it, but he did have the beautiful attitude that you should do anything you want if you find peace. I did that by spending time at Jenny's side and it gave me a contentment I hadn't had for some time. Each day brought with it a greater awareness that she was trying to contact me and I welcomed the attention that a Santeria priest gave me when he realised my devoutness. After a week of brief encounters, during which we exchanged little more than banal pleasantries, he suggested that we should go back to his house for a cup of coffee.

'I willing accepted as apart from Ricardo I was making little human contact to sustain my growing feeling of well being. His home was shared with an attractive woman I presumed to be his partner who he introduced as Cheena, her parents Carlos and Yelina and her younger brothers, both in their late teens and uncompromising in their James Dean look. Cheena warmly took my arm and led me inside to a single room which was immaculately clean but had little furniture. I was ushered into a chair reluctantly vacated by Alfonso, the younger of the brothers who appeared to take an instant dislike to me. The feeling was mutual buddy, I thought. Not that her parents were much better, neither said a word (probably not having any English) and just watched my every movement with a deep suspicion probably resulting from years of anti Western propaganda. I could only see another room leading off this parlour and I could not imagine what the sleeping arrangements were. I was curious but also uncomfortable and wished I had politely declined my priest's invitation. Especially as I was now also doubting his credentials. I had been calling him Father on our previous meetings but I now felt it would be ludicrous to continue with that title and thankfully Cheena called to him as Ernesto, and I followed suit. Despite my misgivings Cheena and Ernesto were very friendly and offered me a plate of meatballs and potatoes that were very tasty. I still had the silent audience of the parents and brothers which was a little intimidating but I consoled myself in that I was probably depriving them of their dinner. I must have been getting better as I could feel my cynicism levels rising. I thought that maybe I'd ask for more, which would really piss them off. Ernesto returned me back to Earth by discussing my vigil and I become ashamed of my thoughts.

'I then began to tell him my story of how I lost Jenny in a night of a wild storm, how Rory had captured us and his death appeared so timely when Jenny's was just the opposite. As I tell Ernesto every detail of that terrible day and he sat transfixed, remaining silent after I have said all I can. I began to say how I wished I could be with her when he lifted his hands to cover my eyes and I felt all my energy leaving my body.

'Quiet child' he said. I later thought how ridiculous that sounded as I must have had twenty five years on him, but at the time I felt total submission. 'You have described the night Oya visited us.' I wanted to ask who is Oya, but had no control over my speech. It didn't matter as he explained all I wanted to know in a definitive lecture.

'Oya is an Orcha, a god. Orchas are the manifestation of Ashe, the life force – the balance of the Universe. There are many Orchas but only seven rule the forces of nature. Oya controls the winds and rain. If she cries torrential rain falls on the Earth. If she flicks her tongue she lashes the World with lightening. Her power knows no bounds. But she is compassionate; she creates chaos to create the way for new growth and carries the spirits of the dead to a new world. If Oya is your Orcha she will look over and take care of you, but she will choose you. You can not ask her to be your Orcha, you can only offer yourself to her. If she does visit you, you must never look at her as she will strike you blind. Some tell the tale she has nine heads like the tributaries of the great river in Africa and never wants to be seen. She is the one that will bring Jenny to you, the dead are always with us, Oya will help you find her. If you want to make contact with Jenny you will enjoy the spiritual uplifting that the communication would bring. Join us tomorrow for our initiation ceremony; we will welcome you with open arms'.

'I looked around at Ernesto's in laws who remained non-plussed and I thought I had outstayed my welcome, but I was excited. The potential metaphysical contact with Jenny along with the curiosity to learn more of the religion in whose name my friends were murdered made such an invitation irresistible and I asked Ernesto where I could stay. Cheena offered me room there but I respectfully declined, I didn't fancy her brothers anywhere near me whilst I was sleeping, so she suggested another house two streets away where they did have a room spare. I discovered later that it meant that my hosts had to sleep in their kitchen but they were very hospitable.

'The ceremony started on Saturday with the crowds gathering early all dressed in bright colours to win favour with the Orishas. Conversations were endless, without any particular structure and whilst many of my fellow worshipers were friendly and inclusive, conversations were of course in Spanish and I felt a little lost but that was not the fault of my fellow worshippers.

'In front of a makeshift altar sacrifices were brought, exotic fruits and vegetables, cooked meats, sacrificial animals and bottles of aguardiente, a lethal concoction made from sugar cane. After an entry worthy of Chris Eubanks, the Bishop entered the room and took a huge mouthful of the aguardiente and spewed it all over the congregation as a sort of blessing. I felt uncomfortable again at this distasteful spraying which reminded me a little of being at a punk concert, but all around me people were ecstatic. The bishop mixed a drink from all the offerings and passed it to Ernesto, dressed in full regalia, who then offered it to all who wished to participate, and everyone did.

'Then new recruits were required to lie face down on the floor and the bishop went through a dance ritual which I felt was harmless enough but was rather unnerving. During this dance the drumming started, a rhythmic, all embracing beat which pervaded all the senses.

'As the beat reached a crescendo Ernesto took my hands and pulled me in front of the altar amid clapping and foot stomping from the crowd. It was hot and I was sweating profusely but I felt at ease, not threatened at all.

'The priest covered my eyes with his hands as he had in his home and the incessant drumming became all embracing. I felt serene and suddenly all was quiet as I dropped to my knees feeling a total peace with nothing on my mind except my consciousness.

'The priest whispered Jenny's name in my ear over and over again and I could hear her talking to me.

'She was whispering that she loved me and that she missed me but warned me to take care; the priest will look after me. Trust him, she said, believe in the Orisha.

'I was in a timeless state as bodies danced around me, maybe for a minute or maybe hours as the blood of sacrificed animals was sprinkled on my face slowly trickling into my mouth. I was oblivious to all feeling as though I was watching myself taking centre stage in a colourful carnival. The bishop faced me with a cut throat razor and I was suddenly frozen with fear. I thought I was going to be the ultimate sacrifice but I still could not move. Two men came from behind and forced me to my knees, with my head bowed. I was ready to find Jenny and my fear melted away. Ready to accept my fate, the bishop pulled my head back and slowly shaved my hair to the applause of the entire congregation. After the ceremonial cutting of the long hair, other priests dressed like Ernesto appeared with more delicate razors and foam and left my scalp smooth and shinning. The audience queued to decorate my bald pate with the colours of their Orcha. Slowly I rose to my feet but felt assaulted. I had no control of spasmodic movements and began to cavort to cheers and wild hoops of joy. I heard a chanting of Oya, Oya, Oya and I knew then that she had chosen me. I was going to meet Jenny.

'The ceremony ended in a cacophony of silence and I was spread eagled on the floor, feeling no embarrassment, no shame, no pain nor fear but also no energy.

'I could not move and was carried to the back of the room by four young men who smiled benignly at me. A young girl was summoned to look after me and she smiled, mopped my forehead with a damp towel and held my hand.

'I tried talk to her and whilst I knew she wasn't Jenny I called her by that name and she responded with flashing eyes and a warm heart.

'Behind us the congregation were chanting as another novice went through a similar ceremony. Cuban Jenny offered me more aguardiente which I knew was silly but I accepted it willingly. Slowly I began to regain my strength and for what seemed like hours Jenny stayed by my side, saying nothing but constantly caressing my cheeks and gently kissing my ears and eyes every so often. I was at total peace, a feeling I had never had before. I didn't want to be anywhere else, be with anyone else, or do anything else. I closed my eyes and drifted into another world where I felt close to the real Jenny and she told me to get out of Matanzas as I was in danger and there was work to be done in Havana. I couldn't believe I had made direct contact and stayed as long as the ceremony lasted and her voice disappeared. Eventually the festivities died away and the congregation dispersed to the sounds of Bob Marley's 'Trenchtown Rock'. It felt so inappropriate, a singularly stark piece of music epitomising urban deprivation and violence at the end of a joyous ceremony, but then what was appropriate. Ernesto and Cuban Jenny lifted me to my feet; he blessed me and my strength felt suddenly restored, though the pain also returned. Cuban Jenny took my hand and I got a horror of being unfaithful and pulled away. I realised her role in my initiation did not stop at care and attention. The hurt on her face brought more guilt but I could not be what she wanted and she ran off. I knew she probably would feel contempt for me for my not being able to return the love and nurturing she had given me and that she may be regarded as having failed in her duty, but I must also be true to myself.

'I looked at my watch and discovered I had been out of my body for nine hours, it could have been nine minutes for all I was aware and I thanked Ernesto profusely for his encouragement to take part. I had meet Jenny, talked to her and was excited and frightened at the same time. He smiled back, bade me farewell and a safe journey though I wasn't quite sure which journey he was referring to, Havana, home or another world. I somehow felt that I had disappointed him. Maybe he wanted me to stay in Matanzas but Jenny had told me there was work to be done in Havana. I had to go.

'Not being too concerned with the quantity of aguandiente I had consumed and feeling Jenny's guiding hand on my shoulder, I decided to drive straight back to Havana arriving just after midnight with the town buzzing with activity. Every corner was alive with drinkers raising their plastic beakers and I went from street to street maniacally looking for the work Jenny has told me of. I didn't know what I was looking for but as I turned a corner into El Floridita, it suddenly appeared.

'I was not sure if I felt excited or horrified as I watched O'Hara negotiating with a young girl who could not be any more than fourteen. I stood in the shadows and calculate they spent five minutes deciding what ever details that had to be agreed. I couldn't believe my luck, my nemesis right here before me caught in a compromising position which just sickens me and every right thinking person in the world. I said a prayer to Jenny and to thank Ernesto, Santeria and Oya for bringing us together. This was my divine right to put things right. My calling, which would cleanse my soul and lift all the heartache of the last year away.

'I followed them around two streets as they turn up a quiet unlit road. This was my chance, I found a half brick lying around the street and ran up to them from behind, screaming 'O'Hara you evil monster' and struck him straight on the forehead as he turned to face me. My first blow hit him with the corner of the brick and immediately felled him, with blood spurting over me and the young girl. She was screaming and turned to grab my arms biting my wrist like a wild cat. The quiet street turned into a momentous discord of sound and people emerged from every door way. With my arms fighting the girl I aimed a few kicks to O'Hara's head, happy in the knowledge that I was doing God's work.

'Eventually I was dragged to the ground by a few rather large men and the girl I have saved disappeared into the crowd that had formed. Within minutes half a dozen police arrive but I didn't fear the outcome. I just had to explain what happen, that O'Hara was an evil man and justice has been done under God's will. A Cuban God at that. O'Hara was head down in the gutter, even more poetic justice, motionless with a blood stream forming a pool in the dust. A wonderful day comes to a momentous end.

'I was marched of to an office where I was left to my own devices for the rest of the night. The only worry, but hardly surprising I told myself, for my own safety, was that they locked the door as they left.

'I tried to get some sleep, but felt elated. At last I had done something positive to avenge all that had happened. O'Hara will have some explaining to do back in Ireland, even if he has survived. But I really hoped the world had seen the last of the greedy, self serving, corrupt, paedophile and evil Irish politician that O'Hara has become. I wandered round the room virtually all night, recreating the Santeria ceremony over and over in my mind.

'It was not until ten o clock that anyone came in to see me and the room was getting decidedly sticky as the temperature rose without any air conditioning, running water, food and toilet facilities other than the ubiquitous bucket.

'I was beginning to feel uneasy when a young officer entered the room and questioned me in perfect English to submit details on an official form, name, nationality, what was I doing in Cuba, where was I staying, passport details and virtually every other detail that they can ask me which was of no relevance to why I was here. I was beginning to tire of the barrage of questions, none of which refer to the incident. I asked to see a superior officer so that I could explain exactly what happened and to organise my release. I told him I could do with a wash and some breakfast. He responded with a nonchalant smile and then left me on my own until the early afternoon with my anger rising as each minute passed. When my hammering on the door brought no response and I could not hear any other sign of movement in the building I began to fear my fate. I was in Cuba, not exactly renown for its fair treatment of Westerners who fell foul of the authorities. And if O'Hara had survived God knows what he had told them. Suddenly I started to think that maybe hearing voices wasn't the best explanation for a fairly vicious assault with a blunt instrument.

'When an officer eventually arrived with the young man who first questioned me, I was as ready for him as I would be. Back to the offensive... 'Can you please arrange that I am released immediately I can explain everything I am the innocent party here. The man I tangled with last night is a child molesting monster...'He looked at me and shrugged, 'Mr Miller, I don't think you quite understand the difficulty you are in. You are being held under Cuban Law for the attempted murder of James Mulroy and I have to officially caution you that you do not have to say anything but anything you do say may be taken down and used against you in evidence.' He motioned to the officer who is ready with pen and note book.

'That shook me a little and stammered 'I'm sorry the man I attacked last night was Dennis O'Hara...' but he was having none of it. 'Please forgive me Mr Miller, the man you attacked and who presently is on a life support machine for severe head injuries is James Mulroy, a businessman from Birmingham, England. If you would like to tell us why you attacked Mr Mulroy we would be most interested.'

'But I don't know a James Mulroy.' I looked blankly through the officer who came to the rather obvious conclusion, 'That would rather imply the attack was motiveless and can I assume, unprovoked?'

'I was fighting for my life now and shouted back 'He was going with a child, obviously to fuck her brains out or even worse, he's a scum bag. He got everything he deserved,' not fully appreciating the damning indictment I was making on myself. He said that they had several witnesses that Mr Mulroy was on his own when I attacked him and suggested that I said little else without consulting a solicitor first. Rather needlessly I asked if he was holding me.' To which he replied, 'No legal difficulties here on that score, we can keep you for as long as we like. And you needn't concern yourself with bail either, we haven't quite grasped that concept yet, we prefer to know where our suspects are by throwing away the key. Some food will be sent into you and I suggest you get some sleep. We will offer you a list of solicitors for you and let you make a call to one of your choice. We will probably want to talk to you again this afternoon. Good day Mr Miller.'

'He was right about one thing I did need some sleep. Part of me felt Oya and Jenny would see me through this, the other part was not so sure and I was beginning to doubt if any of the circus I was involved in yesterday was anything more than hocus pocus. But I was in denial, everything would be all right, it was O'Hara he must have been travelling under a pseudonym. I didn't need a solicitor. I have a guardian angel.

'The officer returned the next day after a series of visits from a variety of guards offering relatively good food, washing and toilet facilities on the other side of the building. I was quite relaxed, beginning to get my faith back. However I did get the opportunity to look around what was obviously a very large police station, and I realised I had the best suite. There were several cells with just air holes in the door as the only light. Other cells were crowded with a variety of inmates of all ages, physical strengths and levels of belief in the merits of personal hygiene. I could imagine myself being very uncomfortable in their company. Perhaps I should start to take these charges seriously.

'On his return my captor almost grudgingly announced a chink of light. 'Mr Miller I believe you haven't contacted a solicitor. Normally that would be ridiculous in your circumstances but strangely, I have some good news for you. Mr Mulroy has come round and is making a speedy recovery. He does not wish to press charges and has persuaded us that it may be good for all of us if a trial was not to take place. However he is concerned that your attack was motiveless and he wants some assurance that it will not be repeated.'

'I thought he's never going to get that and Jenny nods her approval on my shoulder.

'He continued 'He has asked if he can come and see you personally to try to put his mind at rest. Are you happy to see him?' I was joyous 'Most definitely. The sooner, the better.' Apparently it would not be for a couple of days as he had to recuperate. In the meantime I was to be held under guard.'

'The couple of days pass without incident as I waited for my head to head with O'Hara. He couldn't press charges because of the publicity, I reasoned with myself. I'd never give him any assurances. I'd blow his mind away along with the rest of his anatomy if I got the chance.

'As arranged with the officer, the time came and preceded by three armed guards Mr Mulroy hobbled in with a huge plaster the size of his forehead, two deep black eyes and a walking stick to steady his frail stance.

'I couldn't believe it 'Where's O'Hara?' I shrieked and flew up towards Mulroy. Two guards held me down on the ground and I kicked a third in the groin. Mulroy turned round to leave without saying a word, but looked at the officer who follows him out of the room.

'Eventually I collapsed under the combined arm of the law and submitted to their wishes. I understood that they didn't think I'd been too smart. I just didn't know what to think. I cried 'What should I do Jenny?' But I didn't get an answer just questioning looks from the young guards as one went away to fetch a straight jacket. This wasn't too good and I was beginning to grasp how deep a hole I had dug for myself.

'The next day passed without incident but I was more or less numb to anything anyway and the following day an officer called in to see me with good news. Or so he claimed.

'We have contacted the authorities in Ireland and two Gardai are flying over to Havana to escort you home. Mr Mulroy has agreed to drop all charges provided you agree to leaving Cuba immediately and that you are committed into psychiatric care. Fortunately for you, you don't have to make a decision on this, we will make it a condition of your repatriation. You will stay in custody until your escort arrives when your belongings will be collected on your behalf and transferred with you to the next available flight out of Cuba. I would warn you that any attempt to escape deportation will result in proceedings being brought against you for criminal assault. If found guilty, which without trying to prejudge too much, I would think there is a more than an even chance that you will be, you will serve a sentence in a Cuban jail of anything up to life imprisonment. Unless you have a liking for rats and a desire to mix with the downwardly static I would suggest that it may not be the most promising way to spend your pre retirement years. Oh finally I almost forgot, you have been declared an undesirable alien by our Ministry of the Interior and you will not be allowed to return to Cuba. I would say you are heartbroken.' His less than subtle sarcasm was unwanted and I thought rather western. Maybe he was educated in Dublin. I could not think of anything to say to him as I could only think of not being able to talk to Jenny ever again. A realisation that things were turning for the worse was beginning to dawn on me. My guard turned to leave, sensing I suppose that I was not really in the mood for engaging in conversation. Apart from the delivery of food and the escort to the toilet I didn't see anyone else for four days.

'My transfer to Dublin took the same form as the previous two except that I was constantly handcuffed to one of the two plain clothes Garda that accompanied me. Initially they were friendly, asking after the tales of my intrepid adventures that they were aware of, but they ignored my presence when I offered no response at all. All that was going through my head was that I was being committed. Why for God's sake? I knew I had not handled myself very well, but surely I was the victim. And I was not going to be able to visit Jenny anymore. Nothing else seemed to matter.

'Nearly two weeks in a cell in The Bridewell passed without my really noticing anything. The conditions, the food and the good nature of my warders were little better than they had been in Havana but I really had no interest, as day followed night. The only break in the routine was an occasional walk in the sunshine and visits from doctors making a variety of tests on me. Eventually I was informed that in the absence of any supporting testimony as to my mental health I was being committed to the Central Mental Hospital in Dundrum, where I would stay until I could prove to my ability to look after myself.

'I asked about my right to a fair trial and innocent until proven guilty and was told by the sergeant that I was not in prison nor was I charged with anything. So it was entirely up to me when I would be released. I knew that was the furthest thing from the truth he could have said.

'And so here I am. My story is over.' I look over at Aidan for a response but I don't know what I want. 'I want to go home, Aidan but there's something missing and I don't know what it is.'

'That really is one hell of a story. I didn't want to interrupt you when you were in full flow but you must be tired. Physically and obviously emotionally. That was some helter skelter of a journey, Ben. You really have travelled a long way in a short time, possibly you've felt the depth of the pain you have suffered twice. Maybe it wasn't fair to put you through this, but I don't think we could have reached this position any quicker and you are well on the way to a complete recovery. I think you should rest for a few days. You've nothing to lose and a stress free life to gain. I'll come back on Monday and urge you in the meantime to relax. Don't persecute yourself for more answers or seeking ways of to make some sort of retribution. Try to think that you are about to start a new era where your past will play little part. I know that is not easy but you have to turn to the future and purge yourself of thoughts of what might have been. You've a lot of unfinished business with O'Hara, Paul, Dave and Katie and regrets about how your life could have gone with Jenny and Susanna and maybe even Trish as well. But put them all behind you, be positive Ben, we are close to getting your life together. Don't rush it.'

I nodded without commitment. 'Um be positive. Really Aidan, what I have got to be positive about? I'm not feeling sorry for myself but let's face it there is no happy ending here. I'm sure I'm missing something and whatever you say I won't be happy until I have settled a few scores with O'Hara. I want to get out but I'm scared I'll do the wrong thing.'

Aidan stayed quiet for a minute then offered a reassuring smile 'We'll take it at your pace, Ben just rest for now and I'll see you on Monday. I'm really proud of you.' And with that he left.

Chapter 22

The next day Trish visited me. 'Listen Ben I've been thinking a lot about your story. And when I say a lot I really do mean every fucking minute, you bastard. And I've come to a conclusion that you may not want to hear but here goes.'

I sighed, resigned to more bad news or maybe a pep talk. I was wondering if I should relive my final experiences that I had shared with Aidan, but then figured she probably had an outline from him already. I still didn't see why she had to take the bull by the horns quite so quickly. Why couldn't we go through the how are things routine a bit longer? 'Have you been talking to Aidan?'

She smiled and nodded her head 'I rang him up and he mentioned that you had come to terms with all the sequence of events without going into detail. But it's not that I came to talk about. You'll thank me for saying this someday but you've got to let go off this thing you have with O'Hara. It really hurts to say this but he's won, he's beaten the system and you have to come to terms with that; it's over. Even if you did manage to discredit him and even send him to jail, do you think he would get more than six months and after that he would be free to spend the millions upon millions he has salted away? That would only screw you up more. *You cannot beat this system*, you know that, you can only beat yourself up.' She looks at me wondering if she's touched base. I'm not too sure, I know what she's saying, but we can't give up. There has to be some one marking the score.

'Trish, I know what you're saying but I can't just walk away. He's done terrible things, pocketing a fortune at the expense of all of us. He can't get off without someone saying this is not right.'

'Ben, I'm not saying you should give up fighting, but fight battles you can win, not ones you just wear yourself away. O'Hara will answer for what he's done and maybe that will be to a higher court. I'm not particularly religious but I do believe that a judgement day comes. It may be on this Earth or it may be on the next, but it doesn't have to be you who brings him to justice. Just look at yourself, the past six months have been eaten away by a desire to get even but you've been channelling your energy against the wrong man. Let him trip himself up. He may not get all he deserves but his downfall will come, trust me. I've been thinking about this all day and I can't understand how you let Paul away with what he did. Did you never consider going to the police? He really has a lot to answer for. I never knew, I feel kind of dirty working for him all this time. Let's go after him, Ben. Make him pay. Make him pay for planning to murder you, for cheating on you with Katie, for screwing money out of you, which I'm sure he pocketed.'

'I know what you're saying but look at it rationally. I start accusing Paul of arranging a hit job on me on the grounds of a conversation I had with O'Hara, a man who it is well known I have been investigating for several months. It coincides with the time I discover he is having an affair with my wife, also the time when I accused him fairly publicly of ripping me off and walking out on my job. Do you think the police might put all those coincidences down to fate. I think you know the answer to that. And aside from all that you have a good job in the Tribune. That would be compromised, for what. Nothing. If you think O'Hara's won, you must think Paul was in a race without any opposition.'

'Listen I don't care about my job, I wanted to be a journalist to seek out the truth and be fearless in telling it as it is. I don't want to work for a man that has so much to hide he wouldn't know the truth if it bit him. I know that sounds pretentious crap but I happen to believe in it.'

'You give me hope and despair, I'm so glad you came back Trish, but as you said I don't think I like what you say.'

'You're a fine man Ben, and you owe it to yourself to get better. You know you can beat this and live a good life. I'll do everything I can to help you through this. The first thing is tomorrow morning I'm going into Paul's office and rip up my contract and anything else I can lay my hands on. If he mentions notice I'll make him shit his pants and say I know everything about what happened in Cuba. Just because the law can't touch him doesn't mean he doesn't have kittens about it every now and then.'

I smiled at her and contemplate some rebuttal to her offer to resign, but she's right, you can't have principals in this business and work for a gangster. She'll find work easy enough; she's bloody good at her job.

I tried to say something meaningful but I think it's all been said for now. She pulls herself up to leave and I follow suit,

'Thanks for coming Trish; I really will think about everything you've said.'

'You can't get rid of me that easily I'll come back tomorrow and we can go through everything. I'll tell you exactly what Paul said. You know I'm really looking forward to it and you still have to fill me in with all the details of the Santeria experiences. If you feel like going over it again.'

'Yeah, maybe. I'm not sure myself to be honest. Come back tomorrow and we'll talk anyway. Take care.'

I watched her go down the corridor and laughed to myself for the first time for a year. Whoever invented the word sassy must have seen Trish coming.

Trish visited me later in the week and described her head to head with Paul which finished with him completely losing the cool, ranting at her for leaving him in the lurch and saying she'll never work in this town again. His aggression melted away when she let him have every detail of O'Hara's deal with the Chronicle.

'Would you fancy everyone here learning of your murderous streak, I can't imagine too many journalists queuing up for assignments you arrange, not to mention the Chronicle's directors, Katie and the police. So what if it isn't substantiated, there would be so much muck flying around some would stick', she told him exactly how it was. 'And don't think about counter slander claims, with O'Hara and God knows who else prepared to bury you if they have to save their own reputations.' Trish then described that without acknowledging his crimes, he vented a foul outburst on me and pacified her by ushering her out of the office and ultimately out of the building.

'Katie does know about his involvement with O'Hara,' I said sadly.

'I don't believe you, what is she going to do about it?'

'Probably nothing, what can she do. I do know she doesn't want to be in the same room as him now which is some consolation. But how are you fixed now?'

'I got word of two months pay through my bank and you never know I might look for some more. But I think I got fixed up on the Independent as a crime reporter. I'm waiting for word to come through, but the interview with Dominic Graham went well on Monday and I fancy the change. He said I would be given a lot of discretion in following up stories. Just meet the deadlines. You know yourself.'

Trish left me feeling really on top of myself and I think, seeing things in some sort of order. Aidan called the next day and I asked him exactly what does it take to get released from here. Thinking back to O'Hara's threat when he visited me, 'Can a politician really hold up my release?'

He looked horrified and assured me that that would not happen in a million years, the whole system is strewn with safeguards to prevent abuse. Whatever went on in the past could not possibly happen now and my progress was very heartening. Things should start to move in a positive direction in the next week or so. Whilst being a little relieved at his assurances I was still a little cynical as to the wheeling O'Hara could do and beginning more and more to feel that Aidan does not deal in specifics. After he left I started to think more and more as to how I could use O'Hara's threats against me to backfire on himself.

If I could provoke him into committing himself to a course of action that was effectively imprisoning an innocent man for fear of public exposure, he would surely find himself in very serious hot water. I know in the true sense of the word I am not innocent, my attack on Mulroy was gratuitous and appalling, but it was he who decided not to bring charges, and although my return to rational thinking has brought some pangs of conscience, I have begun to justify my position in strictly legal terms. I think of what Trish has said but know she's wrong. I can beat the system. This is one fucker who has to pay.

I knew exactly what I have to do, I have to convince Dr Sissons that I am making steady progress, sufficient that my release is about to be considered but perhaps not too quickly. I want to give O'Hara time to react. And somehow get word of this progress to O'Hara along a stated determination that I'm looking for revenge, that I still have all the details of the Cuban child abuse and that I'm still looking to publish.

On Trish's next visit I tell her what I'm trying to do and to my absolute delight and I admit surprise, she totally supports me. I look on her with a paternal pride. She really has everything it takes to be a very good journalist. She's bright, persistent and knows exactly when to back off and when to strike. And she has moral courage.

'I know I argued against this, but that was because I felt you were eating yourself up with anger. I can see now that it's having the opposite effect. It's fuelling your recovery, it's given you purpose and desire and I'm right beside you. If there's anything I can do...'

'God, you've no idea how much that's music to my ears, if I'm going to try to screw a bent politician to the wall I can't think of a better ally to have in my corner than the best investigative reporter in the whole country' sometimes I make myself sick with the smaltz.

Trish is not far behind, mockingly putting two fingers down her throat, 'Do you really want my help or are you just try-ing to get rid of me?' But she smiles and whilst I know it may have been a little too heavy, it probably wasn't too far from the truth.

'I'll get Aidan to give me a date for my possible release and see if you can get word to O'Hara's office. Best not directly maybe you could get the Indo to run a line in the social col-umn that I'm well on the road to recovery. Someone will read it to pass it on. Then we just wait and see if anything happens. I might have a slight relapse to make sure he has enough time to get the message. Then if he's true to form I think you may have to do some digging in the Department of Health.'

'What do you mean – someone will read it, — we happened to be the biggest circulation newspaper in the country.' I return her smile at her feeling of belonging, but say noth-ing as she continues. 'Just messing, I'm only too delighted to help in any way. Give me a ring when you get word from Aidan and I'll do the business in the Diary.'

I face the doctor on his next visit to give me a definitive date for my discharge. He quite happily suggests in seven days time. He will have to get the discharge papers coun-ter signed by one of his colleagues but judging from my progress that will not be a problem. Finally because I had been committed directly from custody there would have to be some release forms from the guards that charges are not being brought. As any alleged offence was committed outside the state, and the Cuban authorities released me to Irish officers with no evidence or recommendations, he could not see how that could be an obstacle. However I would be required to be discharged into the care of a competent adult who would have the time to give me fairly constant supervision in the first few weeks and to receive regular visits from Social Services.

No problem whatsoever I told him, thinking the exact opposite. Maybe Caroline would do it. Anyway that isn't the issue in hand I've got to get word to Trish so that a train of events can be put in motion.

That done I sit down and wait getting the Indo everyday in anticipation. True to her word, Trish managed to get a couple of lines down at the end of the page of the Social Diary ... *We are delighted to report that the former Chronicle reporter Ben Miller is to be discharged from psychiatric care following a breakdown in the summer whilst on holiday in Cuba. All his friends and colleagues in the business wish him a continued recovery and look forward to working with him again in the near future.*

I smile to myself and wonder what exactly is ahead of me now. I don't have long to wait, a couple of days later Aidan reports that the Department of Justice have requested that a full report has to be made by two doctors and that I have to submit myself to full independent medicals. His report is standard, but the second report must be made by a doctor commissioned by the Department. He expresses his regret at the delay but suggests it is just procedure in cases where the initial entry into the hospital was unusual, to say the least.

I assure him that he is not to worry, another couple of days is of no consequence. What I don't say is that I'm delighted and can't wait to tell Trish to get down to the Department of Justice and find out exactly where this request originated.

PART FIVE

DAMNATION

Chapter 23

October 20 2004

The medical is arranged for a week's time and I am given the third degree by a Doctor Latimer, an elderly man who appears a little bitter. I feel he is very wary of dealing with a potentially dangerous patient, my attack on Mr Mulroy being foremost in his mind. I hope this reputation is carried through to my release, I could see a new era of respect.

His tests are based on psychiatric responses and whilst it is hard to gauge his reaction I'm quite happy in the answers I give. However Aidan surprises me a couple of days later when he informs me that Dr Latimer has suggested that I undergo further tests and they want my permission to undergo hypnotherapy. He explains that Latimer thinks I still suffer from bipolar disorder causing the unusual swings in my moods and which can affect my ability to function normally. It is biological in its origin; however the experiences may be psychological. *Tell me something new!* I assure Aidan that I am quite happy to undergo any treatment Dr Latimer suggests and that he should not feel any way responsible for my release being postponed a few days. I do not tell him that am delighted that it is taking place and can't wait for Trish to come in with something linking O'Hara to these tests.

Next day Latimer calls over with Aodan to explain, 'Bipolar Disorder may be caused by a gene deficiency but is more likely to be a combination of circumstances that the mind has been exposed to. There is a strong indication that ECT can help, but in recent years we have found that patients and probably more significantly, relatives, are generally unhappy to allow patients to under go this type of treatment. Largely due to the way it has been portrayed in the media. One need look no further than 'One flew over the Cuckoo's Nest' to see how reservations have arisen. A great film but a shame the movie moguls forget quite often the responsibilities they have been entrusted with when portraying sensitive issues. Unfortunately nothing has changed on that score recently.'

'The medication prescribed to you, lithium, has been very successful in controlling your mania and Dr Sissons is delighted with your progress. However...' *why did I know this was coming* '.... I do not think we have explored the reasons for your mood swings and to release you now without understanding the causes will only result in a relapse sometime in the future.'

Somehow, somewhere I can feel O'Hara's hand on the strings controlling this situation. I look at Aidan who gives me the open hands, 'What can I do' gesture, but I'm sure he is also trying to convey confidence. I try to reply in silent kind. Nodding gently and raising my eyebrows. Latimer drones on, the more he talks the more I dislike him. I can actually see O'Hara sitting on his shoulder, but I do have to go along with him.

'Consequently Mr Miller I feel you would be more suited to a series of hypnosis sessions to try to establish if there is something in your childhood, adolescence, or early married life that caused you some trauma that may have contributed to the disorder emerging. We would need your permission to undergo this treatment.'

Does this guy not read the case notes, four colleagues get murdered, my girl friend dies in a car crash, my marriage breaks up, I lose my job, I'm conned out of a fortune, I get deported from a country I love for aggravated assault. How much trauma do you need to send you over the edge? Still, what the hell, it may be fun and it does give O'Hara a little more rope to hang himself.

'Of course I've no problem with that' I think I metaphorically knock him off his chair, but it does give Trish a few more days to uncover traces of O'Hara's involvement and this just further convinces me that he is up to his neck in it. Aidan is somewhat surprised by my placid response, I might do his professional instincts an injustice but I feel he hasn't a clue what I'm planning.

Latimer continues 'Initially I would like to undergo three half hour sessions with you and review the progress after that to consider what we have learnt and what we can gain by further research.'

I turn to Aidan 'Are you happy with this, doctor?'

'Ben, the decision has to be yours but Dr Latimer's caution is quite understandable and may even be beneficial in the long run.'

A luke warm blessing, but I note his air of professional annoyance in his speech. What can he say, he is part of the system. He cannot go against Latimer. Fortunately freedom was not my first priority, and the benefits gained in the long run may far outreach anything the doctor has in mind.

Trish returns at last later in the day with a little news. She found out that the order for the second independent decision came from the Minister himself. This is in part good news, he was elected to the Dail the same year as O'Hara, and were part of a young 'Dail Brat Pack' back in the Eighties when as young, gifted and enfranchised, they rode centre stage through the political turmoil of the time. O'Hara had concentrated more on developing his constituency base, where as the Minister, James Brady sought political advancement. But they had remained close friends and often seen sitting together at Party conferences. But in itself that contact is nothing; O'Hara will be on first name terms with the whole cabinet.

The bad news is that precedents have been set for ministerial intervention when patients are deported from another country and that a second independent medical opinion is mandatory. As I am willingly subjecting myself to the hypnosis it really doesn't matter.

I am delighted with her work but obviously we have to get proof of some contact or interference within the process. Trish is amazed to learn of the call for hypnosis, but like me doesn't see it as an issue that is going to delay my release too long. O'Hara is going to have to do something else and pretty quickly. I thank her for her efforts and ask her to keep digging, he's going to trip up soon enough. Rather typically she smiles 'Absolutely no problem.'

'Maybe you should get a private investigator on Latimer, taking note of every contact he has during the next few days and see if there is any contact with any acquaintance of O'Hara.'

'Great idea' I wonder how I got so lucky to have Trish on my side right now, she's just brilliant, not just in the work she's doing but also the boost to my morale with her unfailing enthusiasm.

Dr Latimer contacts the hospital and fixes a date for my hypnosis, in four days time in his rooms in the Mater private. A call from Trish reporting that we have a Private Investigator employed, rather uninspiringly named Myles Hammer. He is working twenty four hours a day at €450 per day plus expenses, so let's hope we get some results pretty quickly. I hadn't thought about it recently but my little News of the World fund has taken a battering. But what the hell, if this comes off the satisfaction will be brilliant not to mention that the exclusive story on O'Hara will be worth a fortune. Trish will be entitled to half that, but she's earned it. I do have nagging thoughts though that anyone calling himself Myles Hammer could possibly be competent. I can visual the belted trench coat, tilted hat and drooping cigarette. I hope he never has to give evidence in court, he'll be all American slang. I amuse myself with thinking his slogan probably is ..Myles Hammer, goes further, hits harder.. oh dear Jesus what have you done Trish.

Aidan drives me over to the Mater, for my first trip outside the stone walls of Dundrum for a few weeks. It does feel good and I tell him that. He takes some pride in getting me to this position and is confident that I cannot trip myself up. 'Be relaxed, be yourself, you have nothing to fear.' He cannot accompany me during the tests to protect their independence but says he will wait for me.

Dr Latimer welcomes me in and introduces me to a colleague who will remain present throughout the proceedings. He advises me that I can request that I can have an observer present if I wish but the whole interview will be recorded on video and I will have full access to the video immediately after the appointment.

'No, everything is fine, Dr Latimer.' I feel confident and have no fears that he would compromise his career by interfering with video evidence whatever pressure O'Hara put him under. He responds to my good will by being as pleasant as he has been to date as he puts me at my ease.

Obviously I have no recollection of the session and what seems like just a few moments, Dr Latimer touches my shoulder and tells me it is time to go. He explains how he successfully explored my childhood, my relationship with my parents. How my father left home for a year when I was nine years old and how I didn't understand why. But Mum and Dad were always fighting about his coming home late, I had rationalised. I did well at school but on going to secondary school developed a stammer and a fear of making a fool of myself. I found great comfort and comradeship in devoting nearly all my free time to sporting activities which I enjoyed proving myself to my team mates, myself and more significantly my father. He appeared to expect success without exerting undue pressure. I lost my best friend to pneumonia when I was twelve and had difficulty forming strong bonds after that. I had forgotten all of that and was surprised it still played a part in my subconscious.

All of what Latimer said appeared to be accurate and I took some comfort from his professional approach, even to the extent that I was looking forward to the next session which he had organised for the next day. I was even feeling relaxed which I hadn't felt for some time and then depress myself with the thought that maybe hypnosis is a good idea and all this has nothing to do with O'Hara. No, no – he has to have his dirty little hands in their somewhere.

I call down to Aidan who appears delighted with my report and says he has no problem repeating the run tomorrow, which duly comes after a restless night with my endlessly going over every possible eventuality. Virtually the same foreplay was enacted to get the second session underway. Strangely I felt some apprehension this time, he is going to explore more sensitive areas. Maybe he'll make me face up to aspects of my marriage I'd rather not think about.

Again it flies through and Latimer explains that the session went well and he explored my career achievements and how I felt frustrated at not achieving the creative heights I felt I was capable of. He found I was deeply disappointed that I never found an editor who would trust my ability to produce quality photo journalism. I needed a challenge. He also explained that my marital problems were longer seated than I had thought. The money difficulties in the early years had left us not willing to support each other in times of crisis. Those pressures led to rows, affairs and the eventual compromise as we put our feelings on hold to accommodate our growing family. Not that there weren't good times, and an underlying belief that we were meant for each other. Just the harsh realities of living and providing for a family brought on too many strains.

As I listened to Latimer I found some contentment in that I saw my own story honestly, as far as I can judge, without trying to blame others for my mid life crisis. I have always felt that I lived on a two way street, where I had the choice to go forwards or turn around, I was always the instigator of my own destiny.

The third session is booked for the next day under the same conditions. After finalising the session Latimer explains that he would like to hold onto the tape and discuss a few details with Dr Sissons before I saw the interview, but I had his assurances that nothing would happen to it.

I was a little surprised by this but more worried by what I may have said rather than any possibility that he might try something underhand. This was the crucial period he was covering, all the stresses of my time in Cuba. Maybe I have said too much about seeking revenge on O'Hara, Rory, Dave Byrne and Paul. I might have admitted to aspirations of being a serial killer. And then what have I said about Jenny. Did I truly love her or was a middle aged man flattered by the attentions of a younger girl... even worse maybe I have revealed some stupid ambitions towards Susanna and Trish. This could be embarrassing, even totally unproductive, *why did I ever agree to it*?

'Fine,' I said rather nervously, 'but could I arrange an appointment with Dr Sissons and yourself as soon as possible. I am anxious to finalise this and arrange my release this week,' I don't even buy the confidence myself.

'Of course, I will contact Dr Sissons and arrange something for tomorrow,' Dr Latimer stated but a little less friendlier than he had been earlier in the day.

I go straight down to reception and give Aidan an out-line of what I remember of the session which is virtually nothing. I further mention the misgivings I have had, to which he echo's my concerns. This wasn't what I wanted – I was looking forward to reassurance.

'I'll ring him from Dundrum and let you know what time we'll see you tomorrow.'

After returning me to my room he disappears for a few minutes before returning and keeping his word and said that they would be over at ten in the morning.

'Is anything wrong?' I could see he wasn't quite as self assured as usual.

'I don't know, but I'm going to look at the video now'

'Won't that compromise your independence?'

'No, it's not my independence that is at issue but I think there may be other concerns now.'

'What do you mean, Doctor...tell me?' my mind starts to race but I know he isn't going to say anything else until the morning, but his tone does leave me a little uneasy.

'We'll talk tomorrow, don't worry so much Ben' but I can see he is only going through the motions.

My mind is racing. I wish I could talk to Trish. I just have a nasty feeling about this. After a troubled night Latimer and Aidan enter my room on the dot of ten and ask me to sit down. I look at them both, and get no relief, both are stony faced, showing no emotion and particularly in Aidan's case, looks tired and drained.

Dr Latimer opens the proceedings without any niceties. 'Mr Miller, your hypnotherapy revealed some aspects of your behaviour that were out of character and to a certain extent shocking. I have a copy of the video here along with a statement of accuracy from myself and Dr. Cummings, my assistant you met yesterday. In the course of this interview I will ask you to watch the session and confirm in so far as you are aware that it was an accurate representation of what went on. I understand you cannot confirm specific details, but you will be able to state whether the time, date, place and positions of us all are accurate.'

To say that I've turned wobbly, makes jelly a building material in comparison. What the fuck is going on here. I don't have long to find out.

Latimer continues 'During the course of the hypnosis yesterday I suggested to you that you were troubled by something from your past and that you might like to talk about it. You appeared quite willing to talk about and in fact I felt you were using the session as a confessional. I had suspected from my previous meetings with you that you were not totally at peace with yourself and that certainly turned out to be the case.'

'Would you get on with it?' I am getting very frightened all at once and feel the blood draining from my face.

'Yes quite, but the implications of what you said are extremely serious and I want you to understand that they remain protected under doctor patient confidentiality. As such Dr Sissons here has no knowledge of what went on, only that the consequences do have a significant bearing on your release. Do you wish Dr Sissons to remain?'

'Yes, of course. Now will you please tell me what's going on.'

'Mr Miller under hypnosis, you gave me a detailed account of the time you spent with child prostitutes in Havana. How, each night you returned from Matanzas after seeking solace from a Santaria priest, you sought out girls around twelve and thirteen years old and had full intercourse with them in hotel rooms you booked specifically for the purpose. Further the assault you committed on Mr Mulroy was perpetrated in a fit of jealous rage. He was with one of the girls you had been with earlier in the week and bore not the slightest resemblance to Mr O'Hara, whom I think you had felt had been the object of your attack.'

I'm numb. Latimer paused awaiting a response and when none came continues, 'Do you wish to see this video now Mr Miller?'

I can't believe it, think it's a character assassination by O'Hara. I hate this with every bone in my body. But he can't have anything to do with this. I slump forward, head in hands not knowing what to think. If this is true, it can't be true, it has to be true. I'm the exact antithesis of myself. I hate all the creeps in the world who do this, and now I'm one of them. I don't want to think. I don't want to do anything. I want the world to go away.

'Mr Miller, do you wish to see the video.'

'No'

'Well it is my duty to tell you that the contents of the video are confidential until such time as you wish to make them public. However in view of the seriousness of the crimes you have committed and particularly as I am employed by the Department for Justice I felt it my duty to advise the Gardai that I suspected that you may be guilty of a serious offence and that your flat should be searched for any evidence that may lead to a prosecution. You may feel that I have stretched the limits of ethical behaviour, and I would like to state that I searched my soul long and hard before reaching this conclusion. But you have to understand if I can't give a good reason why you shouldn't be released then I cannot stand in your way. And I cannot use material gained under hypnosis as reasons for not signing your release papers. I did what I had to do.'

Aidan nods in understanding, but I can see he is changing his opinion of me. I say nothing, but Latimer is in full throttle. I wouldn't say he's enjoying it but he certainly knows that these are probably the most dramatic words he has ever spoken in his life and he isn't going to mess up his performance.

'I believe the police conducted their search late last night and removed your computer for further analysis.' He rests feeling vindicated I'm sure.

'I'm sorry' I hear myself say, looking at Aidan. 'I er.... don't know what to say…. I'm…'

Aidan looks at me with a distant air but gently says 'I'll prescribe a sedative and recommend you get through this day with as little activity as possible. I'll call tomorrow morning to discuss all the implications of this with you, Ben. I know how you're feeling, but understand you were suffering a major mental breakdown when all this happened. You were not responsible for your actions.'

Try as he could, the unbearable guilt of what I have done felt like a steamroller pushing over me. I knew it had to be true. Please God, let me die.

Next day Aidan comes and tries to argue the brighter side to this. What is he talking about. In fairness what can he say? That I'm a repressed pervert who only reveals himself when under extreme stress. Great, that really will make me feel better. He knows he's not going to alleviate any of my troubles with sopheric words and that only medication is going to get me through the next few hours. Maybe years.

My next visitors are two garda who let me know that they have completed the research into my computer and that two hundred and seventy five images of child pornography have been found in my files. Further investigations have revealed that they were downloaded from a web site called Molasses Enterprises and were paid for by my credit card. Payment for these images were debited to my account in June, before I went to Cuba.

There comes a stage in accepting pain that the body takes evasive action and passes out. Any expert in torture will confirm that the victim should never receive excruciating pain, but the thought that the pain that is being applied could get worse must be firmly planted in the victim's mind. The belief being that anticipated agony is far worse than the actual pain inflicted. That is of course true of physical torture. The gardai in front of me were neither experts nor even conscious torturers. However they made it extremely obvious that they didn't like me and that they had no difficulty in adding to my anguish. I felt no pain, but was in agony. I wanted to inflict the physical hurt on myself that I felt I deserved, but couldn't actually raise any limb. Even my head was bowed, I could face my accusers, which they took as admission of guilt. I don't want to argue, I don't want to do anything. I do feel my mind has reached the stage that there is nothing else they can tell me which would make my position worse. Even that allusion is shattered.

The Gardai inform me that as long as I stay under supervision I will not be charged with possession of the pornographic material but once I accept that I am well enough to be discharged then I would face charges. Another real Catch Twenty Two situation. As long as I stay committed there will be no publicity. But as soon as I am released charges will be made and it will be all over the papers for trial by media. And everyone knows how the public feel about child molesters. You don't have to be guilty, just a whisper is enough to destroy your reputation for life. The police leave without any compassion, making it very clear of what they felt of the scum I represented.

Aidan calls to inform me that they regard me as a suicide risk and I'm put on twenty four hour watch. I look back on the last few months. If I thought I had depression then, I didn't know the half of it.

No friends, no family, no hope, no prospects, locked in an institution I can only escape by facing criminal charges for possessing images of child pornography which I have to face up to I am guilty off, even if I only engaged in their procurement whilst I was suffering from acute manic depression.

I have to face the fact that I'm going to spend the rest of my life in virtual solitary confinement, and maybe that isn't so bad, seeing no one else would want to talk to me.

I begin to look forward to my dreams, which because of the shortness of my sleep patterns I recall more and more frequently. Not that they are in any way joyous, but they are a release from reality and thankfully never seem to touch on the elements of my living nightmare. In a hideous way I believe that my knowledge is increasing in the capacity to be able to cope with living in hell. A state I have convinced myself I am soon to be a resident of.

I can recall from my dreams facing intruders armed with sledgehammers. Now I know these are weapons not to be considered when defending yourself. You can make a cup of tea in the time it takes between the start of the wielding motion to the delivery of the blow. I know now that pain can only be inflicted if a body has feeling, if faced with an opponent lacking this quality the only solution is dismemberment. I learn of the element of surprise, you must master a skill or characteristic your opponent does not suspect. Maybe weightlessness or the ability to spew fire. You have to learn to discount any pain inflicted on you by loving the resulting outcome. You want to be deformed, you don't need to be able to see, you like the smell of burning flesh. Whilst quoting these images I'd rather not go into the details of how these lessons are taught.

Whatever evil vision comes to mind I take contentment that my days will be easier in the future by my ability to deal with these situations when I arrive at my ultimate destination and pray that that day comes as soon as possible.

Chapter 24

29 October 2004

Four Miles South of Damnation

In a moment of self depreciation, and they're coming at fairly regular intervals now, I decide that I want to look how low I had slumped in my fall from grace. Could I feel any worse than I do now? No I argue, there may even be mitigating circumstances. I have to watch the tape.

I place the video in the player they had provided for me and set myself to be prepared to hate myself even more than I do.

The snowy screen gives way to Latimer talking directly into the camera.

'Today is October 23 2004. Time fourteen fifteen. Interview with Ben Miller of Dundrum Central Mental Hospital in my private rooms in the Mater Private Clinic. In the presence of Dr Stephen Cummings and myself Brendan Latimer.'

I fast forward through the first two sessions, somehow their relevance seems lost. Another snow fall, then Dr Latimer is sitting in front of me and clicks his fingers. My head goes down instantly.

'Can you hear me, Ben?'

'Yes'

'What is your name?'

'Ben Miller'

'What do you do for a living?'

'I'm an investigative reporter for the Sunday Chronicle.'

'What project were you engaged on when you were last working?'

'I was on an assignment in Cuba to uncover details of illegal payments made to Dennis O'Hara for the past twenty years in return for political favours.'

Everything fairly straight forward up to now, both questions and responses seem natural, without any undue pressure on Latimer's part, nor any hesitation on mine. However I was aware of what was to come and think about fast forwarding to the relevant spots on the tape but I stay watching until the whole situation changes quite dramatically, when I sit up to pay acute attention.

'Would you like to tell us anything that's on your mind about the time you had in Cuba?'

'Yes, I found a great peace there. I found Jenny and we talked. She loves me.' It sounds strange to hear myself making rational statements when I know I'm going to destroy everything in the next few moments.

'Did anything happen to you when you were in Cuba that was out of the ordinary?'

'I felt a compelling urge to kill someone after I had been to a Santeria ceremony. I have never felt that way before.'

'Who was that person?'

'I don't know, but he was with a young girl and he shouldn't have been with her. It was my work to save her. Jenny told me.'

'Did you think they were going to have sex?'

'I had sex with her, she was beautiful, so innocent, so young, I loved her with every bone in my body.'

I closed my eyes in horror. This is really happening. There's no mistake, it's me saying everything. I can't believe what I'm watching on the screen, but it can't be denied.

Latimer continues his questioning. 'Do you know where the girl came from?'

'No I'd never seen her before'

'How did you meet her?'

'A man told me about her in a bar I was in.'

'Were there any other occasions when you had sex'

'I met another girl, she was only twelve, so friendly and sweet. It was her first time, she screamed a little but I held her hand and said everything would be OK.'

'Where did you take these girls?'

'I would always get a hotel room away from my regular lodgings. I didn't want people to see me.'

Despair knows no boundaries when you disgust yourself. I'm numb and can't move as my eyes are locked onto the screen.

'Did you like your time in Cuba?'

'I loved Cuba; I loved the people and the way they look on life. I loved the towns, particularly Havana. I want to go back.'

'But you can't go back, Ben do you know why?'

'Because I hit a man with a stone. But he deserved it. He was an animal. I hated him.'

'Were these the only times you had sex?'

'No, on another occasion a mother came to me offering her daughter for an initiation. She didn't like me and tried to get away but I forced myself on her….'

I turn off the tape, I can't take any more. I know why now I'm on suicide watch. I don't want to live any more.

I lie on my bed, not eating, not speaking to anyone. Just images of myself running through my head endlessly boasting '…..she was beautiful….so innocent…..so young….she was only twelve…it was her first time… she screamed…. She didn't like me….. I forced myself on her….' Over and over again. I know now what hell is. I can't escape from being with me.

I stay for hours on the bed with this thirty second main feature rolling through my brain and eventually fall asleep to suffer I presume more subconscious agony. I wake less than two hours later, sweating, agitated and still thinking exactly the same thoughts.

The nurses, who come in to see me, seem distant and are quite happy to obey my commands to take away the food and drinks. They look at me with some distain; Latimer must have told them my secret. So much for patient confidentiality, but I don't care; the whole world can't hate me as much as I do.

The seconds slow down, as time heads into a cul de sac. I think two days pass when Trish calls to see me, full of enthusiasm. I cannot understand why she is upbeat, but I realise she does know. How can I tell her? She is about to update me on the progress she has made on O'Hara and Myles Hammer's report on Latimer, but before she starts I have to make the most harrowing confession in my life. It was like telling your children you don't love them. I get her to sit down and I run through the whole ugly sequence of events of the hypnosis session, not bearing to look her in the face at any time.

After listening to everything I say, she asks 'Do you think you did everything that Latimer says you did?'

'Of course I did, I'm an animal. It's all there on film' I throw the tape at her but she ignores it and looks at me in a way no one has ever looked at me before. I thought I couldn't think any worse of myself but I think Trish has found a way to heighten my self pity. I think she hates me more than I do.

She leaves without saying goodbye, but I feel better somehow, glad she knows. I'll miss her but I never wanted her to visit me under false pretences. And then another dawning; Trish is a beautiful girl but I never thought of her as anything else but a colleague. I know why now, she's twenty two; she's too old for me! This thought refuses to go away as I torture myself with a review of every thought I have ever had concerning any child of my acquaintance.

Caroline calls the next day and I do exactly the same to her. I want everyone to know exactly what a monster I am. I tell her everything and she is left speechless for some time.

'Is there anything I can do' she asks before she realises how stupid that is. And then she hits me with a killer blow when I was least expecting it.

'Are the kids OK?, why don't they visit you, Ben? Say this isn't happening.' She screams at me.

I'm knocked sideways 'I swear Caroline on everything that's sacred to me, that I never, never, never did anything ever. I love my kids with all my heart; you've got to believe me.'

She stands up to leave without saying anything. I don't blame her for thinking the worst, what do I hold sacred anyway. But it becomes so vitally important to me that she doesn't leave thinking this of me.

'Caroline, please, I beg you, call Katie, ask her, ask the kids. Do anything you want. Oh God believe me please.'

She looks at me silently and goes to touch my arm but thinks better of it, pulling away, nodding in some appreciation that I am a desperately unhappy man.

I watch her down the corridor and as she goes I see my last contact with the outside world fade away. I'm left here now until I die. On my own with only my biting conscience as company. Even my alter ego has deserted me. It can't be bothered to comment.

It is difficult to convey how slowly time goes by when you do not think. If your brain is paused on one image, every minute is a day. Every day, a year.

On optimistic moments I run through the tape in my mind to try to recollect something of the incidents that were played. I try to reason with myself, I am sick, I was deluded, this is a nightmare and I will wake up at any moment.

But nothing, no memory, no justification, I even feel as mentally sound as I've felt for some time, so how can I plead diminished responsibility? And this is real. I cannot escape that life is going on and everything is normal except for the creep that's living inside my body. There is no explanation… I am a monster.

I desperately trawl through my memory banks to find some clue as to what my have triggered my actions. Maybe I was abused as a child and developed mental blocks that I remember nothing of. But I can't reason that way. I am still responsible for my actions. As I toy with these thoughts I notice that less than a minute has passed since I started on this process. I have to get something else to think about before I drive myself completely mad.

But what… I have no interest in anything. The newspapers, so long my life, now are not even worthy of a look. Television passes in front of my eyes without registering. The recreational therapy offered is not attempted. Food comes and goes with only the slightest interference. Only tea and biscuits hold any interest to me.

The doctors' visits, no specialists visit now, are ritualistic. They seem to be less interested than I am. God, they hate me too. Only the occasional ward orderly is anyway friendly and I totally blank him.

I have nothing to look forward to. I cannot see the point of living but I do not know how I am going to die. I hear of people dying of a broken heart, why can't I?

PART FIVE

Deliverance

Chapter 25

November 4 2004

When Trish calls back I really have no idea how long it is since she last called. The nurses do not give an option to decline her visit, they just usher her in and she sits down in the front of me and takes my hand. I am so startled I cringe away from her.

'Ben, I'm so sorry I doubted you but I think I have some news for you which you will find very interesting indeed.'

I'm surprised that she even addresses me by my first name, never mind seems to be at ease with me. But I'm not listening to what she is saying. I really do not want platitudes.

I start to mumble 'Trish, you have nothing to apologise for. I'm sorry you've spent so much time on my behalf over the last few weeks. I really appreciate what a good friend you have been but it's time to move on. I would really prefer to be on my own.'

'Would you shut the fuck up and listen to what I am saying. I want to show you something, just give me a few minutes. I promise you that you will not be disappointed.'

I've no idea what's going on as she gets up to place the tape in the recorder and motions to bear with her.

The tape starts and I immediately get up to stop it. She gets up and physically pushes me back down in my chair. I get annoyed at her physical approach but don't really have the strength to confront her. Nothing is really functioning too well at the moment, but I look away in childish defiance.

'Just sit down there and listen to me,' she bullies in a way I had never seen her act before. I do as I'm told and look at her as she restarts the video. She runs it up to my first confession on child abuse when she pauses it.

'Did you notice anything?'

'No, would you stop this now' I couldn't help myself but I started to cry.

She presses play again ignoring my protestations and pauses after my second admission. 'Now did you see it?'

I'm not interested; Trish for some reason wants to humiliate me more. I'd forgotten how pleased I was with myself in the tape, 'See what?' Like a defiant four year old I sneer.

'Never mind', she restarts the tape and pauses again after the third confession.

'Well'

'I don't know what you want from me Trish. OK I am a pathetic excuse for a human being. Happy now? Leave me alone.'

There is a tension between us, I'm getting more frustrated at being forced to watch this horror show and she is disappointed that I cannot see what she is driving at. She explains 'On each occasion you admit to abusing those kids it is preceded by a question from Latimer which ends in the word sex.'

'So?'

'So he triggered a reaction from you with the word. He must have hypnotised you before he started taping to brag about child abuse whenever he mentions sex.'

'That's crazy, you cannot hypnotise people to make them do things they inherently disagree with. Get the fuck out of here.'

She ignores my command, 'That's right, but you can get round that with a little imagination. If he posed the question properly, for example whenever I mention sex I want you to pretend that you are trying to trap a child abuser into confessing his actions by gaining his confidence. You do this by admitting that you are involved as well. Be boastful to get them to relax. Can't you see that would be a plausible suggestion to anyone under the influence of an hypnotist?'

'You mean...' I pause to consider exactly what Trish is saying to me. The consequences dawn on me in a flash 'You mean I didn't do this. I've been set up.'

'Yeah, you pumpkin, I think you are off the hook and I think we might have just caught the biggest shark in the water,' she leans over and kisses me on the cheek.

I have never ever thought that I would be pleased to hear myself called a pumpkin. Let's face it ten minutes ago nobody would have called me anything but sleaze ball, including myself. I need a few minutes to digest everything. I've known elation and depression so much recently it's hard to describe how I feel now. I've been sick, but the last few days have not been a mental depression. I was living in a state that I didn't want to be with myself. Suddenly discovering that your worst fears have been crushed, is not like a light at the end of a tunnel, it's a fucking bolt of lightening in the deepest coalmine.

There are still loads of loose ends; self doubt starts to wander back, 'but what about Cummings?'

Trish nods knowingly 'I've already interviewed him and given him exactly the same scenario that I have given you. He states that Latimer asked him to get some water and glasses before the last session started and that you were alone with Latimer for around two minutes. He thought nothing of it at the time, you were both relaxed and in exactly the same position you were when he left. And remember he conducted his first consultation with you in private. He had no reason to doubt his integrity. After all he is an eminent psychologist. But on reviewing the tape he does think you were very susceptible to hypnosis and that two minutes would be enough time to put the autosuggestion to you. He does not argue with my hypothesis. Your similar reaction to the questions ending with sex are virtually inexplicable unless he had engineered your responses.'

'But why would he compromise himself like this?'

'Ben, you know why, don't you…O'Hara, he is behind it all and he so nearly got away with it, but we have him by the proverbials.'

'Hang on Trish, do you have anything on O'Hara at all except that we know he has a motive. Thanks for everything but really things haven't changed.'

'Are you crazy? If you hadn't just climbed out of the biggest swamp in the world I'd give you a slap. Ben, there are now five people who know you didn't do this. You, me, Latimer, Cummings and O'Hara. Twelve hours ago there was only Latimer and O'Hara. By the end of next week the whole country will know. Trust me.

'I will get back to you in the next couple of days with something substantial on O'Hara. I promise. Just take it easy and start planning how you're going to spend your first few days of freedom. I look at Trish and start to wake up. She is wonderful. If she hadn't bothered to look at the tape and if she hadn't made the connection I would have been stuck in here for the rest of my life without a friend. If a week is a long-time in politics, an hour in a mental institution is a lifetime. A new lifetime. Trish waves goodbye and I start to thank her, but she presses her finger to her pursed lips. 'You're not the only one whose happy about this, I'm ecstatic.' She turns and walks away whilst I contemplate a hike in the Wicklow Hills, feeling the cool fresh air on my cheeks.

I can't wait for her return now but control the urges I have to discuss Trish's find with Aidan or any of the nurses and orderlies that have not totally deserted me. They do notice a change in my demeanour and try to engage me in conversation. Despite my perceived crimes most of them have treated me well and are happy I appear less depressed.

Trish returns two days later bursting to tell me her good news. Thinking about this whole situation over the past few hours, I realise that I cannot really help Trish, except to show that I'm really supportive and I have to encourage her in every move. Not that she needs much motivating she's on a high herself.

'We've got a direct contact between O'Hara and Latimer' she splurts out barely able to contain herself. 'About two days ago our intrepid Mr Hammer recorded a conversation between them when Latimer asked for the money to be transferred to a Swiss bank account as soon as possible as he has some business dealings to attend to. He would have thought that you would be forever trapped in your Catch Twenty Two and that you would never investigate the tape too much. I think he reckoned you'd probably never watch it. Let's face it, I think you'd do a lot of things for a million euro.'

'A million wow! And you have this on tape.'

'Yeah, you ought to see Myles, he is wonderful. This is his whole life right now, I don't think he has had any work for months and he's like a dog with a bone. I'd say he's working every hour of the day. But don't jump too many fences just yet. Our tape recordings were made illegally, but even if they were above board would still be thrown out in court as inadmissible. That's the bad news, but the good news is Cummings has agreed to give a sworn affidavit that you and Latimer were left alone prior to your video being recorded. He feels Latimer tried to shaft his professional integrity, has discredited their profession and should at the very least be debarred. He is also very concerned that your mental well being, not to mention your freedom, has been jeopardised in some way by his negligence.

'My feeling is that if we face Latimer with the tape and Cummings affidavit he will breakdown. He is not used to facing this type of investigation. He will know his career is over and that he may well face criminal prosecution. And probable jail. He will want to avoid that at all costs. A statement from him that he entered into an arrangement with O'Hara to frame you because of certain difficulties he is having in his life might way somewhat in his favour when it comes to sentencing. And it may not even go that far if a substantial case is brought against O'Hara.'

'You mean a sort of plea bargain; I thought that was for the movies?'

'Well it is perhaps a little dramatic but I think he'll be clutching at straws and may agree to anything when the time comes. What we say we'll do and what we'll do don't always have to be consistent.' Trish has that glint of devilment in her eye which suggests an air of infallibility, I'm glad she's on my side and not against me.

'Which all means...'

'Ben it means that we have two of the most eminent psychiatric doctors in the country prepared to testify on our behalf that O'Hara bribed and falsified evidence to keep you locked away in a mental institution so that the story of his own use of child prostitutes in Cuba would buried forever.'

All of this floods over me like a warm bath. I feel released from the depths of the inferno and then there's the immense satisfaction that we may have at last got O'Hara once and for all. He thought he was untouchable, and perhaps he has been, but not this time. If he goes to jail he will be persecuted by his fellow inmates. No one likes a politician on the make, but throw in a child abuser to boot, I didn't mean that pun but it brings a smile to my face. Knowing the system he'll probably have some strings he can pull to get solitary, but he'll never escape the ignominy and public humiliation. Whilst riding this crest of euphoria a thought rained on my parade, 'Trish, you've forgotten the images on the internet. I swear I never had anything to do with them.'

'Relax Ben, I suppose you've every right to be paranoid but I thought you'd know by now that I know you have nothing to do with child pornography. Listen this plot O'Hara's been hatching hasn't happened overnight. He's been preparing his ground for months. I'm certain he arranged for your flat to be raided, ordered the photographs with your credit card, he could have got the details from an old card lying around, or through previous orders you had made on the internet. Or maybe you even left your card or statement on the table or whatever. I don't know how these guys operate but I do know it can be done. As regards the charges on the credit card account, you would have paid that without thinking. Remember your state of mind wasn't too hot at the time and the Molasses Enterprises isn't immediately obvious. You're not going to say 'hey I didn't order that porno stuff to yourself. Well not in the state your mind was."

'Yeah, and I've just remembered that when I went to O'Hara's office to shake him down months ago I told him that I was on his case and that his name was the first word I saw every day, and it wouldn't take too much of a brain to figure out that....'

'....it's your password, you idiot, and you told him' she laughed so long that I join her in a fit of giggles. It was so good to laugh.

'Trish, I just love you to bits.'

She smiles and says 'It wasn't only for you, you know. I wanted him just as badly as you did, but I'm so glad to be of service.'

She leaves me having raised my spirits again. I smile to myself and think where I was just a few days ago and now I'm back on the Crusade, only this time I really feel we are closing in for the kill.

There's still a lot of work to do though. I really don't know if Trish should see Latimer on her own. He may react like a cornered rat, and God knows what his reaction will be. I try to contact her on her mobile but it's turned off, which means I think only one thing, she doesn't want me to contact her because she has anticipated my worries. The paranoid mind only thinks in terms of self, not appreciating that there are a multitude of reasons why she should switch the power off. Maybe she's just out of battery.

My fears were fully justified however when Trish comes in to tell me of the progress she has made the next day.

'I went to see Latimer, as we agreed' I wasn't quite sure how she came to that assumption but I let it go 'and truth be told he wasn't exactly over the moon to see me.'

'Never!'

'Yes, smarty pants. And he wasn't too happy about what I had to say to him either.'

'I hope you brought a wire with you.'

'Um…, but don't worry about that, just let me finish.' I motion to her rolling my hands over. Give it to me baby. 'As I said he wasn't too happy to see me but was very quiet as he listened to the tape and read Cummings affidavit. He stayed quiet for about two minutes just looking out the window. And then he turned round and said very gently but with a lot of menace, 'Young lady, I don't know if you realise what you are doing. I have spent a lifetime building up my reputation in psychiatric health care and I take great exception to a little trollop, hardly a day out of school telling me how I've committed a heinous crime against man kind. Now if I ever see you or this tape again I will sue you and your newspaper for every penny it's got. I will deal with Mr Cummings myself. Now if you'll kindly leave me alone I have a lot of work to do"

'What did you do?'

'What do you think, I pushed his desk right up against his belly till he flinched and gave him the works. You don't frighten me, I said, with your law suits. Let me tell you about the heinous crime you committed. You abused your position of trust as a doctor to try to twist someone's mind into thinking he was guilty of crimes he did not commit and would never commit in a million years. You are the lowest form of scum I have ever come across. But here's the deal, you go to the police tonight with a full confession of what you did, how Mr O'Hara paid you to do it and how much. Then you will resign from medical practice with immediate effect and retire to some nice little country cottage somewhere and never be seen again except to testify in the trial of Mr Dennis O'Hara T.D.'

'Magnificent... Bravo..., what did he say?' My grin bursting from ear to ear.

Trish paused for breath, but she is really enjoying every minute of it 'Dr Latimer lost some of his composure but still wasn't giving in 'and what if I say no?' he said. Even better I said, I go straight to the medical council with this story and let them decide what to do with it. However if you agree, Mr Miller has assured me he will not make any complaint against you, will not press any charges for criminal neglect of your medical duties, not that they were neglectful of course and will plead on your behalf to the authorities that as the real criminal in this has been caught he would be happy that no action be taken against you. You would have my assurance that all copies of the telephone conversation you had with Mr O'Hara and the video of your hypnosis consultation with Mr Miller will be destroyed. I will also ensure that Mr Cummings rips up his affidavit and drops all actions against you.'

'Wonderful' I applaud.

'Wait' says Trish holding up her hand to silence me, 'You haven't heard the ending'

'Go on'

'He looked at me for a few minutes then nodded his head. 'Lets get all this down in writing' he said 'and then I'll go with you tomorrow to the Gardai.' 'No way I said it's now or never', I didn't want him blowing his head off last night. So off we went without a murmur and gave a full confession to the police.'

'It's over' I pick her up and danced round the room.

'Well not quite' she smiled at me, 'True, O'Hara was arrested last night and was refused bail. I think the fact that he has already offered a million to dump this problem, means there isn't any amount that could be set that would be a sufficient disincentive for him from doing a runner. But I think the problem is that I have made a deal with Latimer that strictly I shouldn't have. I said both you and Dr Cummings would drop all charges and allegations against him. And for the sake of my own personal integrity I would like to honour that.'

'Right now, Trish, I would give you anything you ask of me. And if Dr Cummings doesn't agree I'll … what am I thinking of course he'll agree.'

'I hope so.' But it didn't even register on my radar as a worry.

Chapter 26

Two months later

When I got back to my flat after five months, without any visitors apart from the police who didn't do too much tidying up, the place was a mess. I didn't have too much incentive to clean and though my computer was returned, neatly stacked on the dining room table, the thoughts of reconnecting it up didn't appeal to me.

I recover the post from my post box which amounted to close to a hundred items, bills for the phone, mobile, ESB, cable all standard charges and all taken care of by direct debit the only annoyance is the €45 per month for broadband. There are statements from the bank, insurance reminders also taken care of by direct debit, junk mail one particularly interesting one from the travel agent extolling the virtues of revisiting Cuba. If only...

However at the bottom of this depressing pile of non personal reams of paper is a small hand written white envelope with a Spanish postmark, which I tear open with just a touch of excitement (expectations are fairly limited when you've experienced the emotional roller coaster I had been on).

'Senor and Senora Gomez requests the company of Ben Miller and Partner to the wedding of their daughter Susanna to Dr Sean Bourke at the Church of Our Lady, Via Torres, Madrid on the 22nd January 2005 and afterwards at the Hotel Parador, Toledo...RSVP.'

I expend a lot of energy wondering whether to go or not. Madrid, do I really want to rake up some many memories, and then onto Toledo. What is Susanna thinking of. Maybe it is a search for closure for her, but it's a bit of a risk on your wedding day. My cynicism is creeping back I'm glad to say.

But then again I would rejoice in seeing her happy. We had been through so much together, and of course there were sometimes when we were not together but we've both survived, hers through her lovely doctor, mine through mental triumph over despair of which she knows nothing.

Another problem, if I go, and I think I'm heading that way, who should I go with? Only Trish would really entertain it and it might be a way of saying thanks, but then again we would only know each other and realistically what do we have in common other than an extraordinary story of my desire to bring a corrupt politician to justice and her belief in me. She shared my lowest moments and didn't leave my side, I'll always be grateful, but I don't think a weekend in Madrid covers it. I eventually manage to raise the necessary bravado to mention it to Trish and I'm knocked over by her absolute delight in the thought of meeting Susanna again. I hadn't realised how much of her professional life had been linked in someway with my adventure and how she wanted to put some finality to the whole episode with a happy ending.

The weekend away is a triumph in re-establishing my contact with normality and having a good time. Just to be surrounded by nice people who try to make me feel at home and who have no interest in anything but my happiness was such an excursion into uncharted waters. Trish has a great time too, and got on with Susanna as though they were long lost sisters. They must have bonded after I shamefully attacked Susanna. The thought of my actions making me cringe in embarrassment.

All forgotten now I hope and she truly looks beautiful, not that Trish was too far behind, maybe she'll invite me when it's her turn to wear white. I hope so, life has turned full circle in a few weeks and it would never have happened if it hadn't been for her.

O'Hara managed to pull some strings, eventually secured bail through a security of €5 million, put up by the Minister for Justice himself. I think it's the first time in the history of the state that effectively the Minister for Justice has, on behalf of his Government, accepted a bond from himself.

I would have thought he was too close to events to want to get involved but maybe O'Hara has something on him too. I wouldn't put it past him doing anything. But at least I'm happy that he cannot skip bail without causing an almighty political scandal which would put him and the Government under the microscope of the World's press. Surely even he wouldn't do that.

Anyway the trial date is set for the April and I hear later that he made a full confession to the police to avoid a public hearing. Only the sentence is in question and my trust in the Irish judiciary, despite many moments of doubt, is sufficient to believe he will get his just deserts. Strangely that doesn't seem to matter any more, he is now part of my history, a past I have to leave behind. I am still seeing Aidan and he is pleased with my progress and my ability to departmentalise my thought processes.

Trish is furiously chasing down organised crime through the pages of the Independent, a role they have never played before. She obviously wore them down with her exuberant fervour, and Caroline has re established contact but at a little distance. I don't think I can really forgive her for giving me my darkest moment with her silent accusations. Kate never calls, but I hardly expected her to, we have both turned that corner. However all three of my children regularly visit and I enjoy their company.

Perhaps because I'm not the slush I was through the final days of my marriage, and that they no longer have to take sides has opened up a completely new relationship to us all.

Probably the most surprising discovery since my release has been that after running through the details of my account with Myles Hammer I learn that my debt to him is far in excess of the final balance quoted on his invoice. His surveillance work was meticulous, innovative and his commitment to his client, me, was bordering on devotional.

Over a period of a few weeks we engage in a convalescent comradeship based on opposites. He is quiet, self effacing, a teetotaller, a deep thinker with a gentle dry wit and a respect to everyone which borders on being obsequious. But he is sincere with a deeply held moral conviction that good will defeat evil and I really like him. His early career in the Garda Siochana, was successful and became a detective sergeant within seven years of joining up. His resignation three years later followed a long period of self analysis when he realised the constant confrontation and aggression required was a style he just could not live with. His work now is very carefully selected and will only take cases he feels are virtuous. Whilst his excellent contacts and incomparable dedication meant he had many happy customers, he did find them hard to find and consequently he struggled every month to met his outgoings.

When Trish approached him to undertake my work, he was delighted as his parents had fallen foul of one of O'Hara's scams many years ago and were forced to leave their home as he steam rolled a change in planning zones in their area to the benefit of wealthy patrons. His action halved the value of their property, and they had to move to a much smaller house whilst O'Hara pocketed fifty grand.

He enjoys his downfall with more relish than he imagined himself capable of and we toast his incarceration on a night of alcoholic free celebration during which he informs me that yes, Myles Hammer is his real name. He is surprised I am surprised.

We become good friends and I know he helps me back to stability. My cynicism, still live and well, also teaches Myles that you can earn a living without having to make the world a better place every day.

Despite my saying that I have to put my history behind me, I do feel that I owe it to myself to revisit Paul and Dave Byrne, if only to show them I have survived.

I call to Paul's office unannounced to find him collecting his personal belongings. I am taken aback, but just stand in the doorway waiting for a response from him before I say anything.

'I suppose you're happy now, you prick.' I don't know what he is talking about but he does give me the impression that his leaving is connected to the O'Hara saga which makes me very happy. I nod my head, without a word, turn and burst out laughing as I walk out into the sunshine.

The mood is too good to stop now and I head straight over to Fitzwilliam Square to confront Dave. There's a new Miss World on reception who goes through the same procedure as my earlier visit. This time Dave appears after a few minutes, A little apprehensive. I take the initiative and walk up to him with an open hand. 'No hard feelings, Dave' and shake his hand warmly.

He says nothing as I turn to walk away and give him my translation with my back turned to him 'What I mean is I'll never forget what you did to me until the day I die'. For the second time in fifteen minutes I cannot control my giggling.

After settling everything I have to do I have decided now to follow my dreams. I've no mortgage, no responsibilities, no emotional ties, a little money in the bank and a lot of plans to fulfil. I really want to create something, I have a lifetime of experience in journalism, a passion for photography and a world that needs changing. Even if it's only in a small way, I'm going to make a difference. I owe that to Trish.

POST SCRIPT

8 October 1967

Quebrada del Yuro, Bolivia

Sergeant Bernardino Huanca of the Bolivian Rangers faces a moment in time which rewrites history and forever casts a shadow over his life, which never goes away. Facing him is a wounded rebel guerrilla, caught in an ambush that would leave him immobilised by gun shots to his calf but still in his full senses. The guerrilla's colleague, Willy Sarabia raises his rifle at Sergeant Bernardino but the rebel stops Willy by raising his hand and speaks directly to Bernardino. 'I am Che Guevara, I am worth more to you alive than dead'. Other members of the Rangers quickly surround the two men and Che is carried and Willy is led, tied to a horse, the seven kilometres to a schoolhouse in La Higuera, a small village in the hills in South East Bolivia. Sergeant Huanca hands over his prized capture to the command of General Ovando.

There followed twenty four hours of jubilant mayhem as Che's captors struggle for ultimate authority to decide his destiny. However they all are aware that there are strong influences which cannot be explained. A mixture of fear and respect for an idolised man, many of the troops fall under Che's immense presence. Despite calls for some compassion he is kept bound to his chair throughout his captivity. Feed like a baby and accompanied during toilet calls, his last few hours were an undignified end to a life of great adventure and charismatic revolution.

Coded reports of Che's capture were sent immediately to military headquarters in Vallegrande, but were received with some scepticism. However Captain Ramos, a Cuban undercover CIA agent and Colonel Zenteno of the Bolivian guard immediately travelled by helicopter to question their infamous prisioner, if indeed he was who he said he was.

Captain Ramos was the first to question Che and they shared the mutual respect that sworn enemies have for one another when they are no longer enemies but just two professional soldiers who have been selected on different teams by accidents of birth. Ramos discovered and empathised with some of Che's ideology and saw that his struggle was for the genuine plight of 'His people' whether they were Argentine, Cuban or Bolivian.

Che's claim, that the people of Bolivia live like animals without clothing, housing and hope, was accurate. They were exploited and maltreated by their Government who saw the farmers as no more than work horses. Che was not overawed by his own plight and his only thoughts were to get a final message of support to Fidel Castro and a desire that his wife should remarry. It is theorised in many quarters that war is an expression of love. In the face of the ultimate danger, thoughts of those most dear are those that feature in first in every front line combatant. It is the belief that you are living and ultimately dying for a purpose that creates the adrenalin rush of self justification. Che epitomised that theory.

During the course of several interviews Che was subjected to, Zenteno and Ramos were drifting apart on on deciding what should happen to him. The Bolivian's anxious that he should not be made a martyr and provoke a civilian unrest whilst the American's were keen to ensure that he be kept alive for further questioning to somehow discredit Castro by the revelation of some as yet undisclosed indiscretion.

In Ramos' absence Zenteno received orders from Villegrande that Guevara should be executed immediately and his body disposed of in an unmarked grave along with any other rebels captured. But that his hands should be removed from the corpse to enable his identity be confirmed by fingerprinting.

Zenteno followed his orders and sought volunteers to perform the final act. A Sergeant Mario Teran volunteered to seek revenge for the deaths of three of his colleagues the previous day and was told to shoot Che below the neck as any discovery of the body should confirm that he died in battle. As he entered the schoolroom Che was calm and self assured and demanded that he should be allowed to stand in his final moments. Rising still bound to the chair, Teran suddenly feared he was facing a supernatural creature and ran to the door but realising he would face ridicule if he were to immerge without completing his mission turned and fired at random, hitting Che several times in the legs and groin. As the slain Guevara fell to the ground biting his own arm to prevent himself screaming in pain, the now fearless Teran walks up to the slain body and fires at point blank range at his thorax killing him instantly.

On seeing the blood flowing over the floor Teran leaves the scene without composure and failed throughout the rest of his life to remove the image of Che, blood oozing out of his punctured throat, still bound hands and feet to the chair, prostrate on the ground, his eyes still open in defiance and strong in a piercing eternal impression on Teran's subconscious.

Ramos was informed of Che's execution and furiously sought out Zenteno to demand that nothing should be done to the corpse without before he get in instructions from Washington. He went into the schoolroom and was moved by what he saw. He had felt the presence of immortality when he had spoken to Che and now could not accept that he had played a part, no matter unwittingly, in the final chapter of his life. Again he sought out Zenteno and ordered that in the name of humanity the body should be cleaned up and laid on a bed where he would be entitled to some final rest. Zenteno surprisingly agreed and further ordered a young doctor who had been assigned to the army unit to preserve his body as best he could to prevent the corpse from rotting before a decision on its burial could be made. The doctor injected the body with formaldacide, which left the body shinning with an aura of greatness that most of his captors had learnt to accept over the course of the last few hours.

Word had got around the locality that Che Guevara had been shot in battle and villagers started to appear at the schoolhouse demanding to pay homage to the fighting legend. Fearing an unsavoury conflict with the local civilian population Zenteno allowed the villagers to file past the body as it lay in state. Amongst the mourners several nuns from the local convent arrived and were shocked by the resemblance to Jesus Christ that Che's body had acquired with the preservative.

Realising that such stories would only lead to a pilgrimage and that building up Guevara's reputation to a status of Demi God was not in the Bolivian Government's interest. Not to mention that of the American Government, who just wanted the name of Che Guevara disappear of the face of the earth, Zenteno decided to send his body immediately by helicopter to Vallegrande for a discrete disposal. After a hasty autopsy, General Ovando, the senior officer in Vallegrande ordered that he be buried without his hands, which were finger printed by Roberto Quintanilla for future conformation that he was in fact dead. Che was joined in an unmarked grave by the six other rebels who had been captured and executed during the skirmishes.

ACKNOWLEDGEMENTS

This is my first attempt at writing a novel. My style of self deprecation is not restricted to fictitious events; I am convinced you will not be surprised by my opening statement. However to get beyond an idea to complete this narrative takes a certain will power and a belief in what I was doing was going to be of interest to anyone.

To help me in that belief I needed encouragement and I lacked none of that from my family. My wife Maria, kids Mark, Eva and Gavin and especially my grandson Luke. All of whom I love dearly and offer this book as a dedication.

However writing in a vacuum can be self absorbing. I have offered drafts of the book to several people for their comments and most return with gratuitous praise. Lovely to hear, but not required. Never previously being an advocate of constructive criticism, I changed my views quite dramatically and longed for negative comments and positive suggestions. In that regard I would like to thank Creona O'Connor and Susanna Collery who contributed to my feeling the necessity for numerous re-writes. The major one of which was undertaken after I submitted my work to The Writers Workshop. Professor Ashley Stokes reviewed the story and suggested a completely different approach along with a change of style. I have attempted both, hopefully with some improvement but I thank him for his forthright comments.

I learned of Che Guevara's capture and execution along with the rest of his life from 'Che Guevara. A Revolutionary Life' by Jon Lee Anderson and my knowledge of Santeria was largely taken from 'A practical Guide to Afro Caribbean Magic' by Luis M Nunez though I have studied many other sources on the internet.

Finally I would like to thank Trafford Publishing for the opportunity to publish this book. For those of you who entertain similar aspirations, I offer no better advice than to explore their web site.

MIKE BEETLESTONE
mikebeetlestone @imagine.ie